I0659354

THE EASY WAY OUT

ALSO BY ROBERT LANE

The Second Letter

Cooler Than Blood

The Cardinal's Sin

The Gail Force

Naked We Came

A Beautiful Voice

The Elizabeth Walker Affair

A Different Way to Die

THE EASY WAY OUT

A JAKE TRAVIS NOVEL

ROBERT LANE

Copyright © 2022 Robert Lane

All rights reserved.

ISBN: 978-1-7322945-5-4

Mason Alley Publishing, Saint Pete Beach, Florida

All rights reserved. No part of this book may be reproduced, scanned, or distributed in any print or electronic form without the author's permission.

This is a work of fiction. While some incidents of this story may appear to be true and factual, their relation to each other, and implications derived from their occurrences, is strictly the product of the author's imagination. Names, characters, places, and incidents either are the product of the author's imagination or are used fictitiously. Any resemblance to actual persons (living or dead), localities, companies, organizations, and events is entirely coincidental.

Cover design by James T. Egin, Bookfly Design

He was born with a gift of laughter and a sense that the world was mad.

—Rafael Sabatini, *Scaramouche*

THE EASY WAY OUT

PROLOGUE

It was late May in Saint Petersburg, Florida: summer coming into pitch, the sun in full command of the sky. The bullet, free of its chamber, sliced the thick afternoon air. It crossed the interstate in a meaningless speck of time, cleared a FedEx truck, and entered the airspace above the public park adjacent to the elementary school.

Liana Castillo pumped her legs to urge the swing as high as possible. She loved the precise moment when her body hung motionless before falling backward. At that highest point, Liana envisioned her soul continuing upward, floating from her body before reuniting in a backward arch.

Not that she shared that sensation with anyone, for Liana didn't understand this business about the soul. No clue. She'd heard the word in church—it seemed mighty important. And judging by the mumbling adults who crowded her on Sunday morning, it certainly could use a ton of forgiving. But she'd never summoned the nerve to ask what it was, what it had done so terribly wrong. Liana found only joy inside. Evil had yet to make its presence known in her budding life.

Liana's mother, Theresa, sat on a bench, having relented to her youngest daughter's plea for a five-minute swing. Theresa finished sending a text, coughed, stood, and stuffed her phone in her purse.

"Let's go, baby. If you want spaghetti, we need to stop on the way home and pick up some meatballs."

At age ten, Liana had not sampled the world's culinary delights, but if she had—sampled all the culinary delights the nations could present—spaghetti and meatballs would never be dethroned.

The bullet.

At the top of her arch, just as her soul gained separation, the bullet, on a downward trajectory, grazed her head. Liana's tender body splayed to the ground, where her head struck with a sickening thud.

"Baby!"

Theresa dropped her purse. She rushed to her daughter's rag doll body. Theresa Castillo knew what a hurt child looked like. What a sleeping child looked like. Above all, she was terrifyingly aware that she had no experience, no reference point, for what confronted her—awkwardly crumpled legs and arms protruding in unnatural angles like broken twigs. The god-awful stillness of her daughter's body.

She fell to her knees.

No! No! No!

A crow landed next to the body.

Years later, when the house was empty, the noise gone, Theresa Castillo would credit the bird for squelching her anger with the world that perpetuated so many lies.

. . .

A FEW MINUTES LATER, NICKY RIGGINS CLIMBED OUT of his 2008 Honda Accord like it was a damn Bentley. He strolled into a Circle K and grabbed a pair of hot dogs, a handful of condiments, a Coke, and a bag of chips. He dumped them on the counter.

"These, too." Riggins grabbed a package of Skittles.

Riggins was always jacked after a job. This one didn't go as planned, but fuck it. Besides, they'd paid him upfront. Said he'd give it his best shot. Huk. Huk.

"You like Skittles?" he asked the man behind the counter.

The man kept his face down.

"You know you do," Riggins said. "Everyone loves fuckin' Skittles."

Riggins didn't bother to pay. Nor did the man behind the counter solicit any money. The clerk knew his job was to just bag the items and not to cause any trouble. Not for a pair of wieners. Not for a bag of chips. Not for all the cash in all the cash registers in the world. Besides, in another month he was moving his family to a different neighborhood. Got a new job. Adios, Circle K.

He'd been working twelve-hour days since before his first memory. He finally had enough money for a down payment. A house had come on the market that afternoon, and he couldn't wait to tell his wife. The kitchen had been remodeled with all stainless-steel appliances. His wife craved that gleaming symbol of arrival more than anything. She had just texted him: they were having spaghetti that night, and she was going to stop by the store on the way home, and was there anything else he needed? Spaghetti and a new house. What a day. Their time had come. Hard work does pay off.

His phone rang.

Theresa.

Did she wonder if spaghetti was okay for dinner? She knew it would be. He'd planned on telling her about the house when he got home, but it was all too exciting and gushing out of him. I'll tell her now. Yes. Yes, that's what I'll do.

Manuel Castillo would spend the remainder of his life stuck in the moment right before his finger tapped the phone.

1

It was midway through the second year of my daughter's life that Brittany, my older sister and only sibling, told me her twenty-four-year-old son was missing.

My sister and I were sitting at the end of my dock. A lazy outgoing tide funneled the water through Pass-a-Grille Channel and out toward the Gulf of Mexico, less than a mile from our dangling toes. A pod of dolphins, Monet's underwater ballerinas, gracefully broke the surface. Sheepshead nibbled on the pilings, their striped bodies rising and falling like spirits in the water. A day has never passed when I have not sat at the end of the dock. That's not true, of course, but I'd like it to be true.

"Mom came to me in a dream," Brittany said. "She said, 'Evan is suffering.'"

"Suffering? How so?"

"I don't know, Jake. It was a dream. I don't believe that stuff for a nanosecond. Besides, how would she even know his name?" She glanced over at me. "Crazy, right?"

"Nothing is crazy."

"You're right." She swayed her head. "And *that's* what's crazy."

"I can't be right?"

"You know what I mean."

Whenever I'm with Brittany, I'm reminded of the monorail at Walt Disney World. Brittany and I rode it once, as children, our hands pressed to the glass, gliding through the magic kingdom of youth.

We want to believe life is that monorail. A suspended journey to an enchanted theme park of dizzy happiness, a land of milk and honey. Goofy. Minnie. Mickey. Donald. The gang's waiting for us amid piped-in music, sparkling fountains, postcard palm trees, and flawless green grass laced with walkways cleaner than your kitchen counter. Never mind that a cast member is suffocating inside the costume for union wages to create your glorious illusion. We see and believe what we want to. And in the Sunshine State, we expect to be in a sunshine state of mind.

But my family's life had been violently derailed. During our vacation—a few days after our monorail ride—we were lounging around a motel pool in Florida. Brittany went to our room to retrieve a book. My parents never saw her again.

Matilda.

Everything goes back to that day. Or that day keeps multiplying forward, your pick. The concept of family. The knowledge of evil. The realization that the world, preoccupied with spinning night into day and tilting summer into winter, does not even offer a sympathetic nod to those who struggle to hang on. That's a lot from a one-word-titled book. The kicker? They turned it into a funny movie. The lesson? You take your laughs where you find them.

I'd discovered eight years ago that Brittany was not only alive but married with two children and living three hours north of me. It's a long story. It had a happy ending. Not all stories do. We'd kept in touch since then, but not as much as either of us would have liked. It had been difficult for us to carve time out of our lives for each other. That's what I tell myself, although it is something I prefer not to examine too closely.

After she was snatched from their lives, I became an unbearable reminder to my parents of what used to be. A survivor from their aborted dreams. Kathleen has suggested I see a "professional." My wife is a goddess with words. A wizard of letters, a commander of commas, and an admiral of paragraphs. But even the great ones whiff sometimes.

I asked Brit where Evan was in his life.

"He graduated a year ago from UF with a master's in English lit," she said. "He's working on his PhD and wants to write, but he knows it's a long shot to make a living at it. I think he'll eventually teach."

I'd not seen my nephew, Evan, in three years. Maybe four. Sad, considering people commented on how similar we looked.

"When was the last time you heard from him?"

"Couple months, three maybe? We were in Europe for three weeks. We didn't hear from him the first month or so we were back. He was never one to call much. I talk with Addison every few days. Boys are different, but that doesn't mean we aren't close. We are.

"He did security system work for TOTA Technologies. They're a software company in downtown Saint Pete. They started as a home and commercial security company and still do a little in that space. I think he was more of a free-lancer for them."

"TOTA Technologies?"

"Ever hear of them?"

"No," I lied. I didn't want to needlessly worry her.

Her eyes tracked a leaf riding the ebb tide. "I feel stupid for not knowing more. I called them, but they said he hadn't worked there in months. It's not like him."

"Did you file a police report?"

She nodded. "With no suspicion of foul play, they weren't too interested in pursuing a twenty-four-year-old man who hasn't called his mother in eight weeks. It's hardly a crime."

"Obviously they're not mothers."

Brit flashed a smile. "You got that right."

My older sister was aging well. Crow's feet had sneaked in around her eyes, but her smile was as effortless as it had been when we were children, her soothing voice unmarred by the abrasion of time.

"Imagine if I'd told the police about my dream," she said. "They would really think I was nuts. You'll help me, right?"

"Crackpot like you? No way."

She shoved me in the shoulder.

"It's a shame we haven't seen each other more," she said.

"That's on me."

"No. We both bear that. Let's do better, and not just because of Evan. Deal?"

"Deal," I said. And I meant it.

Our last Christmas together, I stumbled down the stairs three at a time, only to find her in her bathrobe, clutching her green stocking. Mine was red. My mother saw them as Christmas colors. My father as starboard and port. To go from that to her disappearance three months later, witness my family get amputated limb by limb—my mother by cancer, my father by the bottle—was something no "professional" could help me with.

Kathleen calls that a bad attitude.

Brittany needed my help, and I saw an opening. An opportunity to make amends. For as I'd come to build my own family, to author my own life, my anger toward my parents morphed to forgiveness. Empathy. Even compassion. The Latin root of *compassion* is *pati*—to suffer. *Com* means *with*. Compassion is not empathy. It is not understanding. Compassion is to feel another's pain as your own. Now that I have my own daughter, I feel my parents' hurt. I've come to see their downfall as inspiration to create joy from their sorrow.

Joy. That's my daughter's name.

The sailboats *Fantasea* and *Magic* glided past, tourist legs draped over the bows. The taut mainsails glowed yellow as if the sinking sun were beckoning them toward the horizon, willing the boats to the edge of the earth. A pelican smacked the water, uninterested in the poetic world.

"Joy is a beautiful child," Brittany said, as if my hobbling thoughts were stitched on the passing sails. "I couldn't see you as a father—you were pretty serious about that army stuff—but you're a natural around her."

"I'm afraid," I said.

"Of what?"

"That I'll screw up."

"Of course you will. Take it from one who's further down the road than you. They'll forgive you long before you forgive yourself."

Hadley III appeared. She sniffed Brittany, then nestled

between us and folded her front legs underneath her. Brittany stroked the cat behind her ears.

"I think Kathleen wants another one," I said.

"Cat?"

"Kid."

"You think?"

"We haven't explicitly discussed it."

"Ahh. We've all been there. And why would that be?"

"She's afraid I'll say yes and not really mean it."

"We've been there as well. Would you? Really mean it?"

"Damn the torpedoes. But it would have to be a private adoption. We got lucky with Joy. Having someone intersect our lives who happened to be bearing an unwanted child."

"Could happen again."

"That's not a game plan."

"You think there's a game plan, little brother?"

"Tell me more about Evan."

She said the last time they spoke was before she left for Europe. He indicated the owner of TOTA, Edward Giancarlo, had asked him to do side jobs, security cameras for his house and a warehouse the company owned west of downtown. "But he never talked much about his work. He considered it nothing more than a means to put food on the table."

She contacted his friends. They hadn't heard from him in some time. They were concerned, which troubled her. She called the police.

"I knew something was wrong. But at the same time, I desperately wanted to hear his voice on the phone telling me he was swamped, that he had lost his phone. I held on to that wish for too long. Stupid of me."

"What about his apartment?"

She brushed away a few strands of her auburn hair. The

air is always agitated at the end of the dock. "He lived in downtown Saint Pete. His suitcase is still there. So is his backpack, but no computer. He would never take his computer out of his apartment without putting it in his backpack. I'd like you to look at his apartment. Maybe you'll see something I missed."

Hadley III stood, gave me a sniff, walked a few paces behind us, and stared at the water. A palm leaf rode the tide, and a center-console fishing boat with twin engines roared in from the Gulf, its wake scaring the water. The cat didn't heed the noise. Its attention was on the leaf. I've always marveled at—envied—the cat's ability to coldly shut out the rest of the world in favor of what captivates it.

I promised my sister I'd comb through Evan's apartment first thing in the morning. She gave me an extra set of keys.

"Do you still see Garrett?" she asked.

Garrett Demarcus and I had known each other since grade school. Brittany knew him from that time as well.

"I do."

Her eyes rested on mine for a beat. "I thought I saw him jogging when I drove down the street."

"He's here for a few days."

"Don't give me that."

"We got a small job coming up. Mop duty for a man in the Agency."

"Anyone I might know?"

I thought her question was more for her husband, Alex Brackett, than for herself. Brackett, who worked for the State Department, and I were cordial, but that would be the peak of our relationship. I held him partially responsible for some of my sister's lost years. We all knew this, and we all knew that we all knew this.

"Yankee Conrad," I said.

"Hmm. Don't know him. Give Garrett my best. Did he ever marry?"

"No. He's still looking."

"Good for him. He needs to move on."

Garrett's fiancée had been the victim of a drive-by shooting in Cleveland, Ohio, close to twelve years ago. I didn't tell her Garrett was still looking for the man who pulled the trigger, not a new lover. He and I had exhausted ourselves years ago searching for the shooter. He had since hired various private firms to take up the cause, continually rotating new eyes on the case. He had the first solid lead in years.

She tented her hands in front of her mouth and then brought them down to her lap. "I can't stop thinking of the future," she said.

"How so?"

"The emptiness of it. The sadness. The grief." Her eyes drilled me. "The greatest grief we have is not for what is past, but for that which will never be. For future lost. We have bad family blood, Jake. Someone has to break the chain. It's got to be you."

SHE DROVE AWAY IN HER WHITE BMW WITH TINTED windows. Instead of going back into the house, I returned to the end of the dock, a torrent of thoughts accompanying me. The sunset sailboats were gone, and the bay was settling into the night. The soundless, spinning red light of an ambulance rose over the bridge across the bay.

There is no meaning at the end of the dock. No bearded spiritual guru dispersing wisdom and magisterial edicts. I never return a better man than the one who went out. But it is there that I escape the tragic vibrations of my past, for they do not follow me back. The tide and the wind take it all, and I return empty. My mind clean. Unintruded on. Ready to give that monorail one final chance.

2

I met a man named Angel three times. This is the first
time.

It was the night after Brittany and I dangled our feet off
the end of my dock, the sheepshead suspended in the
current.

The man stood in front of a rack of electrical wiring in an
industrial warehouse west of downtown Saint Petersburg.
The security lights created caves of shadow in the aisles. The
air was stuffy. Motionless. It was one-thirty in the morning,
and I was a quarter past dead, hungry, and ticked at myself
for not eating something earlier. Things weren't going as
planned, and a growling stomach and stifled yawns didn't
help matters.

He looked like the devil. Or at least that commercialized,
Eurocentric rendering of God's most famous rebellious
assistant. The devil swayed his head and smiled—a Joker
convolution of crooked horse teeth that came up higher on
one cheek than the other. His greased black hair flared over
his ears like demonic Cadillac fins, his dark eyes sucking in

all the light around him. His body twitched. He was a man eager to leave his stink upon the world.

Garrett and I were there to collect two employees of TOTA Technologies. I hadn't mentioned it to Brittany as I couldn't see how the job was in any manner connected to Evan's disappearance. We were given the two men's names, the location, and nothing else. One of those men now lay on the floor, having taken a blow to the head from a butt of the devil's revolver. The other man stood next to his captor, afraid to breathe. When the devil had announced they were free to go, the man in front had taken the first step. The devil had whipped him in the back of his head with the butt of his gun. That unlocked the gun cabinet. Garrett pointed his gun at the devil, and one of the devil's two henchmen returned the favor to Garrett. The other—he was smaller—cowered behind the devil. Both those men wore black face masks with cutouts for their eyes. The devil did not. He kept his gun deliberately aimed at the floor. At this point, either we'd all get out alive, or there would be one man left standing. Probably the coward.

I voted to see the sunrise. That's why I kept my gun holstered and drew my mouth.

"Now why did you go and do that?" I directed my question at the devil. "We were getting along great here, weren't we? We give you the package. We get our boys back. What do you say, big guy?"

"You are lucky I did not kill him," he spit out. "You were supposed to come alone."

"Are you talking about that Black man behind me pointing a gun at your head? Never saw him before. Lucky for me, though, he was in the 'hood. How about you allow my other passenger to cross, or are you going to bully him as well?"

The devil snorted. "Bully? You think this is bullying?" He took a step toward me. "You want to know what a bully does where I come from?"

One hour—that's what Yankee Conrad had said. We had been clicking along nicely on that pace until this cat played Whac-A-Mole with one of the men. That had brought the guns out. Garrett never took his eyes off the devil. And although the devil liked to flash his fangs, his jittery eyes were aware of the tall, muscled man pointing the barrel of a gun at his forehead.

"I appreciate the offer," I said. "But let's conclude the business that is beneficial to us both."

"Beneficial," he said. "What is beneficial for me is that I kill them both. I do not negotiate. You tell them. You tell them they are lucky. Next time, they get their people back in a box. Amazon. Prime. A head. An ear. Things are different now."

"You know, I didn't catch your name."

"Angel."

"Well, listen, Angel, it's been a lovely cruise. Now if you'd like the money in the briefcase, allow the man to walk to me, and, if I may kindly add, please refrain from striking him."

"You tell the *cobarde* men you work for that I'm in charge now. I run the show. When you leave in your car, you do not forget what I tell you."

"Truck," I said to Angel.

"What?"

"I came in a truck, Angel. Not a car."

He opened his mouth and rolled his tongue inside his

lower lip. The small man behind him shuffled his feet. The man on the floor groaned.

"I don't care if you rode a donkey's ass," he said.

"A donkey is an ass. Listen, Angel, I'm leaving with these two men. Seeing as how you're not interested in the briefcase, how about if I take it as well?"

"I don't trade money for lives."

I took a step toward him, careful not to impede Garrett's line of fire. Angel smelled like he just got out of the shower, and that seemed so wrong.

"Take the money," I said. "Give me the men."

"First you promise me."

"I don't make promises."

"You don't even know what I want."

"I don't give a donkey's ass what you want."

He chuckled. "I like your humor." His face contorted. "But I don't like you. You see my face? My eyes? I wear no mask. I fear no man. I deal on my terms. Anyone who crosses me?—there will be no negotiations. You tell them. This is the lesson you leave with here tonight." He turned to the shorter of the two masked men. "Get the money."

I retreated and reached to the floor without turning my back on Angel. I picked up the briefcase just as the smaller man approached me. He took one step more than was necessary and planted himself directly in front of me, his back to Angel, blocking his view. He thrust his left hand out. But as I extended the briefcase, his hand kept coming. I started to react, but something in his eyes caught me. Caribbean-blue eyes with fine eyelashes, and if God ever created prettier eyes, he kept them for himself. I breathed in the Tennessee hills after a morning rain.

It was he who smelled like a shower, not Angel.

And he was a she.

I kept my ground as she snatched the briefcase with her left hand. She thrust out her other hand and palmed me a crumbled piece of paper. I balled it in a tight fist. Only then did she step away.

"Walk," I said to the wrist-bound man behind Angel. He took a wide step around Angel and hustled behind me.

"Remember what I told you," Angel said.

"I don't even remember your name."

His gun had been hanging casually at his side. Without taking his eyes off mine, he pulled the trigger and shot the man on the floor. The man screamed in pain.

"That's so you remember my name."

He spit on the man.

"And that is for your smart mouth. You remember me now?"

"I got a tip for you, Angel."

I paused, forcing him to come in.

"What?"

"Remember me."

He gave another snort and sauntered off. The masked man holding the gun lowered his weapon and followed him. The woman who had given me the briefcase knifed me a look before she, too, turned and walked out the pedestrian side door with a red exit sign above it.

I dropped to my knees and turned the man over. He writhed in pain.

His friend spoke. "Is he dead?"

"No. He shot him in the leg. If he wanted him dead, he'd be dead."

"But why—?"

"Quiet," Garrett said and dashed to the exit door. He

would stand guard. We wouldn't take any chances that Angel and his crew weren't done for the night.

I punched 911 on my phone. The femoral artery runs down the thigh and, if struck, can be fatal. I tore the man's shirt off his back and applied pressure to his wound, which did not appear to be as bad as I feared.

Twenty minutes later, the man who had been shot was in stable condition and on his way to a hospital in an ambulance. I called Yankee Conrad and explained the situation to him. He said he'd dispatch someone. At two-thirty, a woman with short, silver hair and a commanding presence arrived. She huddled with the police in the warehouse and showed them a business card. She left without making eye contact. The lead detective walked over to me. He was disturbingly crisp and attentive for that hour of the day. I bet he wasn't hungry.

"When did you start working for the feds?" he said.

"Wasn't aware I did, sir."

"Don't 'sir' me. You're Rambler's buddy, aren't you?"

Detective Rambler and I had gotten acquainted while working several different cases—one in which he considered charging me with a murder I didn't commit.

"Tell him I give him my best."

"I'll tell him you can't keep your damn nose clean. I'm turning this report over to him. I don't need this in my life."

"Am I free to go?"

He turned and sauntered away.

As I made my way to the door, I noticed a piece of paper on the floor. It was the scrap paper the woman had given me. It must have dropped out of my hand when I fell to my knees to help the victim. I'd forgotten about it in the rush to save the man's life.

I bent over to tie a shoe that didn't need tying, scooped up the paper, and stuck it in my pocket.

As we drove away, Garrett said, "If I returned fire, we'd all be dead."

"I know."

"He spit on him."

"I know."

"I'd like to meet him again."

"If dreams come true."

"What did he give you?"

Garrett misses very little. But I wouldn't expect him to have known the smaller of the two men was a woman.

"He was a she. Recently showered and with eyes that would spin your heart."

He nodded. "I can see that. The note?"

"That, I don't know."

I dug in my pocket and handed the note to Garrett.

"What does it say?"

"I am Rachel," Garrett said.

"That's it?"

"That's it."

"I am Rachel?"

"Apparently."

"Want to catch breakfast someplace?"

"No. But I could use a burger."

"Even better."

3

Yankee Conrad's wife, Constance, was on the phone when I entered his office the next morning. Despite her decades on me, when we'd first met, we'd engaged in a harmless flirtatious exchange. She gave me an it's-good-to-see-you-I-can't-talk-now-but-he's-expecting-you-so-go-on-in-and-we-would-have-been-a-great-pair-if-our-lives-had-overlapped look. But before you commit me, consider this: Women can pen novels with a twitch of their lips. Conduct symphonies with a bat of an eye. Flatten armies with a flutter of a hand, and peel a man's skin with the touch of a fingertip. God might have created man in his own image, but he was banging a bong when he did women.

Constance and Yankee Conrad had worked for the Agency for the entirety of their adult lives. Constance's father had been a member of the CIA's predecessor, the OSS. They operated in their own quiet theater, with the mantra that the less you knew, the better off you were. Obscurity is your friend.

Garrett had gone home to Cleveland. Yankee Conrad and

Garrett had never met, and both desired that that continued to be the case.

Yankee Conrad rose from behind his massive desk, stretching his angular frame until he threatened the ceiling, high above our heads as it was. His office was cut from the captain's quarters of his great-grandfather's freighter. Gnarled wood that had once ridden the waves under the Southern Cross and now sat in air-conditioned solitude. But an indistinguishable smell remained. A decanting concoction of sea, sun, and salt aged by the tannins of time.

He rounded the corner of his desk, and we each claimed a burgundy leather chair. I sank an extra six inches more than I would have expected. I gave him a recap of the previous evening's events. He listened with a forward lean to his body, his eyes alive with humorous curiosity. Today's bow tie was pink with monkeys on it.

"And this man—Angel—claims to be in charge?"

"In a vague sense. How did TOTA get involved in the CIA?" I knew little other than my orders to facilitate the exchange.

"TOTA sends men abroad to collaborate on software with companies in which they partner. Companies in Russia are known to have ties with the SVR, the former KGB. As you know, they have repeatedly hacked both corporate and US government computer systems. We asked TOTA to go in with antennas up and learn what they can. Cyber War is the new Cold War. Leon Panetta, the former head of the CIA as well as Secretary of Defense, warned us about this almost a decade ago in his famous Cyber Pearl Harbor warning. That time has come. We also believe the SVR actively assists drug cartels in laundering money."

He paused to see if I was on board.

"What is to prevent TOTA from profiting from what they learn?" I said.

"Indeed. What is? I've received word this morning that TOTA, due to the recent scare with their two employees, has decided to withdraw from cooperation with the Agency. It is certainly their prerogative, and one can hardly blame them in light of recent events."

I inquired how long the two men Garrett and I collected had been detained.

"They were scheduled to come back over a week ago. TOTA received no notification of their whereabouts until the exchange for cash demand. A million dollars. Play money, really. Intended, I would think, to send a message. TOTA provided us with the funds, which you handed off." He tented his hands in front of him. "We cannot be taken advantage of. But more than reputational damage, we need to ascertain what, if any, harm has been done. As they have severed the relationship, we are no longer welcome there.

"The company is controlled by Edward Giancarlo. The relationship was handled by an associate of mine, Eugene Levinson. Gene has stepped away on his own accord to allow a pair of fresh eyes to examine his work."

"Is Levinson straight?"

"He has a weakness for the dice, but it was he who suggested we put a pair of eyes on Giancarlo. He's a solid career man, married with two grown children. If Levinson was hiding anything, the last thing he would want is someone looking under the hood."

"Or that would be the first thing he would suggest."

Yankee Conrad nodded. "I'd like for you to be those eyes. Start clean. Unswayed. Meet Edward Giancarlo. Enter his circle. Don't be afraid to shake him. You can't harm our relationship—as I said, he has already cut the ties.

"There is a gala at the Mahaffey in a few nights. Giancarlo and his wife are hosting it. He is a man about town, although he is rumored to have started his career in questionable company. I've secured a pair of tickets for you. If Edward Giancarlo used us to gather information that he then sold to others, he stands as a rich testament to our misguided attempts. Like doctors, we bury our mistakes. Unlike doctors, we prefer a shot at retribution before we shovel the dirt."

"Could you make it three?"

"Pardon?"

"Tickets to the Mahaffey fundraiser. My neighbor is useful on such occasions."

"Certainly."

He stood, and I did likewise.

"Are you familiar with the name Evan Brackett?" I asked him as we headed toward the door.

"I am not. What of the man?"

"He's my nephew. He's missing. His last employer was TOTA Technologies. He also did personal security work for Giancarlo."

"When did you learn of this?"

"Yesterday."

"Do you have any reason to believe his disappearance is related to his work at TOTA?"

"I do not."

"I'll keep my ear to the ground. Meanwhile, let me know if there is anything I can do to assist you."

"I will. One more item. One of the men who accompanied Angel was a woman. She handed me a note that said, 'I am Rachel.' Does that name mean anything to you?"

"I'm afraid it does not. And you?"

"No idea."

He paused, as if arranging his next words. "If your nephew's disappearance is in any manner related to his work at TOTA, you will need to exercise faultless aplomb. You will be on your own. That is the only way to ensure that we are not held accountable if it blows up in our face."

"That is hardly a vote of confidence."

"Merely stating the facts, Mr. Travis. It always blows up in our face."

4

The treat of my evening while attending a performance at the Mahaffey Theater is savoring a Jameson on the rocks while enjoying the solitude of the rear veranda. The veranda overlooks a lighted fountain and marina. The tick-tock metronomic beat of sailboat masts marks the time, while the fountain gurgles liquid diamonds that sparkle in the black night.

That was not the case tonight.

The reception hall's doors were open, and the buzzed crowd spilled into the (my) veranda. The air was thick like a musty Bordeaux. It was a breezeless evening, as if the wind had no interest in joining the festivities. A Latin-combo band played at one end of the reception hall, and a mile-long banquet table spewed treasures from sea and farm. Men and women dressed in black, their hair tied tight behind them, circulated among the crowd holding round silver trays of hors d'oeuvres skewered with toothpicks with colorful frills. A frumpy man wearing glasses riding low on his nose bent over the table, loading up his plate like it was Thanksgiving. There's one at every party.

That afternoon, Yankee Conrad had forwarded an encrypted email detailing the relationship between TOTA and the Agency. Levinson would debrief employees who went to foreign countries concerning their meetings: Who else was present? Are you sure it was this woman? This man? Did she leave alone? Did they touch each other? Appear intimate? In all, six employees had been debriefed by Levinson over the past eighteen months. The email indicated that nothing of substance was gleaned by their efforts. But a report only states what the writer is willing to share with others.

The email also noted that Edward Giancarlo had been married three times and had no children. He was a major contributor to the arts in Saint Petersburg. The Dali. The Mahaffey. The Museum of Fine Arts. His name topped the donor's list of each organization. His picture, along with his trophy wife, Erica, graced every web page. The centerpiece couple of the who's who in the Sunshine City. Giancarlo was also a nonpracticing lawyer.

I'd gone to Evan's apartment and found nothing of interest. I'd let Brittany know. I also contacted Detective Rambler. He said he'd keep his ears open, but, as Brittany had said, with no foul play, there was little the police could do. I felt bad that I had no encouragement for my sister. I refrained from telling her that I was looking into TOTA. Her days had to be excruciatingly long.

There was more.

What if my nephew was not the innocent young man his mother thought him to be? Would she resent me if I were the one to expose an unknown, and perhaps ugly, truth about her son?

"The world ends if I don't have a whiskey soon," I said to the most important person in the world, who, as luck would have it, stood next to me.

"Champagne for me," Kathleen said.

"Make it two," Morgan added.

"The bar to our port side is a few feet closer than the bar on our starboard side," I pointed out.

Without further discussion, the three of us threaded our way to the port-side bar, where we queued up behind fellow desperados. Kathleen caught a circulating waiter's eye, and we each snatched a cube of beef tenderloin cooked in a Thai sauce.

Morgan started chatting with a woman with tomato-red hair wearing a flowing robin-egg-blue dress. Her face had the lashless look of redheads, her skin unflawed and pasty white, as if she was raised in a country house in the heather moorlands under a November sun. To this day, I do not recall her approaching us. Her soft eyes raked Morgan's face.

"Tell me," she said, her voice soft, "about the first time you ever cried in a theater."

Morgan never flusters, but his hand trembled as he brought the flute to his lips.

As Morgan and the woman from the moorlands stepped to the side, I spotted Edward Giancarlo perched by an open door, minions flocking to his side. I was suddenly washed with boredom. I'd attended similar functions, and they all smelled the same. I tried to rally myself by rehearsing a few opening lines and—

"Hey, buddy, I'm talking to you."

I shifted my attention back to my wife, who, with Everest

heels, was nearly my height. Kathleen had sworn a blood oath numerous times never again to indulge in high heels. She broke her vows with the regularity of a young monk who promised never to touch himself. Her excuse? They were good a few times a year for her vanity. The monk's excuse? He touched someone else.

"Did I miss anything?" I said.

"I'm expecting twins."

"Help me out here—is that one or two fathers?"

She punched me in the shoulder. She was feisty tonight, high heels and fists. Something else was gnawing at her, probably the whole *another kid* thing, but I didn't ask because—well, I just didn't.

"Do boys ever mature beyond the knuckle-dragging age of fourteen?" she said.

"Not that I'm aware of."

"His wife's name is Erica, correct?"

"She's in the gold dress. Standing over next to—"

"Gold? Were you a golden retriever in a previous life?"

"Do you see her?" I asked testily. Outside of black and white, Kathleen and I rarely saw the same colors, and, I might add, whatever I saw was wrong.

"Down, boy. I've been watching her. She's number three, right?"

Across the crowded floor, Erica Giancarlo threw her head back in silent laughter.

"She is," I said.

"I'll report back."

The mystery in my life sashayed toward Erica Giancarlo, leaving me with my shriveling cubes of ice. I dropped a ten on the counter, introduced myself to the bartender—his name was Bryan—and requested that he add a little juice to my tumbler, remember my name, and honor our special time together.

The band took a break, and Giancarlo stepped over to the stage. He thanked everyone for their generous support and rambled on about how the arts are the heartbeat of society, and we must keep the heartbeat strong. His face fell as he stepped away to applause.

I was waiting for him.

"I appreciate everything you do for the arts," I said before others had a chance to close in on him.

Giancarlo had a small mouth and tight lips. His slender frame exuded uranium density. He stood on the balls of his feet. He reminded me of FDR's quote, "Never underestimate a man who overestimates himself."

"Thank you," he said, for what I could only guess was the umpteenth time that evening.

"We're lucky to have people like you willing to step forward," I said, applying a little more butter.

"We do what we can. If you'll excuse me."

"I'd rather not."

"Pardon?" A hint of irritation laced his voice. Shuffling feet behind me told me that others were biding their turn.

"I facilitated the exchange for your two men."

His eyes widened. The first glimpse of humanity. "I understand it was not as smooth as we wished it to be."

"Such things seldom are. Is Marcus doing better?"

"Who?"

"Your employee who took a bullet."

"Oh yes. Thank you again."

"Did your employees tell you anything about their captors?"

"They were debriefed by your employer. I believe you have that information."

"I'm more of a freelancer."

"Then you likely know what you're cleared to know. Again, my deep gratitude on behalf of the men and their families."

He started to slide to my right.

"I heard some disturbing words that night."

He stopped and angled his face toward mine, taking a moment to appraise me.

Me: A salmon shirt. (I'd called it pink, and Kathleen, who purchased it, had sternly corrected me while I was preparing *her* dinner.) Beige slacks and a blue blazer. That apparently fatal combination led to Kathleen accusing me of looking like a "1980s cardboard cutout from a fly-over-state country club." Guessing that wasn't good, I'd offered to change. With a peck on my cheek, she retorted, "Don't even think of it." See why I drink?

"I didn't catch your name," Giancarlo said.

"Jake Travis."

"I hardly think, Mr. Travis, this is the time and place."

"Name the place and time."

"Is it necessary?"

"Considering my life hung in front of my eyes that evening, I find my simple request both harmless and justified."

"Do you have a card?"

I handed him my card.

"My secretary will call you. Now if you'll excuse me."

He didn't wait for a reply.

. . .

KATHLEEN STEPPED AROUND Frumpy Man, who'd taken up residence at the banquet table. She plucked something out of a steaming pan and awkwardly maneuvered through the crowd before tottering to a stop beside me.

"How's that vanity?" I said.

"Vanity is my folly," she said, butchering Jane Austen. "You do know, high heels were originally worn by men."

"We wisely ditched them."

"The *only* blemish on the ascent of women."

"Ascent?"

"Certainly you realize we're living in the last hurrah of men."

"Right. I keep forgetting. What do you have for me?" I nodded at a plate she held in her hand.

She handed me the plate. "Shrimp and cheesy grits. I grabbed all the sausage I could without being escorted out of the building."

"You are the center of my soul." I took a bite, using a black plastic spork. "Anything else?"

"Things aren't well in the Giancarlo household. Edward —not Ed—works and sleeps. There is no in-between. He is under considerable stress."

"How do you know this?"

"Erica—she is number three—said the stress level has skyrocketed the past few months. He's home less often, always dashing to Naples for business. She added he doesn't share why or who, but something or someone is turning the screws."

A man with a domineering voice had moved close to us. He incessantly attacked those in his conversational circle, an unfortunate group of drooping smiles, tired eyes, and plastic faces pretending they were having a good time. I took Kathleen by the elbow and steered her outside. While still crowded, the noise level was more conducive to conversation.

"Tell me more," I said.

"I'm tapped out, ace. To answer your earlier question, I followed Erica the Third into the women's room. I thanked her for hosting and blubbered condolences for suffering the endless parade of people, like me, who wanted to talk to her."

We had stopped at the rail overlooking the fountain. Kathleen faced the reception hall, her back to the fountain. I faced the fountain, my back to the reception hall. She turned so that we both faced the fountain, our arms resting on the metal railing. The breeze, like a starlet who'd kept her fans waiting, finally made an appearance.

"Do you think she confessed Edward's state of mind to everyone with a pair of ears?" I said.

"I'd like to think I bring more to the game than that. No. I caught her with her dress up and her guard down. She doesn't strike me as a whiner."

"Who does she strike you as?"

"An actress. The whole Erica the Third character. When I first entered the women's room, she was slumped in front of the mirror. When she saw me? It was cue the cameras. Head up. Eyes bright. Shoulders straight."

Kathleen turned her face toward me, the light from the fountain glowing her cheek. Age had started to plant its flags, but the joke was on age, for it only added to her beauty.

"What type of woman would want to be Erica the Third?" she said. "What's she in for? To be able to strut around the Mahaffey, queen of the night, toast of the town?"

"Are we automatically trashing love?"

"That's always a contender. But I sense it's a few lengths back, fading fast."

"Anything else from your restroom rendezvous?"

She considered my question, although she wasn't prone to indecision. "It's like her dream is slipping away, but she's still fighting for it."

I knew enough not to challenge her further. I yawned, not being fond of late events, or, for that matter, thinking after dinner. My body aches to be on the beach by six a.m. That inarticulable pull, that clockwork anticipation, starts the night before. I took another sip of whiskey, relishing the dissonant chords in my mouth.

I filled Kathleen in on my conversation with Giancarlo and that I planned to call him in the morning if he did not reach out to me.

"Did Erica give any indication of the pressure he faces?" I asked, circling back to a comment she'd made previously.

"Talk to her yourself," she suggested. "Tell her you're with me, the woman who rudely stalked her into the powder room. Ask her what she meant by her comments."

"That's a little strong."

"Think so? I asked her if she regretted saying yes to Edward Giancarlo's request for a second date."

"You did no such thing."

"I did."

"What possessed you to—?"

"I don't know, Jake. Maybe it's these damn high heels. I felt like it. I said it."

She rarely called me by my name, let alone salt her language. She placed her hand on my chest. That wasn't a standard move, either. The night was turning into a wheelbarrow load of firsts.

"Don't let her fool you. She works hard to be tough. I don't think it comes naturally to her."

I took another sip of whiskey and set off to meet a woman who was fading out of love, leaving behind a woman who had confiscated my heart.

5

Erica the Third.

An accredited tease and an authentic fake, she greeted each person with unwavering attention and unwarranted excitement. I was plotting how to make my final approach when she sprang free from a group of women and strolled to the bar.

The crowd was thinning, and some of the luckier patrons had slithered out the exits. No one followed Erica to the bar, which itself was deserted except for my buddy Bryan, who, God save the Queen, had not wavered from his post.

"May I have another water, please?" she asked Bryan.

"Ice?"

"Please."

He plucked two cubes of ice from a metal bucket, dropped them in a glass, and spurted water over them. He handed her the drink and shifted his eyes to me. "Another one, Jake?"

"I'm good."

Erica, a flawlessly coifed brunette with infectious dimples, turned to me.

"First names with the bartender?"

"It's good to know the important people in the room."

"Then you wouldn't know me."

"Don't sell yourself short, Erica."

"You have me at a disadvantage, Mr. . . . ."

"Oh, I'm hardly important."

Her lips curled up. She cut Bryan a look before flicking her eyes back to me.

"Now, Jake," she said. "You don't impress me as a modest man, and it's much too late to engage in flirtatious warfare."

I introduced myself.

"Erica Giancarlo," she said. "But you know that, don't you?"

"Guilty. Thank you for hosting the event and enduring the evening," I said, copying Kathleen's line.

"It's my pleasure."

"How is your husband holding up? He seems to be under considerable stress."

She tilted her head. "Is there something I can do for you?"

Erica the Third was worthy of her title. Her gold— yellow, lemon, whatever—dress was tight enough to show her figure but loose enough not to broadcast it. She gave me the same attention she'd given everyone else she'd talked to that night, which made me wonder if she even saw me. For her eyes were like the seashells Kathleen brought home from the beach—beautiful and empty. We'd keep those seashells for a few days and then toss them, leaving grains of sand on the kitchen counter. I would clean the counter before Kathleen, unable to resist the urge, would relieve her pockets of more seashells. She never walked the beach in a garment without pockets. She never returned from the beach without a few treasures, which I rinsed, displayed, and eventually tossed. That circular activity made perfect sense to us, and for some reason, I saw seashells in Erica the Third's eyes. The beauty. The mystery. So easily attained. So casually discarded.

"If you stare at me any longer," she said in a husky voice, "I'll have to charge rent."

"My apologies."

"No need. It's just an old line I like."

"My partner and I facilitated the ransom demand for your husband's two employees."

She took a moment to digest my abrupt statement. "I see. Edward was greatly relieved when they were safely home. I understand one man was shot, but nothing serious."

"I talked to your husband earlier. He is watching us now. He'll ask you what we talked about."

"What makes you so sure?"

"Don't most marriages work that way?"

"Half of marriages don't work at all."

"Which half are you in?"

Erica's eye melted past mine to where her husband was conversing with two other men.

"I'm sure he expressed his gratitude for your effort. You'll have to excuse me, for I know little more than that. Not a woman's place, you know," she said coyly.

"Walk with me."

"Why?"

"Walk and find out."

She sucked in her cheeks, and we strolled shoulder to shoulder until we were clear of the bar. We stopped at the open door leading to the patio, and stardust stirred within me. It always does when I stand next to a woman I do not know. Some men stare into telescopes searching for God; others burn their eyes into microscopes seeking to unlock the universe. But I? I am tripped by women.

"You indicated to my wife that someone is putting pressure on your husband," I said.

Her face went cold.

"The blonde in the restroom? The woman who has no right wearing heels?"

"She does struggle with them."

She arched her eyebrows. "Struggle? She stumbled around like a drunk giraffe."

"I'll pass along your observation," I said, thinking it would be good payback for Kathleen's country club slam. "What more can you tell me?"

She paused a beat.

"Did Sally send you?" she asked.

"Sally?"

"Did he?"

He?

"I don't know a Sally."

"Never mind." She bit her lip. "I'm afraid I spouted off some nonsense to your wife. It was the booze talking."

"You asked Bryan for 'another water.' You haven't had a drink all night."

"My, my. Aren't you the observant one?"

"Why—?"

"Don't," she rushed out.

"Don't what?"

"Look into anything. Stay away from us."

"Who is Sally?"

"Nobody."

"You need to trust me or your husband."

"Are you nuts? I don't know you."

"Me or your husband."

"You're jesting."

"I may need to confide in you and you in me. But this conversation never took place."

"What an inflated opinion you have of yourself. Why would I trust you?"

"Because you're Erica the Third. You try to ignore that, but you can't. It's there every time you look in the mirror."

"You're an ass."

"I mean no disrespect. It's your decision. He's coming. Show me what you got, Erica the Third."

She slapped me across the face. Edward Giancarlo pulled up behind her.

"Keep your paws off me." She spun part way around and then feigned surprise to see her husband.

"You should be more careful who you invite to these shindigs, Edward. Let's go. I'm tired."

She marched off, leaving me to face Giancarlo. I rubbed my cheek, swelling with heat.

I shrugged my shoulder. "Can't blame a man for trying."

"I expect better manners the next time we meet," Edward Giancarlo admonished me.

WE WERE READY TO CALL IT A NIGHT, BUT WE WERE missing Morgan. Neither of us had seen him since the woman raised under a November sun had turned a page in his life.

"These damn heels," Kathleen said. "What was I thinking?"

"Erica said you had no right to wear heels."

"She did not."

"Some reference to stumbling like a drunk giraffe."

"Bullshit."

Kathleen had unleashed the dogs tonight. She had nothing against swear words—telling me once that a well-placed blasphemy trumped a thousand thesauruses—but accepted the challenge of speaking without them.

She scanned the lobby. "Where *is* Morgan? I'm ready to split this safari."

"I know."

"Where?"

"Follow me."

"Yes, bwana."

As I took her hand and led her toward the theater, she asked, "What happened to your cheek?"

"Erica the Third slapped it off my face."

"Sorry I missed that. What earned you the honor?"

"I think she did it so she could lie to her husband about what she and I were discussing. Now she can tell him that the sole aim of my posturing was to get my hand up her dress."

"She that fast? 'Cause I know you're not."

"I'll find out. But if I want to investigate Giancarlo, it would be beneficial to have her cooperation."

The first two doors to the theater were locked, but the third accommodated us. Morgan sat alone in the middle of the concert hall. Kathleen wedged past him and sat on the other side, interlocking her arm into his. She kicked off her heels and crisscrossed her legs underneath her.

"How long have you been sequestered here?" she asked him.

"Most of the night. Eleanor—she goes by Ellie—and a few others joined us."

"She's the woman you met when we first arrived, who asked you when was the first time you cried in a theater?"

"Yes. We took turns taking center stage. Someone tossed out a subject, and you had five minutes to act it out."

"*Damn* it," Kathleen said, and I wondered if I even knew my wife. "Don't ever do something like that again without me. Where is Ellie?"

"She has a young son, and her sitter was good only to eleven. And your evening?"

"I've sworn off heels until the end of time."

"I recall you've had similar epic aspirations in the past."

"Please. Encouragements only, not reminders."

"I can carry them home again." He turned to me. "Did you run into—what happened to your cheek?"

"It got in the way of the swift and just hand of Erica the Third."

"She was in here."

"Erica?"

He nodded. "Popped her head in the same door you came in. Asked if any of us was Sally."

"Sally," I said.

"Mean anything?"

"She asked me if Sally sent me, but referenced it as a man's name."

We were quiet for a moment, the weight of the long day taking its toll. I wondered if my pillow missed me as much as I missed it. As we stood to head for the aisle, I said, "You forgot your shoes."

"Piss on 'em."

Who is this woman?

Morgan collected Katheen's shoes, and we marched out of the theater, across the pavement, and up the steps to the second level of the parking garage where my truck was parked, Kathleen padding away on her bare feet.

At the top of the stairs, Kathleen said, "Let me have them."

Morgan handed her shoes to her. She raised them high above the trash can and ceremoniously dropped them into the can.

"Feel better?" I said.

"Hell, yeah."

"Your once-impeccable language has suffered a galactic setback tonight."

"My language is *damn* impeccable."

Rachel. A man named Sally. Evan. Erica the Third. Salty-Tongue Kathleen. I had a whole list of people who were a mystery to me.

But only one shellacked my heart and stripped me to the studs.

6

My oar stirred a dead fish, its glassy eye staring incoherently at the heavens. I was so intent on the broken-down beauty of death that I almost missed a dolphin as it broke the surface on the other side of the kayak. Its body gleamed in the sun like wet cement. I was kayaking around the island, which was like paddling through a ceilingless museum. Confused clouds were more vivid on the water than they were in the air. Moored sailboats stood at attention. Birds perched on pilings and snuggled in dense mangroves, whitewashed by their droppings. A woman sat at the end of her dock drinking coffee. Or was it tea? Her feet were bare. A closed book rested on her lap. She stared over the water.

I put the paddle down, touched the water, and pinched a cloud between my fingers.

I'd done five miles on the beach earlier, but the morning, monstrously brilliant, was too grand to allow it to slip away. I never want to surrender a Florida morning, for whatever follows will not be as good. And so, I stretch it as long as I can, knowing that one day it will be my last.

Non basta una vita.

One life is not enough.

I STACKED THE KAYAK ALONG THE SIDE OF THE HOUSE, tucked Joy under my arm, and carted her to the backyard, where I nuzzled her between my legs. Waxy-green palm fronds clattered in the sunlight, dancing shade on the ground. Hadley III slunk toward us. Joy took a stab at the cat with her floppy arms. It cat-walked away, much to Joy's dismay.

Kathleen taught English at a college a few miles from our home. The abbreviated summer session was underway, and she had a midmorning class. She shouted goodbye from the screen porch and hustled out the door—late as usual. My wife struggles mightily with two things in life: punctuality and the kitchen. Make it three. She's never cracked the cardinal directions. North, south, east, and west. Just doesn't get it.

"I mean, the world's round, right?"

Our sitter, Bonita, arrived. I gave her my daily edict to speak as much English to Joy as Spanish. With a glitter in her eye, she ran off a torrent of Spanish I didn't understand. She knew this. Bonita had raised her own four children and, at age forty-five, was not surprised to find that she missed the occupation. She took very little, if any, of what I said seriously. Strangely, that endeared her to me.

"*Arrivederci,*" Bonita said. "I teach your daughter Italian today. That is what you want, right, Mr. Jake?"

"*Oui,*" I said.

"Au revoir."

"Auf Wiedersehen."

I coughed as I got in my truck. A red tide was lurking offshore, and it tickled my throat, for I am more sensitive to it than others. A red tide is an algal bloom, a natural phenomenon of which the exact cause is unknown. It is lethal to many living organisms. I always know it's there before reading about it. Before a hundred dead fish float off my seawall, a hundred glassy eyes to heaven. Kathleen and Morgan are not as affected by the early stages of the bloom. But if it gets bad, it affects everyone, and there is no way to ignore it.

I headed to Harbor House, a give-me-your-tired-your-poor refugee center that Morgan and I operated. We had one full-time employee, Domingo—a name that means born on Sunday—who lived there. He had texted me that a family had arrived last night while Kathleen was bemoaning high heels and reneging on a decade of cuss-free language. While on the road, I called Brittany and asked if she'd heard anything new, inconsequential as it might seem. She had not. She added that her husband, Alex, had called in some favors from the State Department, but there was little they could do and no reason for them to be involved.

An hour later, while I was making lasagna that could be heated up for consecutive dinners, a man who identified himself as William Standiford, Edward Giancarlo's secretary, rang. He requested that I drop by "Mr. Giancarlo's house" at four-thirty that afternoon.

THE BLACK IRON GATES OF EDWARD GIANCARLO'S house swung open at a crushingly slow pace. The asphalt lane gave way to topiary-lined paver bricks that formed a circle in front of the house. A burly, neckless man stood waiting for me.

"I'll take your keys," he said, extending his hand. He had the grizzliest pair of forearms south of the Canadian border.

I tossed him my fob.

"Follow me."

He paraded me into a pretentious grand foyer with a round marble table under a chandelier the size of my boat. An expansive circular staircase that could hold a football team for their annual picture curved off to the left. My hirsute guide hiked us through an equally wide hall that ended at the rear of the house. He swung open eight-foot French doors, and we entered a covered outdoor living area. Beyond the couches, chairs, and kitchen, an elegant swimming pool stretched. The gray, incomprehensible waters of the Gulf of Mexico lay beyond the property. Grass trimmed to putting green standards encircled the pool. Erica the Third, wearing a one-piece bathing suit—originally designed, I believe, to be paired with a top—was stretched out on a recliner next to the pool. Her curvaceous body glistened under the murderous sun.

Edward Giancarlo nodded a few times, instructed someone to "get it done," tapped his phone next, and unplugged an earpiece.

"Mr. Travis."

"Mr. Giancarlo."

He snapped shut a laptop that sat next to a sweating tall glass on a coaster.

"Sit." And then, as an afterthought, "please."

I dutifully complied, taking a seat on a flowered couch across from him. He pushed back his chair and angled it out to face me. The man who had confiscated my keys stood off to the side, hands folded in front of him.

"Thank you again for taking care of my two men. Clarify for me in what capacity you are here today."

"Pardon?"

"You're a freelancer. A strongman. Hired by the CIA to conduct an exchange. If they had any issues with intelligence we gathered, my contact would have reached out to me."

"Strongman?"

"I'm not being disrespectful, but you were hired for a specific job. That job is completed. Besides, I have disengaged from the Agency. I will no longer be putting my people at risk."

"Would you prefer my inquiry come from your regular contact, Mr. Levinson?"

"That would be fine. Now, if there is nothing else, Leonard will show you out."

I stood and strolled over to a bar cart. The ice bucket was filled with sharp, unmelted cubes. I'd arrived at cocktail time.

I glanced over at Giancarlo. "Levinson's out. I'm in. Can I fix you anything?"

"You are a presumptuous man," Giancarlo said as I turned my back on him. "Not to mention rude. My wife said you made a crude advance on her the other night."

It was good to know that Erica had protected our conversation. I poured a shot of single malt scotch into a heavy glass tumbler and added ice from the bucket. I dipped my head toward the third Mrs. Edward Giancarlo. "We each took a swipe at each other, but hers stung more."

"State your purpose. My gratitude for you saving my men only runs so deep."

"Barely wets your toes from what I can tell. Why did you disengage from the Agency?"

"I'll indulge you. It was time to move on and focus on my businesses. Their requests were becoming a distraction. If there had been any issues with my decision, I would have been notified."

I raised my glass. "Consider yourself served. I had the pleasure of meeting a man who called himself Angel. Name mean anything to you?"

I thought he blinked out of sequence, but he was a hard man to read.

"No."

"He was the man who shot your man. Spit on him, too."

"I know nothing of him."

"He said he runs the show now. I'm supposed to pass that along. Any of this ring a bell?"

"Must I repeat myself?" Giancarlo glanced at his watch. "I'm sure you've been briefed, but so we are on the same page: My company deals in many countries. In this case, our team was in Russia. Our government has asked us, from time to time, to report back who we see. What we hear. All very low level."

"Angel was no Soviet agent. I'm guessing he was cartel muscle."

"That Russia, and their despicable SVR, supports the cartels is hardly surprising."

"How's business?"

"Pardon?"

I scanned his property. "You seem to be doing well for yourself."

"Are we finished?"

"I'll be talking to the two employees."

"Why?"

"Is that an issue?"

"Is answering my question one?"

"I'm not interested in a second-hand rendition."

"I understand they both took early retirement. I can hardly blame them. They didn't sign up for a life-threatening mission. Leonard can put you in touch with our HR director."

A woman dressed in a maid's outfit came out and presented Giancarlo a cocktail with a cherry in it. She cleared a small dish that had crumbs on it.

"Thank you, Missy," he said to the woman. He turned his attention to me. "Why wasn't I told that Levinson was being replaced?"

"This is how you learn. Tell me about Evan Brackett."

Concern swept his face. "Who?"

"The man who worked here, at your house, and at your company."

"Why do you ask?"

"He's missing."

"I'm afraid that—"

"Evan Brackett is my nephew," I said, interrupting him, although I wish I hadn't.

"I see," he said, in a tone I couldn't place. He balled a hand into a fist. His face, incredibly, tightened even more. "I'm sorry to hear this. Is your relation to Evan in any manner connected to you being chosen to conduct the exchange?"

Evan.

"No. But it intensifies my efforts. I understand he worked as a TOTA employee and did side jobs for you."

"He did some work on this house when I added a wing. He was in the home security division, not the software division. Although that was how I started the company, it is no longer a significant part of our business. He was a pleasant young man."

"Why did you select him to work on your personal residence?"

"Who said I selected him?"

We were bluffing each other, and I couldn't decide which card to play.

"His mother."

"Evan must have misinformed her. Evan, along with others who performed work for me, were selected by my general contractor."

"Were you on a first-name basis with the other employees your general contractor selected as well?"

"I try to know the names of my employees."

"Except those who get shot."

"Is there anything else before you leave?"

I surveyed the backyard, worthy of a Shropshire County castle.

"I would like to apologize to your wife."

He took a sip of his drink. "I'll pass it on."

"It's a personal message."

"Do as you wish. I believe you are aware of my wife's ability to defend herself."

"What does it stand for?"

"Excuse me?"

"TOTA."

His dead eyes rested on mine. "Theater of the absurd."

"'The dignity of man lies in his ability to face reality in all its senselessness.'"

He tilted his head, a slight curl in his lips. "Good for you, Mr. Travis. Enjoy your evening."

He stood, collected his phone, and strolled into his house. I hiked out to Erica, the full force of the summer Florida sun pressing upon my back.

Earbuds were nestled in her ears. I positioned myself so as to shade her face. Her eyes popped open but registered no surprise or embarrassment. She groaned, took out her earbuds, and propped herself up on her elbow. Leonard stood in the shade on the back patio, well out of earshot.

"You're blocking the sun," she said.

"It's bad for you."

"Maybe I like things that are bad for me," she said caustically.

"That was a nice move, slapping me. It was an effective way to bury our conversation."

"Is that what I did?"

"Tell me about Sally."

She squinted at me. "Never heard of him."

"You sought him in the theater."

"I told you. No one."

"Everyone is someone."

"Good to know. Why are you here?"

"I wanted to poke your enchanting husband and let him know I'll be talking to the two employees. What can you tell me about them?"

"Me? I'm the fuck-pad number three, remember? Midway to five."

"I never said that."

"Didn't need to."

"Is your husband involved with drug cartels?"

"What on earth are you talking about?"

"I rescued those two men from a drug cartel."

"I'm not privy to his business deals."

"I'm sure you overhear phone calls."

"When he's home. He's in Naples a lot for business. Besides, why would I tell you?"

"Keep yourself out of jail if it all falls down."

"I have spousal immunity."

"Someone's done their homework. Ever hear the name Evan Brackett?"

"No."

"Think harder."

"What are you going to do, Jake?" she said in a breathy voice. "Beat an answer out of me?"

I stepped to the side. The sun seared her face. She sat up, put sunglasses on, and crossed her hands over her knees. I turned my back to the house, reached into my pocket, withdrew my card, and let it flutter down on her chair.

"When you need a friend," I said.

She let her eyes rest on mine for a hot second. She took the card and slid it under her pink-and-white-striped towel. She put her earbuds in and lay down on her back, begging the sun to make love to her.

On the way out the front door, Leonard gave me the contact information for the human resources director at TOTA Technology. As I executed a smooth turn out of the driveway, my thoughts ran ahead, a search engine looking for the most viable match to my discontent. Giancarlo knew more about Evan then he indicated. Maybe Angel as well. But my thoughts settled on Kathleen. It's always Kathleen.

Something was brewing in her. Something she'd kept

hid that was threatening to explode. If it was the whole another-kid thing, I wanted to tell her I was fine with it, but I couldn't say that unless I believed it to be plausible, and I couldn't see how luck would strike us twice. If I said yes and it never happened, it would have been better to said no and have her mad at me than to have her live with busted hope.

I didn't understand any of that, and that is why I knew I understood it perfectly.

7

The human resources director at TOTA Technologies said she was expecting my call. Jay Parini, one of the two men we exchanged the money for, and his wife had bolted to the Keys for a few days. Marcus Knowles, the man who had taken the bullet, "has a ranch south of Lakeland," she said in a tobacco-curated voice. "What he sees in the scrubland escapes me. His partner, Duane, does sculptures. Maybe he gets inspiration from all the nothingness. Beautiful place, though. We had a Christmas party there once— that's a holiday party now. You could lose your job if you don't keep up with the new labeling system."

That scrubland was south and then east, in the prairie land that comprises much of Florida yet receives so little attention. As I drove with two fingers on the wheel, I thought of taking Joy on her first kayak trip around the island. It was a recurring image I'd been having. Why couldn't I shake it? It was as though, if I delayed for too long, I would in some manner maim her for life. But, for an inexplicable reason, I didn't feel I deserved to take her. Hadn't earned it. I shifted mental gears. Garrett had called that morning and said the latest firm he'd hired to find who killed his fiancée over a decade ago might have a name any day. I wondered if closing that dark chapter of his life had anything to do with my kayak obsession. They didn't seem related, which only served to reinforce that, in some manner unrevealed to me, they were.

I arrived at the address and pulled into a narrow driveway. It curved for no purpose, for its terminus point was a straight line from where it had commenced. A sculpture of a cowboy on a horse sat in front of a garage. Behind the sculpture, two double garage doors were raised. The house, to the left of the garage, had a deep front porch running its length. A man with his back toward me was sketching on a large sheet of paper on an easel. He did not appear to be Marcus Knowles. Loud music played.

"Excuse me."

He turned, reached for his phone, and lowered the volume. I introduced myself and said I was looking for Marcus Knowles.

"Are you Jake?" he asked.

I had called before committing myself to the trip.

"Jake, I am."

He thrust his hand out, and we shook. "Pleased to meet you, Jake I Am. I'm Duane the Sculptor. Marcus the Magnificent is inside. I'll let him know you're here."

He slipped into the house, and I surveyed the garage. There were bronze sculptures in various degrees of completion. Sheets of paper, similar in size to the one Duane was working on, were tacked to the wall. Cowboys gathered around a fire. A rancher, bent with years, hauling a fence, his hat dripping with rain, his spine curved—

"Mr. Travis?"

A man in linen pants and a flowered, untucked short-sleeve shirt stood at the door. His protruding stomach was indicative of a man who did not shy from culinary pleasure. His eyes indicative of those who find a song in every conversation. A poem in every person.

Marcus Knowles looked far more relaxed than the last time I had seen him.

"Thank you, again, for getting me out of there alive," he said.

I asked him how his leg was.

"Much better. Can't say I care for being shot, though. Let's get something to drink. It's disgraceful to be without a glass in one's hand this time of the day."

He turned, and we trudged through the side door of the dusty garage into the house. Two Pomeranian dogs circled me with comical enthusiasm.

"Sorry," he said. "They love company."

"They're no bother."

"Oh, they will be. Come on, Magenta. Columbia. Room time, girls."

The dogs followed Marcus down a hall. He returned a minute later. "I can't stand to cage them, so they have their own wing. Come. I'll give you the ten-cent tour—it gives me a chance to brag—and then we can have drinks on the porch."

The rough exterior of the humble house belied its curated interior. Pictures were artistically framed, the frames demanding as much attention as the pictures. One grabbed my attention. The frame was massive, the words within it small to understate their weight. It was Leonard Matlovich's epitaph. Matlovich, a Purple Heart recipient,

was the first openly gay service member. He served in the
Vietnam War.

When I was in the military, they gave me a medal for killing two
men and a discharge for loving one.

I complimented Marcus on his home.

"It's comfortable," he said. "Duane and I go from just
the two of us to hosting large parties. It serves both
occasions."

We arrived at a crowded bar cart.

"What's your dream?" he asked.

"Scotch. On the rocks."

He fixed me a drink and handed me a heavy glass
tumbler.

"The ice will melt quickly, of course, but I detest drinking
out of plastic. Duane and I toured this distillery a few years
back. Moray is a delightful town. We had a B and B in Bish-
opmill and set off from there each day. Come. There's
usually a breeze this time of day. If not, I'll refund your
dime."

I followed him out to the porch. Wind chimes tingled in
the breeze of which he foretold. We each claimed a stuffed
chair facing the manicured yard.

After more idle chat, which I sensed he could run with
forever, I told him that Angel's words had disturbed me.
That the CIA had reservations about their former—now that
TOTA had withdrawn—partner. I was careful not to frame
my remarks in a manner that could be construed to question
his actions, but rather stressed that we were interested in
making sure we had his story right.

"We didn't do anything wrong," he said.

Marcus was better at framing pictures than I was at framing questions.

"I didn't suggest that."

"You didn't need to. Have you met Edward?" he asked.

"I have."

"What do you think of the little snake?"

"Charming."

"And?"

"He claims to have no clue why Angel said what he did. What was requested of you on those trips?"

"We made observations. That's it, dear."

Marcus spoke as if each word was a finely crafted object deserving his best frame.

"What did you observe?"

Instead of answering, he said, "Why do you think the foreign companies we corroborated with were so eager to work with us?"

"So they could observe you. Perhaps even recruit you."

He glanced down at his feet. "A stupid game really." He looked back at me. "We all knew why we were there. Both sides wanted the same thing."

I asked him if he ever lifted any piece of information that he thought might have been of interest to the US government or advantageous to his company.

"No. And that's just it. The mantra was tight lips and big ears win the day. Both sides played a good game." He shrugged. "It always ended in a tie."

"Tell me how you ended up in the hands of the cartel."

He took a sip of his drink and pinched his lips together.

"Jay and I were detained at the Moscow airport. No big deal. They'd done that before. You know, a scare tactic. Those prissy little Reds are into that sort of thing. But this was different. They kept us in a room—a deplorable cinder-blocked space. Honest to God, I thought I would never forgive myself if that was the last thing I ever saw of the world. We missed our flight. A man came in and said we'd be going home on a different flight. We were relieved. They booked us through LA. When we got off the plane there, we were told a private jet would bring us back to Tampa.

"But they blindfolded us on the jet. We spent two days in some Mexican hut—at least that's what the spooks told us—and then they blindfolded us again. The next time my eyes were free was a few minutes before we met you in the warehouse."

"That must have been terrifying."

"I could comment that it wasn't what I signed for, but that in no way conveys my experience. The firm's been pushing us older guys—I'm —out. I took the offer."

"You could have just said no more travel."

"Oh, my discontent had been brewing for some time. I just needed an excuse. That's it. Unfortunately, dear, I have nothing else to offer you."

"How many trips did you make abroad for your employer?"

"The last was my third. Pity. I did enjoy the infusion of another culture. Really? I used the trips to collect art."

I asked about his debriefing with Levinson, the CIA man in charge of the operation.

"A droll, colorless man. He drilled us on who we saw, who said what, tedious at best. He would show us flash cards with pictures, that sort of thing. Nothing at all Bondish."

"Did Levinson ask any questions that seemed out of line?"

"Such as?"

"You tell me."

He gave that a silent measure.

"No. To the contrary, Gene the Machine—that's what we called him—almost seemed relieved when we didn't have anything useful to say, which was most of the time. He struck me as a tenured bureaucrat whose interest, and whatever minor personality he'd been born with, had long deserted him."

I asked him more detail about his captors and experience, but nothing appeared to be relevant.

"Can I refresh your drink?"

I gave him my tumbler, which I realized was etched with nude men hanging from trees. He went into his house, taking his drink as well. He returned a moment later.

He handed me my drink. "Do you plan to interrogate Jay? I believe he and his wife escaped to the Keys for a little R and R."

"Interrogate?"

"We both know you're sniffing for dirt. I can save you the effort." He leaned forward in his chair, a gold necklace breaking free from under his shirt and swinging out in front of him. "There is zero connection between TOTA employees and drug cartels. You didn't ask my opinion, but here it is: Everyone knew we played a game, and the Russians decided to scare us. They called their cartel friends—we all know they help them launder money—and told them to rattle us." He popped his eyes wide and did a face shrug. "Surprise. It worked."

"One of the hooded men that night was a woman. She handed me a note saying her name was Rachel. What do you know of her?"

"We were blindfolded. I don't recall hearing a woman's voice."

"Does the name Evan Brackett mean anything to you?"

"No. Should it?"

"One more. Did Levinson ever make any unusual requests?" I asked.

Marcus Knowles exhaled. He hesitated, as if at a cross-roads, and then reached across and touched my hand. "Excuse me."

He stood and went into the house. A few minutes later, he returned.

"I've got homemade pasta with Bolognese sauce for dinner," he said. "Why don't you join us? Duane should be out of the shower by now. Let's pick out a good red, shall we?"

"Are you going to answer my question?"

His hands fell to his side. "Oh, Jake. Really? We were doing just lovely here. Let's eat first, shall we? I've been looking forward to this hour since the moment I crawled out of bed."

MARCUS PAIRED A DELICIOUS BOTTLE OF BOROLO TO accompany our dinner. We ate on the back patio, the humid air clinging to my skin like a drowsy lover who didn't want to leave the bed. We were discussing Duane's work.

"My first heartthrob was painting," he said. "In response to an obvious lack of talent, I took up sculpturing. What talent I do possess lies in that area."

"And I," Marcus said, "adore food and am mad about cooking. Unfortunately"—he patted his stomach—"you can literally see the problem those twin passions create. But I'm up to fifteen thousand steps a day. I read that David Sedaris was clocking in at sixty thousand. I don't know how the man does it. If I gain a pound or so a year, I can live with myself, assuming I'm not Methuselah's descendant."

I asked Duane if he had a studio that displayed his work.

"I show at a place in the warehouse district in Saint Pete. I've also sold two pieces to the James Museum of Western Art. Have you been there?"

"I have."

"They recently had a gay cowboy photography exhibit. It was good to see that art out there."

I added a spoonful of Bolognese sauce to perfectly cooked capellini noodles. "We were discussing unusual requests by Mr. Levinson."

Marcus dabbed his mouth with his cloth napkin and placed it on the left side of his plate.

"Okay, so here it is: Levinson dropped by about—maybe six months ago? He purchased one of Duane's sculptures."

"Why was that unusual?"

Marcus folded his hand in front of him. "Well, Jake, it's not so much an unusual request as we think—that is to say, there is a possibility—that a bull Levinson bought from Duane was used to move cash to Mexico."

"How do you know this?"

"We suspect it."

I flipped open my hands. "Why do you suspect this?"

"We were blindfolded until you came. But you can't blindfold your ears. While we waited for you, I heard men talking. They were joking about a bull with brass balls. How much money can you put in a ball? That sort of thing."

"What makes you think it was your bull?"

"They called him by his name."

"You named your bull?" I directed the question to Duane.

"I name all my work. Inscribed on the inside. That one was after a children's book I read to my niece."

Marcus reached over and touched me lightly on the arm. "What I heard that night was, 'Ferdinand's getting a grand in each ball. Now *those* are brass balls.' Can we prove it? No."

"Did you and Jay both hear this?"

Marcus fidgeted in his seat. "We did, but I was indisposed part of the time—the little boys' room. Bad time for the runs. Jay could well have heard more or heard things differently."

Eugene Levinson, the CIA handler, had purchased a sculpture that ended up stuffed with money. That did not indict him, but he would need an ironclad explanation.

"Have you sold more sculptures to Levinson?" I asked Duane.

"No."

"Did you mention what you heard to Levinson?"

"No."

"No?"

Marcus patted his lips with a napkin and then placed it on the table to the right of his place setting.

"You see," he said, "Duane's an artist. I'm a cook who faints over crushed velvet serpentine sofas. You, on the other hand, are a man who makes light conversation when someone has a gun pointed at him. And your friend? My, my. He never even flinched. Scary, really. I know it's lame, but we don't want to be involved." He winced a smile at me. "That's your job."

"And you're sure the name Evan Brackett means nothing to you?"

He shook his head. "Sorry. Who is he?"

"He did some security system work for TOTA and then for Giancarlo's house. He's missing. I'm looking for him."

"A total blank."

I looked at Duane.

"Nothing," Duane said.

"And you're sure that neither of you know of a woman named Rachel?"

"Well," Marcus said, letting his breath out. "I took Rachel Welding to prom. We double-dated. The other girl's date was dashing in a tux. His Rock Hudson coat snuggled his shoulders without a fold or crease below the neck. It tapered just beautifully down his sides. Exquisite, really. That's when I knew, but I don't think you're searching for that Rachel."

"No."

"Neither was I, dear. Neither was I."

8

The following morning, I returned from my beach run to find John Wayne perched on the end of the dock. I'd become acquainted with Wayne, a US marshal, years ago when we worked on a case together. Wayne had saved Kathleen's and my life, his six-shooter blazing as he charged over the dunes on the beach where she and I were strolling. He dropped an assassin who had just passed us, spun, and drawn his gun.

It would have been the day of my last morning.

I'd called him on a whim when I left Marcus and Duane. It was a long shot that he could help me, but he had his own network and I was begging for leads, both in finding dirt on Giancarlo and, more pressing, finding Evan. I'd also contacted Yankee Conrad. He recalled reading a white paper stating that Levinson, in an attempt to track drug money and working in conjunction with the DEA, had requested money be planted in the system. If that were the case, Duane's bull was bugged in an effort to find where it went and, more importantly, who received it. Yankee Conrad had called late last night and confirmed that the purchased bull had been an unsuccessful attempt to track money. He added that he would try to confirm it with the DEA agent who ran the operation.

I rinsed off under the outdoor shower, changed, and then grabbed two cups of coffee and a hat. Kathleen and Joy were still asleep, although Joy would soon be up and my responsibility. I strolled out to the end of the dock, dead fish staring up at me.

"Coffee?" I asked, taking a seat beside him.

Wayne's wide-brimmed hat shielded his face from the strengthening sun. His thick hair flared out of the back of the hat but came up short of touching his collar. He gave his signature single nod and popped the lid on his Styrofoam cup. I added hot coffee to his cup. A swirl of steam escaped, losing its identity in the air. I adjusted my baseball cap as the sun had yet to climb high enough to be blocked by the awning.

"I forgot what a special spot you have," Wayne said, his eyes studying the distant shoreline. He coughed twice.

"Red tide," I said.

"So I've read." He took a sip of coffee. "We might have a link for you concerning Edward Giancarlo. We put a man in witness protection not long ago. He infiltrated the cartels and presented other agencies with valuable information."

The US Marshals, the oldest federal law enforcement agency, are best known for operating the witness safety program, commonly referred to as the witness protection program.

Wayne continued. "He claims to have overheard a conversation about a sculpture of a bull used to launder cash. The same bull you mentioned. He also claims to have met people who knew Giancarlo."

"Did you question Giancarlo?"

"Not in our jurisdiction."

"Tell me about the man in the program."

"He wasn't my case. But my understanding is he worked for Giancarlo, or his company. He was taken to Mexico against his will to perform security work at a cartel compound."

"I can't imagine the cartel allowing an outsider to walk away," I said, my mind pinging a dozen directions.

"That is a mystery. He was feeding us information, and then we lost him. About two weeks ago, we picked up his trace. The cartel dropped him off in the States. We debriefed him and set up a new identity. He resisted at first, but we stressed it was for his protection."

"My nephew, Evan Brackett, did some work for Giancarlo. He has not been seen in months."

"I wasn't directly involved, nor do I have the man's prior name or a description of him. As much as possible, those things cease to exist. From what I know, he doesn't sound like a normal civilian. Our guy turned out to be pretty smooth. Spent close to two months inside. That takes a pro."

I didn't know whether to be relieved or disappointed.

"It might be best if you talk to our source," he said.

His offer surprised me. "The man in witness protection? In what regard?"

"We're not sure we ever got the whole story of what happened while he was in Mexico." He paused. "I was informed that when we debriefed him, he talked about the cartel as if they were family. He was almost despondent to be free. His demeanor raises questions about his forthrightness."

"Any theories?"

"None that we've concocted yet. Maybe you can help us there. With luck, he may even have information on your nephew, although that's a stretch. But that's a line of questioning we had no reason to pursue.

"We've contacted him. Told him you had a few questions. That he could trust you. Said you'd be by tomorrow morning —he's a little less than two hours south of here. You'll have an alias. Mick Underwood. Do not reveal your real name. Do not ask him his former name. Our man had a DEA handler. That man is missing and presumed dead. You can never reveal his identity or where he lives. No one can know." His traveled eyes rested on mine. "Do you understand?"

I wondered if the deceased DEA agent was the same man Levinson associated with and who Yankee Conrad was searching for regarding confirmation on Duane's bull, Ferdinand, being used to track money.

"I do."

He took out a piece of paper from his shirt pocket. It had the name Walker Percy, an address, and this: Baby Jesus is fishing.

"That's my line?"

"It is."

"You got it?"

"I do."

Wayne tore the paper into small pieces and leaned over the side of the dock. He opened his hands. Baby Jesus floated away and down, growing smaller until it disappeared in the dark green water.

9

An hour later, Detective Rambler called. I'd just finished batting down a hornet's nest with a broom outside my front door, scurrying out of harm's way.

"Remember the shooting a few weeks back?" he said. "Took the life of the girl on a playground?"

It took me a moment. A young girl had been shot, her head grazed by a bullet while she was swinging. She'd fallen and died, her head striking the ground. The media referred to her as the swing set girl. The cause of death was an ongoing debate.

"The swing set girl," I said.

"She's got a name," Rambler said tartly. "Liana Castillo. I met with her father, Manuel Castillo. I suggested he meet with you."

I leaned the broom against the wall and took a seat in a shaded front porch chair, keeping a wary eye for irate wasps.

"Why me?"

"You're looking into Edward Giancarlo. Giancarlo's daughter, Kylie, was at the playground that day. We suspect she might have been a target. Castillo's daughter most definitely was not."

"Giancarlo doesn't have any children."

"Kylie was—is—the daughter of his second wife. He adopted her for a while."

"The killer would go after the adopted daughter?"

"It's just speculation. If it was a hit, whoever ordered it might not have known she wasn't his biological daughter. Thugs are stupid."

"I still don't see—"

"Think you can make the time?"

Rambler was a few years older than me, and at times, he intoned those years. He gave me Manuel Castillo's number and said Castillo was expecting my call.

"A deserted lot on the west side of the interstate."

"Come again?"

"That's where we think the shooter was. On a crane. That's the only way the angle works. Kylie Giancarlo—the ex kept the name—was in line had it not been for Mr. Castillo's daughter. The department won't investigate her death. If we call it a murder, it'll just be one more unsolved homicide. Makes us look bad. The homicide business is up twenty percent this year, and we're running under fifty percent closed cases. The brass needs to keep it over fifty."

"And you want me to . . .?"

"Just give a damn. Christ, can anyone do that anymore?"

He disconnected. I stepped on an injured wasp, and for some unimaginable reason, was struck by guilt. Was it for killing a wasp? Or was it that a man I admired had just accused me of not giving a damn?

10

Give a damn or not, Manuel Castillo would have to wait. I wanted to interview Wayne's man. He was my best lead in finding dirt on Giancarlo, and while I had no reason to believe Evan's vanishing act was related to his employment at TOTA, it was all I had.

I told Kathleen that I had a rendezvous with a lover and that I'd be gone most of the day. She said to give my lover her best, and why and where was I really going? After I said I couldn't tell her, she reminded me that we were out of bananas, and if you come home without them, buddy, then don't ever bother walking through that door again.

You get a woman like that—buddy—you don't let her go.

I drove south on I-75, listening to rock music on low volume. It struck me that Rambler did that every day: gave a damn about people he didn't know. Sure, he got paid, but it's the manner in which he chose to support himself. That rationale made me feel like a lesser person. Maybe I was. Maybe we all are.

I tried to exorcise my depression by focusing on taking

Joy on a kayak ride. That just ramped up the anxiety. What if, before that kayak ride, some trashed drunk front-ended me, and that's all folks? The world would never know my pitiful, unspoken desire. Never know I lay in the ground an unfinished man.

The address Wayne had given me was marked by a mailbox on a stick stuck in a milk can. There was no drive. I pulled next to a clump of oleander bushes, clambered out, and followed a path in the sand. The path veered along the water's edge. Five minutes later, a cabin on a circular bay came into view.

Walker Percy's cottage, 107 Pine Island Road, was on a strip of land that fronted a saltwater inlet. Coconut palms bent hard against the west, prepared for the storms that had structured them and would test them again. The front porch gave way to potato-lumpy sand that turned smooth, like fine-grade sandpaper, at the edge of the still bay. A gold two-door sedan sat to the side of the cabin. There appeared to be just enough clearance in the shrubs to get the car out.

A young man came out. The screen door slammed behind him, bouncing twice. He had a week of whiskers and tousled brown hair. He stopped midway across the covered porch.

I knew that man, for he was a younger version of me.

"Evan?"

"Uncle Jake?"

"You're Walker?"

"You're Mick Underwood?"

"What are you doing here?"

"What are *you* doing here?"

"We're making no progress here."

"No, we're not."

He'd changed in the days we'd not seen each other. Not just in years, but he'd crossed that threshold into adulthood. That unmarked year, different for each of us, where age is no longer a measurable leap from the number that preceded it.

"How did you find me? My mom, right? I knew she'd be worried."

"She is worried, but I was sent here by a US marshal who doesn't know your real identity."

"You got the code?"

"Baby Jesus is fishing."

"Mom always said you were a strange bird."

"That's how she described me?"

"*Enigma* was the word, I believe."

"Walker Percy. You pick it?"

"I did."

"You admire his work?"

"Not as much as the name. When they told me I could pick a new name, I wavered between Walker and Levon."

"Like the song?"

"That's right."

"I thought Jesus blew up balloons all day."

He chuckled. "Fishing, blowing balloons. Whatever. The point is, his head's not in the game."

"Your mom's worried, Evan," I said, suddenly irritated at him and our mindless banter. He was holed up in an idyllic cottage while his mother prayed on raw knees. "What's your plan? The people who put you in witness protection can't expect you to be dead to your family forever."

"They told me I need to keep low for a little longer, then I can tell my parents. I think she'll understand. You know the family history, right?"

"I do."

Here's a part I omitted earlier.

My sister had to "keep low" for years after her abduction, which is why she was presumed dead. It was during the early 1990s, and relations with the former Soviet Union were finally thawing. Her kidnapping from the motel, by a Russian diplomat's son, was considered too minor an affair to risk derailing political goodwill just as glasnost was taking hold. The US government threw my family under the bus, my parents an unrecorded Cold War casualty.

Déjà vu shivered me in the Florida heat. Brittany wanted me to break the family spell, but like planets in space, we were trapped in a dark orbit.

"Grab a seat," he said. "I'll fetch us a couple of beers."

He slipped back inside while I paced his front porch. I was in a pickle. Evan—Walker Percy—was safe. Something I'd want to communicate to my sister as soon as possible. But I would have to clear that through Wayne, and Evan was likely in danger, or they would not have stuck him with a new identity. There was a good chance Brittany would need to be kept in the dark for a while longer.

Evan returned with two cold bottles of beer. He plopped one on a wood table. We each took a rocking chair.

"I like your ring," I said, dipping my head at his hand. Set in a gold band, it was deep green with speckles of red on it. "Is it bloodstone?"

He nodded. "The blood of Christ. My mother gave it to me when I was thinking of entering the seminary."

"The seminary?" I realized how little I knew of my nephew.

"Bizarre, right?"

"Did you enroll?"

"Naw." He took a long pull from his beer. "Me and the

Great One did a couple of rounds and then called it a day. I just dig spirituality. It's easy to get that confused with religious dogma. Here, take it." He twisted it off his finger and handed it to me. "Maybe you can show it to my mom, you know, sorta as a way to let her know I'm fine."

I wasn't sure that was advisable, but I accepted the ring. I took a sip of beer. It was ice cold. Evan took another drink, synchronizing the lifting of the bottle with his body rocking back in the chair.

"I like your spot," I said, thinking of Wayne's similar appraisal of my place.

"It's a good spot to write, and that's what I tilt at. I do my work on an old Smith Corona I picked up at a garage sale. The typewriter slows down the words. Makes you work for them. Monks used to complain about writing—said it was tortuous work. Writing was meant to be hard." He shrugged and paused, as if he'd lost his way. "Not that it matters; the real stories can never be told."

Evan spoke with a weariness indicative of an older man. As if the waning days of his moonstruck youth had been abruptly jettisoned.

A duck waddled up to the front porch steps. It stopped and stared at Evan with puzzlement—which takes considerable effort for a duck. I sensed it would have continued had it not been for the stranger occupying what was usually an empty rocker.

Evan asked what led me to his "toe of sand." I told him I was looking into Edward Giancarlo's ties to the drug cartels. That a young girl had been shot at a playground, and her death might be related to a drug war. I recapped my night in the warehouse and my visit to Marcus and Duane. I did not mention any names. Nor did I mention the note from Rachel.

I inquired how he'd gotten connected with TOTA.

"Pay the bills," he said. "It's all wireless cameras and phone apps. Easy for me and hard for a generation that didn't grow up with that stuff. But it's not like I went looking for what happened. What happened happened."

His eyes slid off mine and got lost over the bay. A boat skimmed the surface, heading toward the shadows of the mangroves.

"Want to know what I wrote last month?" he asked.

"Sure."

"I burned it yesterday."

"Good. It's out of you, and you can move on."

He cast his eyes on me, eyes that I wanted to believe still held that unreplenishable potion of hope gifted to us at birth.

"I appreciate the pep talk," he said. He let his breath out. "Maybe I picked the wrong venue. Words are clunky. The sticks and stones of our emotions. Or maybe I just don't have the talent for it, but I am sure you didn't come here to discuss any of that."

"Leave no detail out."

He gave me a sorrowful look, realizing I wasn't there for his company, although he had admitted as much. I wished I'd rolled the dough with him for a few more minutes. But that was behind us now. Besides, part of me still wanted to bash his head in for worrying his mother.

Evan explained that while working part time at TOTA, he ended up talking to Giancarlo at an after-work gathering. "Some expensive bar on Central—can't think of the name— but they've got a whiskey menu second to none. The company took the back room, and a woman conducted tastes of different flights. I thanked Giancarlo for the invite. I mean, I was just part time, right? A nobody. We hit it off."

I was about to protest that I couldn't imagine anyone hitting it off with Edward Giancarlo, when Evan, as if reading my thoughts, expounded.

"The guy majored in theater. *Theater.* I didn't know theater majors went to law school and started businesses. Fascinating guy, really, once you break the veneer. Super bright. Very cerebral. Christ, we could have talked all night. I sensed I was the son he never had. He was interested in my graduate studies, whether I was married, all that stuff."

Giancarlo had spoken to me disingenuously about Evan. But people see relationships differently. Maybe the whiskey warped Evan's senses. Or this: Giancarlo lied to me.

I asked him how it evolved after that evening.

"He asked me to help with his house. Adding new cameras and stuff. I popped over there for a few days later—not really much to do, though. Then the foreman asked if I could do some work at a warehouse. That's where the wheels fell off." He swung his head. "I knew the first day I'd made a big mistake."

"Why was that?"

"The warehouse had armed guards, and I don't mean rent-a-cops. These sombreros carried machine guns." He took a pull from his bottle. "Machine guns. The hell am I doing there? I wanted out. Told the foreman I appreciated the job, but I didn't have the time for it any more. They asked me to stay on to finish it, about a week.

"During that week, a man approached me in a grocery store where I was buying bagels. They were out of Asiago, and I was ticked. To think that was a concern in my life.

Frickin' Asiago bagels." He swung his head and took another pull from the bottle. "He had a scar on his nose—his right nostril, like someone had taken a blade to it. He flashed a badge. Asked me for a few minutes and wasn't interested in my answer. He took my elbow and directed me to a café area.

"He was with the DEA and wanted me to do whatever the men at the warehouse wanted me to do. Said if I played along a little longer, they could get me out, but if I wanted to disengage now, they couldn't help."

"They bullshitted you."

"Absolutely. I could have walked anytime. But his request had an element of danger to it—good fodder for a book, right? I told him I'd play along." His eyes widened. "Who knows, Uncle Jake. Maybe we're as common on the inside as we are on the outside.

"My last day, two guys I'd never seen corralled me into a black SUV. Said they had another job for me. I wasn't able to get a message to the DEA agent. They blindfolded me and put me on a plane. I asked why I was blindfolded. The guy said if he didn't blindfold me, he'd have to kill me, and they made him pay for his own bullets. I found God real fast then."

"He wasn't fishing?"

He snorted. "Not that day."

"Did you ever see Giancarlo at the warehouse?"

"No. Far as I know—and I've thought of this—he didn't have a relationship with those guys, or, if he did, it was hidden."

"But you heard his name in Mexico?" I said, recalling Wayne's comment.

He nodded. "I'll get to that." He took a long pull from his beer. "I was there nine weeks."

I let out a low whistle. "Hardly a three-hour cruise."

"They had me tinker with the compound's security system, but it was BS work. Their system was fine and more sophisticated than anything I'd ever seen. When I inquired about going home over dinner one night, they asked me to pass the beans. I kept on the alert for a message, signal, anything from my handler, but zilch. My captors didn't tell me squat."

"Who is 'they'?"

He rubbed his chin. "A man named Vargo was in charge. It was his home. His compound." He arched his eyebrows. "Nice guy, really. That's the shit of it. Said while he was from Mexico, he lived in Tampa for years before the family business beckoned him back. Said he still had contacts there."

"You ask who?"

"Didn't need to. I mentioned Giancarlo's name. He didn't admit or deny. That's all I needed to know."

"How did you pass nine weeks?"

"Read. Walked. One night this black SUV pulls up. The cartel loves black SUVs. Two men pop out. One of the men is holding a box, about this big."

He formed a square with his hands.

"A guy with slick black hair combed over his ear like devil's wings tells everyone to gather around a firepit. He and Vargo exchanged a few words in Spanish. We—me, the guards, the cook, Emilia who ran the house—gathered around." He paused. "Slick Hair tells the man holding the box to give it to him. He gets the box. He opens it."

We were silent for a beat. A palm fond rattled in the breeze, vying for our attention.

"I knew I had to show shock but not recognition. That if ever I wrote a role for myself, this was it, and I had to nail it."

"The DEA agent?"

"You know when you're on a stage and they tell you to look above the audience's faces? Once I recognized the head, I lasered in on a corner of the box. Slick Hair asked if anyone recognized the man missing his body. We all said no, but I could feel their eyes burning me. They packed it back in the box. Took off."

"Slick Hair—did he have a name?"

"Angel. But we're talking Satan, not Gabriel. The game started a day later."

"Game?"

"I played it with another American who showed up."

"What was the prize?"

"My life."

11

―――――

"I'm grabbing another. You want one?" Evan said.

"I'm good."

"You're going to make me fly solo?"

"Another would be great."

He rose and went into the cabin, leaving me with the duck, who had not relinquished its position.

"Looking for food, pal?" I said.

The duck winked at me. Swear to God.

My eyes wandered out to the water where the flats boat lowered its anchor pole. I ached to be on the water, my mind focused on dropping a live shrimp on the edge of a shadow, keeping the line tight should the fish take the bait, nothing else in the world mattering, and I wasn't about to learn how lucky my nephew was to be alive and how close I'd come to delivering devastating news to my sister.

Evan came back out and placed both beers on the table between us.

"The game with the American," I said.

"Right. He popped in the day after the head-in-a-box

stunt. I've never considered myself much of an actor. But I'm here today because I'm good enough.

"I was relieved to have another American in the compound. Each day, No Name—I never learned his name —spent a little more time with me. We had a lot in common: music, books, sports. It was good to talk to someone. Said he heard they came by with the head in the box. Said they weren't really those sorts of people."

"You certainly asked him his name."

"He said I could call him Fred. I didn't push it after that."

"Did the others in the compound ever address him by a name?"

"No. Nor did I care. I'd decided my lack of curiosity directly corresponded to my chances of getting out of there alive."

"Describe him."

"Tall. Angular face. All forehead. Lincoln ears. And pale, like his ancestry roots ran deep in the British Isles, and he had no right walking on Mexican soil."

"Did he give a reason for being there?"

"He said he did accounting and auditing for Vargo. He and Vargo seemed friendly. Professional, though. We're not talking golfing buddies."

"Go on."

"We had lunch one day, just the two of us. He said he was a friend of the man whose head was in the box and that I must never tell anyone what he and I discussed. He said we'd be driving to an airfield in a few days, and I'd be back in Florida soon. He asked me how his friend whose head was in the box had approached me."

Evan kept his eyes locked on the water, but I didn't think he saw it.

"You did the right thing, didn't you?"

He swung his head. He sniffled. The duck, as if concerned, took a step forward. "Man, oh, man. I wanted so bad for him to be good, but he was *so* bad. And *so* good. I saw it clearly. We liked the same music because he asked me first what music I liked. Same with books. We'd traveled to the same places because he'd lead by asking where I'd been to. He was there to get me to confess. He'd been working me for days."

"What did you tell him?"

"That I'd never seen that severed head before."

"His reaction?"

Evan drilled his eyes into mine, his lips curling into a thin smile.

"You'll like this part. No Name—Fred, whoever—studied me for a long moment. He knew. Know what I mean? He knew that I knew that he knew. The whole world knew. I didn't blink. I was a goddamn rock. He patted my shoulder, stood, said, 'Okay, then,' and walked away. I figured they sent him to get a confession from me. You know, butter me up with one of my own."

"I don't want to be insensitive. But why not just kill you?" Although I tried, I was unable to unfasten the tone of incredulousness from my voice.

He swiped a finger under his nose and across the top of his upper lip. "Search me. I mean, Vargo was a decent guy—you know, notwithstanding the drug trade and all. And it was his place. Honestly? I think I caught a break."

The cartels don't grant breaks, but I didn't want to push him or openly question his narrative. I changed tack.

"Why do you think they took you there?" I asked, for I

still didn't understand how he filled nine weeks. "You admitted you had nothing to add to their security system."

He flipped his palms open. "They thought I was better than I was. That's the best I can come up with."

He continued, not eager to dwell on my question. "Two days later they put me on a plane and sent me home. The feds must have been tracking my credit cards. Within twenty-four hours after a trip to Publix—still no Asiago bagels, I mean how hard is it?—there was a knock on the door. I opened the door, and there's two suits standing there. One said he was with the DEA. The other a US marshal. They flashed their badges. Asked if they could come in as they walked past me.

"They, too, were perplexed why the cartel didn't shoot me." He snorted a laugh. "Makes you feel good—people wondering why you're still vertical. The marshal offered witness protection. I asked him if it was necessary. He said he recommended it if I wanted to sleep at night. Told me when things quieted down in a few months, I could tell my family. He knew about my mom's history. Said she'd understand."

I asked Evan a series of questions about what names he heard. But he added little of substance.

"What did the feds do when you fingered Giancarlo?"

"Ask them. I don't mean to be curt, but they're big on receiving information, not so hot on handing it out."

Angel's demonic smile came back to me, baiting me to tie it all together.

"Did you ever see Angel again?"

"No. Show my mom the ring, okay? Details to follow. I thought they'd keep me apprised, but for all I know, they forgot about me."

"I'll take care of it." I didn't know how I would back up those words, but it was what Evan needed to hear. "And you? Sounds like you have more than enough for a book, as long as you don't expose yourself."

He nodded. "I used to think that. That to write you had to travel. Have experiences. Have someone pop open a box with a head in it."

"That's not the case?"

He grunted.

I couldn't pin the source of his remorseful tone, the sorrowful manner in which he cradled his beer. Wouldn't he be jubilant that he was alive? Or was the loss of his name, coupled with a fear of a knock in the night, strangling him?

We stood. The duck waddled up the first step of the porch.

"Keep burning pages," I said, searching for words of encouragement. "One day you'll arrive at a page you can't burn. And then another."

"I appreciate the words. No matter how dismal my previous efforts were, I wake up each morning with the promise of an Irish spring." He peered down at the duck. "But now it's time for chores isn't it, Patty Rachel?"

"Patty Rachel?"

"The duck. She follows me when I potter around the property. People don't think ducks make good friends, but they're wrong."

"Why Rachel?"

He hesitated, as if he'd forgotten how to hitch words together. "It's just . . . a name from an ex-girlfriend. Her name is really just Patty." His jaw quivered. He waved his hand in a dismissive gesture. "I'm talking junior high, man. Long ago and far away."

"Bullshit."

"Hey, easy, Uncle Jake. Sorry, but that's—"

I stepped into him. "Does Rachel have Caribbean-blue eyes?"

Evan's face pinched with fear. "Why do you ask?"

"I met her last week. At the warehouse. Where I picked up the TOTA employees. She gave me a note."

"A note?"

"It read, 'I am Rachel.' Nothing else."

Evan collapsed back into his chair. If it hadn't been there, he would have hit the floor. He swung his head side to side and kneaded his hands.

"She's with Angel?" he said.

"She was."

"Oh, fuck me, man. Just fuck me."

I sat back down in my chair. I reached out and placed my hand on his back.

"Tell me the story that can never be told."

12

This is the story my nephew, Evan Brackett, told me.

Vargo had one child. A daughter, Rachel. Vargo's wife, Sophia—Rachel's mother—had died years before. Father and daughter were close.

Rachel was twenty and had been tutored her whole life. She wanted a crash course to prepare herself for graduate classes in literature. Evan had told Giancarlo—at the whiskey bar—that he was working on his doctorate in English literature and was unattached. Giancarlo passed that along to Vargo. Vargo sent for him—kidnapped him—to tutor his daughter. That is why Evan was in the compound for so long.

"Nothing to do with security work?" I interrupted him.

"Naw. I was blowin' smoke up your ass, Uncle Jake," he said in a disturbingly casual manner. "Vargo didn't want to raise his only child to be the queen of pop culture. Didn't want her to lead a life tainted with drug money. I'd never met a woman like her. So mature. So *wholesome*. She had no interest in the culture of immediacy, the youthful obsession of here and now.

"And it was her and Vargo. That was the family. Vargo took lovers, but he told me once that a heart could only hold so much love. He said even though his wife 'was unfaithful to us for one night,' he loved her and Rachel so much, there was no room in his heart for anyone else. He laid that down over breakfast one morning when we were alone. But that was Vargo. I know he's a bad man—but there's something very human about him. A man can do bad things in the world but still love his daughter more than life."

He paused, and I wondered what memory had picked that moment to resurrect itself.

"The morning we were supposed to start lessons? Rachel kept me waiting three hours. But when she walked in the room? She capsized my heart. Just drowned me.

"She rode every day. A white stallion named Cervantes— a beast of a horse. The ubiquitous black SUV shadowed wherever she went. She told me she wanted to go to England and ride across the open shires, a mist of rain on her shoulders. She was stuffed with dreams, geography, her mind beholden to a topography of fantasy."

"Did Vargo know you were in love with her?"

He bobbled his head a few times.

"It was pretty obvious to everyone."

"And her?"

"It was definitely two ways, if that's your question."

He combed his hand through his mussed hair, his face twisting into a frown. My eyes scanned the bay, for I did not want him to feel the pressure of my gaze. The flats boat had maneuvered closer to the mangroves.

"We'd read to each other under a white cedar tree in the mornings before it got hot. She loved Gabriel Marquez and got emotionally lost in anything Daphne du Maurier wrote. Her mother named her after the protagonist in *My Cousin Rachel*. When I told her that du Maurier herself was haunted by her character for years after she finished the book, it only endeared her more to the power of words. We'd pack a picnic. Stay until the heat was unbearable, stay longer, and then leave."

He took a long pull from his bottle and kept it in his hand, rubbing it with his fingers.

"Vargo educated her right out of his life. She saw the corruption—that wasn't hard; she visited her mother's grave every day. She was a drug war victim. She told me her father had his revenge, but she feared it had destroyed him as well. But despite the blood he rained on the world, he showered her with nothing but affection."

"How did Vargo feel about you?"

Evan arched his eyebrows. "Conflicted? You tell me. He couldn't kill me. He couldn't let me live. He knew by releasing me that I would cease to exist, that I would be given a new identity. That his conscience would be clear—he did not kill the man his daughter loved. Although he might have thought of me as her first heartthrob, I wasn't. Not even the second."

"Why didn't you just tell me?"

He thumbed his whiskers as if digging to get to his skin. "I don't know. I should have. I thought it might come back to hurt my chances of seeing her again, and seeing her again is everything. I'm glad you know, though. I can't bear the thought of dying and no one ever knowing the most impor-tant person in my life. I don't think I realized how much that bothered me until just now."

I thought Evan would pull up, but he plowed ahead. Fearful that at any moment, he would be silenced by double death: his body and his unshared memories. Like me, Joy, and the kayak—forever stricken from the record.

"Our first time was in The-Middle-of-Nowhere, Mexico, on the bank of a shallow stream." He flicked his eyes to me. "Afterward? I thought of death. I didn't know why. And then it hit me; death was thinking of me, like that Dickinson poem. Death was jealous. Envious. That's why he came. But he couldn't have me."

We were quiet for a moment, the lushness of silence filling the air. A great white heron glided in, folded its ballerina wings, and settled in the shallow water.

"She asked me what my favorite memory was. I told her my family lived in New York before Florida. We'd go into the city a week before Christmas to see the Rockettes, catch a Broadway show, join the buzz of shoppers—the whole kit and caboodle. One day, we ducked into Saint Bartholomew's to escape some icy spit from the sky.

"The choir was conducting a dress rehearsal, Beethoven's *Missa Solemnis*. We listened for a long time. There is something about an empty church with a full choir. She wanted to know what it was like—living in New York. I told her it was like living in four places. The long gray winters, the slow greening of spring, the short, hot summers that broke into heartbreaking falls. The sadness when October goes. She wanted to go to the city in winter. Ice falling from the sky. An empty cathedral. A choir singing in a language we did not understand. We pledged we would do that, and please tell me I'm not boring the shit out of you."

"Not at all."

His vacant eyes settled on the weathered gray floorboards.

"We knew we needed to get out. The guards roamed the grounds at night, but we weren't afraid of them. Her room was in a separate wing. We pushed it a little more every day. We knew we shouldn't, but it was bigger than us.

"I was having breakfast. Rachel was supposed to be there, but she hadn't shown up. Vargo came in. He said he talked to his daughter that morning and that we would never see each other again. 'It is over,' he said. 'Ended. *Terminado.*' He told me to pack my bags, that I was leaving in ten minutes."

He swung his head. "What did he think? The heart's got a damn delete button?"

"It takes time to—"

"We talked last night. In my dreams. She was wearing her green dress with the yellow flowers. It was the dress she wore the first morning, when she'd kept me waiting. I wanted to touch her but couldn't." He gave me hard look. "Did you ever notice that about dreams? You can't touch. Feel. Why? Is it because touching is the only thing that is real? Anyway, Vargo, there's your goddamn ending."

He reached down and opened the lid to the wood box. He took out some seed and let it slide through his fingers. The duck took two duck steps and pecked at the floor, no longer concerned by my presence.

"You said Vargo couldn't kill you or let you live."

He nodded. "Vargo said the man who questioned me—Freddy No Name—thought I recognized the head in the box. I started to protest, but Vargo held up his hand to silence me. He said he talked the man down. But I think Vargo knew.

"He said he'd been waiting for his daughter to fall out of

love with me, but he realized that was not happening. Because she loved me, I would live. But I must leave and forget about her. I took the deal. He shook my hand and said, 'You would have made a fine son-in-law.' That's the last time I saw him. They stuck me in an SUV."

Evan sniffled and swiped a finger under his nose. I looked away. The man in the flats boat caught a fish, his pole curving to meet the fight. I couldn't see the fish but hoped it was a good eating fish, and if he ate it alone, that was fine, but I hoped he had someone to share it with. Someone who was glad that he'd gone fishing and come back with a fish. Someone he could touch.

"I got out of the SUV at the airstrip," Evan said. He spoke in a mechanical tone. "I was maybe ten, fifteen feet or so from the stairs to the plane, when she came over the hill, whipping Cervantes. She never did that. You should have seen her ride. You should have seen her, man. She could have vaulted a Roman phalanx. She dismounted and rushed into my arms. She told me she'd find me. That we would go to the cathedral, feel sky ice on our faces, but her tears were hot and salty and nothing like ice from the sky."

"That had to—"

"We tangled in some frantic embrace, our words and tongues making a mess of everything. The men picked her up. She kicked and screamed—just an animal sound. Another man dragged me on the plane. All I wanted was the damn plane to crash so I could die with her salt on my lips, and it was the second time that death came to me, but it wasn't jealous. It was pompous. That son of a bitch. He knows it's only a matter of time."

"Did you tell this to anyone who debriefed you?"

He didn't answer, and I feared he'd become too comfortable with death. No wonder he set his words ablaze.

"No," he finally said. "It's better for her this way." He straightened up. "Your turn."

I told him about the exchange. About the smallish guard with blue eyes who smelled like rain on a Tennessee morning. The note she thrust into my hand.

"Where was this?" he asked.

"A deserted warehouse off Thirty-fourth Street." I thought of a question but couldn't hold it.

"Thirty-fourth Street. Yeah, that's the warehouse I worked at." He reached over and squeezed my arm with far more strength than I would have anticipated. "Let me see the note. I'll recognize her handwriting."

"I don't have it on me."

"But it's still in your possession?"

"It is."

"Bring it to me. No phone, man. Internet either. Part of my protection. Don't you see? She talked Vargo into going out with Angel so she could make a break."

"Make a break? I don't think it works that way."

"None of us have a clue how it works," he admonished me.

"You indicated that Vargo and Angel didn't get along."

"Maybe they patched things up. You'll help me, right?"

"Evan, she's likely back in Mexico."

But my cautious words fell on deaf ears, for hope had taken hold of him. And hope can be an empowering friend lifting you out of the rapids or a heinous traitor creviced in the shallows waiting to pull you under, and you don't know which, and it is often both.

"No. She's here," he said with urgency. "Find her, Uncle

Jake."

"I'll do my best," I said, mustering confidence I did not have. Then I recalled what had flashed through my mind. "Do you think Angel worked for Vargo?"

He rubbed his jaw. "I don't think so. Angel was his own drummer. I got the impression that Vargo would be fine if he never saw the man again."

"But Rachel was with Angel."

He shrugged. "Maybe they patched things up."

"I'll bring you the note. Maybe it wasn't her but someone sent to flush you out."

As I spoke, I wondered if Angel would attempt such a trick. He seemed more of a brute force guy. But underestimating your enemy is a cardinal sin.

"Tomorrow?" he said.

"Day after," I replied, remembering that I'd made arrangements to meet Manuel Castillo—the father of the girl who fell from the swing—tomorrow.

"Mandarin Hide. That's the name of the bar on Central I couldn't remember."

We tramped along the path that led to my truck. He asked me what I planned to tell Brittany when I showed her his ring. I replied I'd have to work that out with my contact, Wayne. As I climbed into the truck, he reached out, seizing my shoulder.

"You'll be back. Day after tomorrow, right?"

"Day after tomorrow."

"Promise?"

"Promise."

I drove away, ignorant of the terrible, god-awful, bone-headed mistake I had just committed.

Plus, I forgot to get bananas.

13

RACHEL

Must my father know everything?

The note had been her idea, a last-minute opportunistic type of move that, in retrospect, she thought, came off rather sad. Silly, really.

Rachel had overheard Vargo talking to the man who had questioned Evan. Fred. The American. He seemed harmless, but Vargo had warned her not to talk to the man, and she hadn't. But that had not kept the man from talking to her when they passed in the hall. *Or was he waiting for me?* It was the first evening after Evan had been escorted off the compound. Evicted from the country. Deported from her life.

"We are exchanging two men for money," he said. He spoke as if they were veteran business partners discussing an ongoing deal.

"Oh?"

That fell within her father's policy, for more specifically,

Vargo had ordered his daughter not to utter "two words to the man."

"We have a business arrangement we need to disengage from." He evoked the same casual tone. "Angel will be conducting the operation for us."

"Why are you telling me this?" Rachel said.

"It is to take place in Florida. The same area, I believe, where Evan is from. I talked to him before your father had him deported. I thought him harmless, but I don't count."

Evan had been telling her about his encounter with the American when Emilia had interrupted them. They never got a chance to finish the conversation, and now Rachel wished they had, for she had no reference point from which to judge the man's comments. She knew Angel, of course. But that was a mark in the wrong direction.

"What do you know of Evan?" she asked anxiously. Her heart's desire to trust the man outweighed her intellect's not to.

"I thought it cruel of your father to banish him. Vargo, like many fathers, is too protective of his daughter. I know. I, too, have a daughter. If you'd like, you can accompany Angel."

"And what? Find Evan?"

Rachel was almost ashamed of the gullibility in her voice, but she'd do anything to be with Evan.

"At least try. Work it out with Angel." He spoke as if he hadn't a care in the world, which is how Rachel knew he cared a great deal.

There it was. Did she believe him? Not really. Could she afford not to go? Absolutely not.

I have no choice.

Angel.

He'd started as one of the bodyguards, became *her* body-guard, and then seemed to ascend to an unnamed throne. Vargo and Angel swung between old comrades in arms and wary adversaries. She secretly urged her father to make up his mind. That she and Angel had a history was something she had never shared with her father. As far as Rachel could tell, Angel had always upheld his end of the deal.

"Why would I bring you?" Angel said. Rachel had just cornered him and asked to go along with him to Florida.

"To find Evan." Then, feeling the need to pad her case, she added, "I want to learn the business."

"To learn the business," he said, as if testing the phrase. "I don't think so. Find Evan? Yes. But I'm not sure I know where he is."

"But you think you do?"

"I might."

"Where?"

"Why does this matter, Rachel? Your father will not allow you to go."

"Must my father know everything?"

That, of course, had sealed the deal. Angel's smile told Rachel that she had played into his hand. By going with Angel, she would have fence mending to do with her father. But consequence and repenting were for another day.

The moment the plane touched down at Albert Whitted Airport in downtown Saint Petersburg, Florida, Angel had confiscated her phone and assigned guards to her. He told her he'd promised Vargo that he would keep her safe. Her plan had been to flee Angel once in Florida. But despite her house arrest, Rachel was far too enthusiastic about life to be disheartened. At least she was closer to Evan. *Be on alert for an opportunity. Do not hesitate to act.*

Angel approached her the afternoon of the day after they landed. "You want to learn the business? You come with us tonight."

"Where to?"

"No questions. In or out?"

"In."

Rachel had just taken a run—accompanied by a guard. She showered before they left.

Rodrigo, Angel's right-hand man, fitted her with a hood and told her to be seen and not heard. The two men they were to exchange had been treated well, although one of them, the heavier one, was beyond nervous and constantly asking to use the restroom. But another man had arrived, not with their party. That man and Angel had gotten into an argument. Angel had ordered one of his men to escort Rachel out of range. He sat her on a metal chair under high steel shelves in the warehouse. She heard Vargo's name tossed around, and something about "ten million was supposed to settle this."

The man assigned to guard her was curious as well. He turned his back on her, straining to hear. Rachel glanced around. Next to her was a pencil on a dirty string and a small writing pad. She ripped off a piece of paper and grabbed the pencil.

I am Rachel.

She'd meant to write more—practicality being unbeatable—but the bored guard suddenly remembered his responsibility. She balled the paper in her hand. It would have to do. She tightened her fist and marched up to Angel.

"Give me a role here."

"Don't talk."

"Give me a role or I'll scream."

Angel gave that a second. "You can accept the money," he said with revelatory enthusiasm. "Then you will have drug money in your hands."

She nearly gasped when she saw the man who was to hand her the money. *He looks like Evan.* Older, for sure. Blonder hair. But a freakish resemblance. When she handed him her note, she was certain he knew that she was a woman. *It rests on him*, she thought. It's not much. Pathetic. We left silly a long time ago.

When she was ushered back to her hotel room, she couldn't sleep. She stood with her back to the room, her face to the sea, and beyond that, the home she could not see. She had been so eager to leave, and now it was gone. But Rachel was not one to dwell on what might have been. That was Evan's sweet trait. What made them so strong together. One unfolding the future, the other guarding the past. They saw life that way and didn't get caught up too much in one direction. Evan had told her of Hemingway's observation: that all stories, if taken to the end, end in death. Rachel believed that two people in love, walking away from each other, if taken to the end, will meet again.

14

All men weep alone.

They weep at the guardrails of ships in the night. They weep in their car before starting the engine. They weep in front of a mirror, struggling to take a tie off, and they weep on the pillow of their empty bed. And so, when Manuel Castillo cried the heart out of the blue Florida sky— even though he sat next to me at a crowded bar—he was alone. He had gone inside himself, to a place no one could follow. There was nothing to do but remain silent and wait for him to return to a world that was not the world he once thought it to be.

Rambler had asked me to meet with Manuel Castillo, proffering little more reason than someone had to "give a damn." I understood that Manuel's daughter had recently died, having tumbled from a swing after apparently being grazed by a bullet. But I was befuddled as to what Rambler expected of me.

Manuel and I were sitting at the new beach bar at the

pink Moorish hotel less than a mile from my home. The hotel was built in the 1920s by an Irishman from Virginia, named after a character in a play by a French dramatist that was turned into an English opera and is set in a town named for its Russian counterpart.

It's a grand place. But it is not a good place to cry.

Blenders roared, a singer crooned, and the twin pools splashed with screeching children. The air was drenched with the sultry concoction of sunscreen, perfume, salt, and sweat—Florida's saltwater gospel. And that gospel is on no finer display than at the hotels that front the warm band of water that laps her sandy and eloquent shores.

Manual Castillo was a teddy bear of a man. He had a round face. Chestnut skin. Buckeye-brown eyes and baby-fat fingers. I chastised myself for my egghead decision to meet him in such a celebratory place. Fifteen minutes ago, I'd asked him to tell me about himself. Manuel Castillo had uncoiled a gale force of words and tears.

He shed a tear for his father, who perished before Manuel could rush to his side. A glistening drop for his mother, who was never the same after the man who had made her laugh since they were both thirteen suddenly vanished from her life. For Stefanie, his oldest daughter, who had tried so hard to make the cheer squad. She was the only girl in her circle of friends to be rejected, and then her friends were too good for her.

A large pearl tear, sliding down his golden cheek, was for himself. When he was young and had dreams of an education. Now he felt inadequate. Another slog in history who made a living with his body, sacrificing all for his children, now cut in half.

He leaked a tear for the house he and his wife did not get —it was to be their home, their stainless-steel appliances— and he couldn't imagine ever having that dream again. I was a little fuzzy on that part, but I think I got it right.

And then great uncensored sobs for his youngest daughter, Liana, who had plummeted from her swing without a sound. She had his eyes. His personality. His soul. He knew these things as only a father can know such things.

Those were tears of the past. Then, the soldier tears of the future marched with communist efficiency.

Tears for the songs he would no longer sing, for their pretty melodies had turned into arrows of pain. Manuel Castillo cried for the boy his deceased daughter would not meet. A young man who would never know that his true love beat him to heaven. Except, Manuel explained, at night, when the young man would witness the sun dipping into the sea. God would allow his daughter to slip out of heaven and stand next to him, and the young man would feel her presence. I had to turn away when he said that. Jesus, the place was loud.

He cried for Liana's future children, who would never sit on his lap.

He cried for his empty lap.

And then a liquid chorus for his wife, Theresa. She had just started taking the girls shopping together. She'd been too excited even to sleep the night before. Now one of them was gone. A third of their posse that was starting to burst womanhood upon the world. The giggliest of them. The laughingest. The goofiest. He feared his wife was permanently damaged.

"We went to our church, the big brick Methodist church

downtown. My wife loved that church. The senior minister is kind, and she tried. But there is little she could say to help us."

Manuel insisted his daughter, an excellent swinger, would never have fallen on her own. The state refused to do an autopsy, so he and his wife had invaded their savings for a private autopsy. The official cause of death for Liana Castillo was a blow to her head. The fall was perhaps due to the bullet grazing her skull. No way of really knowing, don't you see?

"Skull," he said. "They called my daughter's head. A skull."

The attorneys had descended on the Castillo household, eager to sue the city on his behalf. Swing sets are vanishing from the American landscape. This is why. That swing killed your daughter. Sign here. We'll work for free. Just take a sliver of the award.

Manuel Castillo wasn't seeking financial restitution. He didn't trust men who worked for free, for he found work to be hard. Nor did he want swing sets to disappear from the American landscape. Liana loved to swing.

His barrel chest heaved and collapsed. He punched his breath out. "We are people of color, immigrants. We do not ask for anything. We do not break any laws. I work jobs no one else wants."

"What can I do for you?" I asked, feeling a little perturbed that Rambler insisted I meet him, and then feeling ashamed of that feeling.

"The man who fired the gun? Who killed my Liana? He must be held accountable. What kind of country turns its back to such tragedy?"

"You've talked with Detective Rambler. He's a good man. He will do everything within his power."

"*Si*," Manuel Castillo said. "But he suggested I see you. They do not have the time. They do not need another crime. My daughter—they have no interest in her."

"Even if they find whoever shot her, he might not stand trial for murder."

Manuel Castillo had been rubbing his swollen fingers together for most of our conversation. That stopped. He placed his hands on the bar, his stumpy fingers separated as if he was balancing himself. His eyes, under lush eyebrows and bangs that clumped together, leveled on mine.

"I need justice," he said.

"I don't perform retribution," I said. "Nor is it what it's made out to be."

"That's not what I'm asking you." He scooted forward on his stool. "Please. I beg you. To care. To look into it."

"I'll do what I can," I said, for I did not want any man to beg for his daughter's life to hold meaning. "But the chances of us finding who shot your daughter are low. You understand?"

"You will work for her? Remember her?"

"I will."

He wiggled his hand into his pants and extracted his wallet. He laid a picture on the bar. He nudged it toward me.

"This was her last school picture. She will age no more."

Liana Castillo beamed up at me. She wore a blue plaid dress and the excitable smile you only have when it's picture day, and your mother had spent extra time with you the evening before, laying out your clothes and, in the morning, doing your hair. Yes, you look great. Just smile. How you always smile. Don't worry about that. You have such a nice smile.

"She is very pretty," I said.

Manuel Castillo wiped a tear from his cheek. "You take this. You take my Liana."

I delicately placed the picture of Liana Castillo in my wallet. *Christ, is this place always this loud?*

15

K now when you can't remember a name or a place, and then, at the oddest time, it snaps back to you? Like Evan and Mandarin Hide, his Central Avenue bar? So it would be with me and my terrible, god-awful, boneheaded mistake.

Morgan was conducting an ESL class in the main room of Harbor House. Domingo and I were in the kitchen unpacking groceries. We were discussing the family of five, although I was pretend-listening. I was preoccupied with how to approach Brittany with Evan's ring.

"I told them they could stay as long as they needed to," Domingo said, pulling an orange out of a plastic bag. "They will work hard to get their own place. I am cooking them a big dinner tonight."

Domingo was a thin man who spoke in short sentences and carried a long knife. He'd used it once to kill a man before that man killed two women and me. Now he used it to slice an orange, handing me a wedge that I stuck in my mouth. He gave me a second wedge when, doing my best Oliver Twist, I extended my hand.

Morgan's class ended, and a group of giggling and singing women stampeded to the parking lot crammed with late-model cars.

The three of us settled on the rear porch, facing the stagnant pond. The air was so still, I feared it might have eaten itself.

"Did I hear your class singing 'That Lonesome Road' on their way out the door?" I asked Morgan. I coughed, for the red tide bloom was spreading.

"Yesterday, one of the women came in singing that song. We needed a break, so I taught them the lyrics. Domingo played guitar."

I cast my eyes to Domingo. "I didn't know you played guitar."

Domingo nodded. "I do. My mother taught me. She was a gifted musician. We would sing at night on the sailboat. My father danced. He was a man of few words. He spoke through his dance. I've never seen anyone dance as well as my father."

"Are they still alive?" I asked, embarrassed by my realization that I knew little of his family.

"My mother passed four years ago. Not long after my father. I held her hand as she crossed. That is how our memories are passed down. She sings now in my dreams. My older sister is with her. She passed when I was young. For a long time after that, my mother did not sing. One day, she started again. I asked her why she stopped and why she started. She said it is good to mourn. It is better to celebrate."

I flicked a fly away and wondered if Manuel Castillo would ever reach that point. If Evan would ever get over losing a girl who rode a white stallion and read to him under a white cedar tree.

"Does your father dance in your dreams?" Morgan asked. Morgan believed the realities of the day and the emotions of the night are different movements of the same symphony. That dreams are the heart and the mind singing together. If so, they are often outlandishly off-key.

"He does," Domingo said. "Even more so recently. I do not know why."

We were quiet for a moment. "I will finish dinner," he said. "After that, I will lay a fire. Our new guests would like that."

He rose and walked into the house.

"He's been quiet lately," Morgan said. Morgan possessed an uncommon antenna, picking up things beyond my range.

"Anything we can help with?"

"He believes he might join his father soon."

"He thinks he's going to die?" My comment sounded as if I was mocking Domingo. I was not.

"The tomb of time is also its womb," Morgan said, quoting Thale. "We've discussed it. He is worried that all his memories will cross with him, for he is the last of his family."

"You know I'm more of a meat-and-potatoes guy."

"So you say. Domingo feels his job is close to being complete."

"I hope he's not thinking of leaving us."

I knew that was not what Morgan was referring to, but I wanted to steer the conversation to terra firma.

"Any leads on Evan?" Morgan said, granting my wish.

I wanted to tell him that I'd found Evan. But I dared not

jeopardize Evan's safety. To keep something so important from Morgan seemed so wrong.

"No."

"*Some*thing is haunting you."

"I think Edward Giancarlo is involved in the drug trade, and I can't pin a thing on him."

"That's a problem. Problems don't haunt you."

How does he know such things?

"I've met a sad man," I admitted. I couldn't shake my meeting with Manuel Castillo. I told Morgan how Castillo's daughter had fallen from a swing. The thousand tears he had shed.

"I wonder if Domingo's dreams are related to the pain you speak of," he said.

His last comment was more than I wished to tangle with.

"I'll fix dinner," I said.

As Domingo and I prepared a smorgasbord for eight, he told me more about his family. Growing up on a boat, with water under his feet and blue sky above his head. Horizons that defied words. Storms that defined anger. As I listened, it occurred to me that he and Morgan shared similarities, which I attributed to spending the first few decades of their lives at sea.

I called Kathleen to see if she wanted to bring Joy over and join us. She said she had just taken Joy for a stroller ride, and they were going to picnic on a blanket. Mother-daughter time.

We—Morgan, Domingo, the family of five, and I—ate banquet style at the big kitchen table. I talked little and listened much. I jumped up whenever anyone needed anything. Afterward, we moved to the fire. Domingo serenaded us with his guitar as the flames licked the air, the yellow and orange tongues dancing in the dark.

The flame and song massaged my mind, and then they slapped me with the quickness and sharpness of Erica the Third's hand across my cheek. I'd told Evan that I'd met someone who passed a note saying she was Rachel.

"And this took place where?" he'd said.

"A deserted warehouse off Thirty-fourth Street."

What would I do if someone told me that? I doubt Evan was more than ten minutes behind me on the highway.

Stupid. Stupid. Stupid.

I thought of leaving that moment, but I knew it was too late. I left before sunrise the following morning, and I was right.

16

RACHEL

What do I have of yours?

Vargo paraded his riches into the house of God, a
baron unintimidated by his lord.

Sophia led the procession. Tall, yet unintimidating. Then
Rachel. Vargo lagged a few paces, as if to grant appreciative
space for the women in his life. Heads turned when the
three of them entered the stone church with its weathered
buttress and bell tower holding a cross with a circle in it. But
no parishioner would dare hold Vargo's eyes. If he met their
glance, they would quickly abort.

It had not taken long for young Rachel to notice that
not everyone in the church—in fact, no others—arrived
and departed in an SUV, trailed by another SUV. Rachel
had seen the men in the other SUV around the compound.
She had never given them much thought. They always
seemed to be nailing this, drilling that, painting what
didn't need painting, and polishing their shiny black vehicles. They had taught Rachel how to throw a mean knife.

One of those quirky things that no one would ever expect of her.

After the service, Sophia engaged the priest in conversation. She did this every Sunday. Sophia Estrada was not a woman to let words go unchallenged.

"Why don't the men sit with us, Papa?" Rachel said, walking ahead with her father.

"They prefer to sit alone."

"You should at least invite them to Sunday dinner."

"They prefer to eat in the barrack. You know this."

"And do they prefer not to worship with us?" she asked, returning to her earlier question.

Vargo had learned that his precocious daughter rarely made just one pass at something. He admired her for this trait, which she shared with him. But he'd recently started to question what good it had done him. He worried that one day she might find herself with his doubts as well.

"They are fine where they are."

"But—"

"It's business, Rachel."

"It's business, Rachel" was Vargo's tool for terminating a conversation with his only child. And everything was business. Business had no boundaries. No time zones. No ceiling. No floor. It was the air that Vargo breathed. The sole reason to rise out of bed in the morning, the closing prayer of each day.

She'd given up asking her father what *exactly* he did for a living. Why she didn't go to school with the rest of the village children. Why they rarely left the compound, and when they did, why they were constantly shadowed by the men who lived in the barrack. Not that life in the compound was dull. Between her revolving tutors, Emilia—the cook and Rachel's de facto second mother—the gardeners, and the constant parade of "just business" visitors, the estate teemed with activity. For a long time, Rachel considered it the best place in the world.

Until she realized she couldn't leave.

Her home became a splendid prison and her only way of escaping through the endless books she ravaged. Her tutors fell by the wayside, none of them able to go toe-to-toe with her in literature, and literature was *all* that girl craved. Vargo wondered if the world held enough books. If the human race had penned enough words to appease his daughter's insatiable appetite. She refused beyond age twelve to engage in math and science. When her father challenged her on this, she replied that she saw literature in everyday life but had yet to trip across an algebra problem that touched her heart.

"Tell me if I'm wrong, Papa."

"What if you wish to be a doctor? Or an engineer?"

"They are fine occupations, but not for me."

"Still, it's good to know science."

"Nihonium, moscovium, tennessine, oganesson."

"What are those?"

"The last four elements to be named. Numbers 113, 115, 117, and 118, in case you're wondering. You paid someone to teach me that. Tell me, is it good to know?"

"You did well."

"That's not the point. It's my mind. My time. I won't waste it on subjects that don't stir me."

"You're thirteen."

"Twelve. And we should have had this conversation two years ago. Before I wasted an hour on nihonium. Moscovium was easy; I thought of Moscow. Tennessine was Tennessee, and oganesson was orgasm, or organic, depending on the mood I was in. But nihonium?"

Vargo wasn't sure what to do with that. At (apparently) twelve, Rachel looked eighteen and acted twenty-four. It seemed meaningless to Vargo to quibble about her age. She was a young woman.

"You have your mother's heart. She loves books, too."

"What do I have of yours?"

"Me?" He asked as if it was the most peculiar question ever posed to him.

"Yes. What do I have of yours?"

"My heart, too, I suppose."

"Really? I think I have your business acumen. Not that I have an interest in business. But your obsessive focus, although we choose to be focused on different things. You and I are very similar in that regard. I like that I got that from you."

"And my heart," Vargo said, as if the point was too important to him to surrender, and by repeating it, he could will it into being. "When I was young," he added.

Mature as she was, twelve is still twelve. Rachel was unable to detect the note of forlornness in Vargo's voice. Incapable of seeing past her father and into the man. A man whose solitary lust for money and unpardonable sin had long ago mortared his soul. But also a man whose love for his daughter would unbrick his heart so that she might live the dreams of his youth. This, Vargo knew, was his only redemption.

17

Patty the duck took a step back as I bounded up the front porch. I'd been a fool to tell Evan where the warehouse was. He would stop at nothing to find Rachel. The warehouse would have cameras.

A shaft of sunlight darted ahead of me into the cottage. Evan's blue Smith Corona typewriter sat on a small table facing a front window. A chair with a cushion on it was pushed tight under the table. A kitchen was off to my right. A plate with a half-eaten sandwich. A partially full glass of what might have been iced tea. A chair lay backward on the floor.

I sulked back out to the porch and made one of the hardest phone calls I'd ever made.

"I lost your witness," I said when John Wayne answered. My voice was shaky, my heart thumping. I took a deep breath, stepped off the porch, and paced the salty land, the sand shifting under my feet.

"Are you sure?"

"No. But I know."

"Don't blame yourself." It took a big man to say that. "How did it happen?"

I explained my previous visit and how I'd slipped and told Evan where the warehouse was.

"Why did he care about the warehouse?"

"Because that is where I met Rachel. Evan and Rachel are in love. He went looking for her."

"Evan? Rachel?"

"Walker Percy is my nephew, Evan Brackett."

Pause.

"I see." The tone of forgiveness was gone. "And Rachel?"

I gave him the story of the woman thrusting a note in my hand and concluded with revealing that she was apparently Vargo's daughter, and Vargo had wanted Evan in Mexico to tutor her, and she and Evan had a Shakespearean love affair, and that blew everyone's plan to hell. As I spoke, I realized Evan's love for Rachel might have saved his life. Vargo's original intent might have been to bury him after the final English class.

"It's all conjecture," he said. "We'll send a team to Walker's—Evan's—cottage. Do not disturb or take anything. I need you there until they arrive. Less than an hour."

"I understand."

We disconnected. I slogged back inside. I wrapped my hands in a dishtowel, searched the cottage, but found nothing of interest. There were no pictures of family—that would be taboo in the witness protection program. I took a seat at his desk overlooking the front porch and bay. It did seem as fine a spot as any to collect one's thoughts and try to put them into words. A small blue wood box sat on the floor next to the desk. Uneven edges. Caster wheels. Hinges, already suffering from the proximity to salt water. I lifted the lid.

Inside was a thick stack of papers with a rubber band around them. The first page read:

The greatest desire we have is not to want someone, but to have someone want us.

The rest of the pages were empty. Why rubber band blank pages? I stuck them back in the blue chest.

They came ten minutes later as I was feeding the duck. Two career men who had little interest in me and made Patty nervous. They took pictures. Dusted for prints. They boxed all Evan's personal items, including his typewriter. After a half hour, the taller of the two came out to the porch where I sat in the same seat I had sat in when talking with Evan.

"You're free to go."

"Any clues?"

"You're free to go."

I moped off to my truck. The duck followed me.

"Buzz off."

I opened my door, got in, and slammed it shut.

The duck stood on the ground, looking up at me. I fired up the engine and rolled down the window.

It was a quiet duck. A studious duck. A duck that did not back down from my challenging gaze. When you think about it—and I did—that is much to admire in a duck.

Oh, for Pete's sake.

I climbed out of the truck and opened the back door.

"All right, Patty. Let's see if you got it in you."

Patty took two flaps with its wings and landed in the back seat. The heck? Did this duck think it was a dog? Had Evan taken it places? I had spoken to the duck to alleviate my guilt. Now I had a duck in my back seat. I slammed the door shut and headed home.

BUT I DIDN'T GO HOME. I COULDN'T GO HOME.

I did a U-turn and drove over the causeway. After a few hard lefts designed to put me closer to the water, I located the marina across the bay from Evan's cottage. I wanted to talk to anyone who might be familiar with Evan—although they would know him as Walker. He hadn't been in the cottage long, but certainly he'd ventured out and met a few people. But most of all, I didn't want to leave Evan's home. Such an act was an admittance of defeat.

Boat rentals and bait were handled at a shack by the water. I told the sun-crinkled-faced man behind the counter that my friend who lived across the bay was missing. Shrouded by mangroves and palm trees, the cottage was not visible in any detail.

"You talkin' about Walker?" He kept his eyes locked on his computer screen on the high desk used to conduct business.

"You know him?"

"I do."

I waited for more, but he'd answered my question.

"He's missing," I said.

"You said that."

"I was supposed to have breakfast with him, and he's not home. That's not like him."

"You call him?"

"He doesn't have a phone."

The man looked up from his screen, meeting my eyes for

the first time. "No. He don't. What did you say your name was again?"

I gave him my name and asked when was the last time he saw Walker.

"'Bout three days ago."

"Did you see anything suspicious this morning or yesterday?"

"Nope."

"Is there anyone else I should be talking to?"

"Nope."

"Do you have a problem with me?"

He took his glasses off. They fell around his neck, tied together by a fish line.

"You don't look like no friend of Walker's."

"What does a friend of Walker's look like?"

"He didn't have any. Until yesterday."

"Who else dropped by?"

"Why should I trust you?"

"A man's got to choose."

"I can remain neutral. Didn't the Swiss do that during the second war?"

"Both wars. No invaders wanted to attack a mountainous country."

"So why'd we go to Afghanistan?"

"We're talking about helping a man you know. A man who may be in trouble. A man I care deeply about."

"Pretty good friend, huh?"

"He's my nephew. The other man who came looking for him? He is not a pleasant man."

"So you say."

"There are no mountains in Florida. You need to choose."

He sucked in his left cheek between his teeth.

"You and Walker do look like kin. Guy yesterday also said he was a friend of Walker's, but he didn't look like no friend to nobody."

"Describe him."

"Hair greased over his ears. A coiled-snake smile that put you on edge. Wanted to know if some guy I never heard of lived around here. I told him how the hell would I know someone I don't know. You see?"

"Did he give you a name of the man he was looking for?"

"I don't remember it. Barn something?"

"Last name or first?"

"Last."

"Brackett?"

"That's it. Ethen—maybe Eli, one of those names. I told him I didn't know anyone by that name. He asked who lived in the cottage across the bay. I said that was Walker's place." He paused a beat. "Why do you wanna know all this? Walker's a nice young man. Why's he so popular all of a sudden?"

"The dark-haired man. Tell me more."

"Just told you all I know and all I ever want to know 'bout him."

"Did you see Walker the day the man was here?"

"No, sir."

"Did you see any commotion at Walker's place?"

He swung his head.

"What's your name?"

"Alan Powell. But everyone calls me Deuce."

"Deuce?"

"We're not going there."

"Thanks for your time, Deuce."

I took a few steps toward the door but then turned around.

"Did Walker ever mention a girl by the name of Rachel?"

"Matter of fact, he did. We was talkin' once, reminiscing, you know? He said he had a girl by that name, but he lost her. I told him that I let a girl slip away a long time ago, and he'd get over her."

"Did that help him any?"

"Hell, no. I was lyin', and he knew it. I never could tell a lie, good or bad."

18

I checked my dark attitude at the door. I had no desire to infect my family with my plague mood.

"Honey," I said, entering my house later that afternoon. "I got us a pet duck."

Kathleen came out our bedroom. Her bright face, always anticipating the next moment, elevated me off the floor.

"Hot dog! I'm hoping for another child. And you waddle home with a duck?"

"We do what we can."

"You're serious."

"I never kid about ducks."

She blew her breath out. "No, you do not. All right, Daffy, let's hear it."

"Her name's Patty. Would you like to meet her?"

"Boy, would I."

She trailed me to the front door. I opened the door, and Patty stood gazing up at us. Was I mistaken, or was there a hint of hurt in her eyes for not being allowed in the house?

Kathleen lowered herself to the ground. The duck took a step back.

"Hey, there, pretty girl," Kathleen said. "Are you hungry? What does she eat?"

"Let's find out."

I went into the house and returned with a slice of bread and Joy tucked under my arm. Upon seeing the new visitor, Joy flapped her arms and legs with glee. Kathleen tossed a few crumbs on the ground. The duck pecked at them.

"Let's take her around the back," Kathleen said. "We'll see if Hadley Three lets her be."

"I planned to take her to Harbor House."

"Patty will have two homes. Let's go, girl."

Patty waddled behind as Kathleen Hansel-and-Greteled bread crumbs along the way. Hadley III slithered out from underneath a hibiscus bush. I never know where the cat is. I suspect the cat always knows where I am.

Either this would work or not. Patty eyed Hadley III. I passed Joy to Kathleen and picked up the cat. She was not fond of being held. Kathleen placed the rest of the bread on the ground next to Joy.

Patty took two steps and started pecking at the crumbs. I put Hadley III down. The duck stopped eating. The cat cautiously approached the duck. Patty took a step back. The cat sniffed Patty, the bread crumbs, and then sauntered away with that superior attitude inherent in all cats. Joy quacked in what I'm pretty sure was Spanish.

On the drive away from Evan's cottage, I had blood on my mind. Revenge. Now, it was Robert Browning: "God's in his Heaven; All's right with the world."

. . .

THAT EVENING WE SETTLED IN OUR ASSIGNED SEATS in the screened porch under the ceiling fan. A high-octane moon sparkled the windswept bay. Kathleen had made a bed for Patty next to the screen door while I put Joy—who had inexplicably decided to go gently into that good night —to bed.

Kathleen had gone to the college soon after I'd brought Patty home. We hadn't had time to talk. She took a sip of red wine and asked me about my day. I insisted she go first. As cars climbed the bridge on the far side of the bay, as a sailboat drifted by trailing laughter, as the underbellies of clouds flamed fall colors, and as dolphins broke the surface for air, the world closed down, and Kathleen opened up. She recounted her hours since the last time we had touched. But she did not mention where she went. What she taught. What she said or what she heard.

"I worried that Joy will be missing something by not having siblings. I know we talked about it, but we have no direction. And I have a student who is shy, but she writes impressively. Oh, that's just terrible. She writes like a winter storm and we've gotten quite close. On top of that, I think we should pay Bonita more. But what really happened today is I found myself in the middle of a lecture staring out a window, and I wanted to fly through that window. I wanted to fly out so bad and just fly and fly."

It was a windy dissertation for her. It didn't escape me that she'd said *siblings* and not *sibling*.

"Where did you want to fly to, Wendy?"

"Paradise. Where else is there?"

"It will have to be a private adoption," I said, homing in on what I thought was the nucleus of her rambling. "There's no way to put that on the calendar."

Public adoption agencies locked themselves in fallout shelters when I rapped on their door, my radioactive resume having preceded my visit.

"It worked out with Joy," Kathleen said.

"That was coincidental."

That brought a thud of silence.

I saw our daughter as blind luck—being in the right place at the right time. But I dared not breathe that to Kathleen. She, like Morgan, believed she could dream her life into existence. That she could bestride the world with her will, imagining all we are into being. It had worked once. When Anna Vargas's daughter, Kimberly, decided to give up her child.

Anna Vargas had been Elizabeth Walker's housemaid and friend. Elizabeth Walker had been a former lover of my friend Andrew Keller. Keller had wanted me to find Elizabeth. It's a tragic story, and I'll tell you a little bit more later. In getting to know Elizabeth, we'd become friends with Anna. We were lucky. Kathleen is unable to get pregnant, and our daughter was born from Andrew and Elizabeth's misfortune. Kathleen saw the drama as one long preordained Greek play. The future events of our lives lined up, waiting for the director's cue. I saw randomness. We both accepted that the other might be right. (I might have pretended a little.) I will concede this: Who is to say that breathing the fumes of dreams won't take you further than pedaling the bicycle of logic?

"We are made to touch others," Kathleen said. She spoke as if, halfway through her thoughts, she'd decided to go public with them. "To create families. You rarely see a dolphin surface by itself. Think how large the water is and yet how close they are to each other. They touch each other. Rub each other. *We* are made to rub each other."

"No argument here."

"You're not listening."

"I am."

"Life's an open door. Doors. Let's walk through them."

"No."

"No?"

"Let's run."

"Run," she said. "Dash. Vault. Dance. You can tell me more about Patty now. I know she's just the tip of the iceberg."

"What makes you say that?"

"You always ask me first how my day was when you've had an exceptionally poor one."

I dumped on her. I'd have to tell Morgan as well, as I could no longer keep it from him.

"It's not your fault," she said, after I'd rushed through the disastrous and distasteful conclusion of the story.

"Can't blame the duck."

She stood. "Come here."

I stood, and she draped her arms around my neck, pressing her body into mine. I wanted to place a child in her hand like a rose starting to bloom. What good was I if I couldn't do that?

"I'm proud of you," she said.

"For what?"

"Bringing Patty home."

"It's killing you, isn't it? The urge for another child. That's why you carpet-bombed the Mahaffey with profanity. You wore high heels so you could conveniently blame them. You want to fly because when we fly, we do the impossible."

"Think you figured me out?"

"No, ma'am."

"Let's carve our initials in the ruins. Let 'em know we were here. And as for Evan?"

"Yes?"

"'Honey, I got us a pet duck?' Pitiful. Ditch the Barney attitude. Saddle up and find Angel."

As it turned out, Angel found me.

19

RACHEL

Eyes wide open

Rachel's mother would bestow a special gift upon her daughter. This unwrappable present would grant Rachel the means, the coping mechanism, to survive the unpardonable sin of her father.

Sophia Estrada was revered by all. When around children, she had the heart of a third-grade teacher. With the elderly, she had the patience of a saint, granting their wish to savor and extend the moment, no matter how trivial the subject or how rushed her time. For the poor, she gave shelter and food, for she knew the inadequacy, the shortcomings of the heart, when the days were lengthened by empty stomachs. Cold nights. Ragged clothes worn with shattered dignity.

All that is good. Admirable. But those traits were not the gift from her mother that would propel Rachel through her darkest hour, when she learned the inalterable truth about her father. That life-ring gift arrived over a period of three weeks. Three Sundays, to be exact.

The first Sunday.

The priest commanded the parishioners to bow their heads. Rachel complied without thought. But after squeezing her eyes shut, she surprised herself. She popped them open. She stared at the floor. Why now? Was she smitten with curiosity? Had she forgotten to check her rebel streak of youth at the door? Or was it just time?

She felt a giddy sense of pleasure, staring at the stone floor. She and the floor shared a secret. She closed her eyes. No need to tempt fate.

The second Sunday.

She not only opened her eyes, but she also raised her head, fully aware that it might be severed by the quick and just sword of the Lord. It was not. She peered around. And there, beside her—lo and behold—stood her mother. Head held high. Eyes wide open. As the priest implored God for forgiveness and groveled for compassion, mother and daughter locked eyes. They were the only two people in the church with their heads up.

Rachel snapped her eyes shut. She lowered her head.

What is my mother doing? Certainly, her mother had a reason not to obey the priest. Maybe she had a cold and found it hard to breathe with her head down. But she knew her mother didn't have a cold.

The third Sunday.

Rachel did not look away from her mother. Mother and daughter stood like two magnificent white egrets. Chins up. Shoulders back. Eyes alert while those around them bowed, a defeated and ashamed assembly.

Sophia brought her finger up to her lips. Rachel saw the

smile on the other side of her mother's finger. The bonfire in her mother's eyes.

THE FOLLOWING DAY, SOPHIA took Rachel shopping in the city. They'd been before, but now daughter was nearly as tall as mother. When they strode together, the air bristled. All men lusted for them, for that is what men do. All women envied them, for that is what women do, although they pretend not to, just as men pretend not to lust.

They were sitting at an outdoor café under an umbrella, the sun pouring light around them. Their two bodyguards sat four tables away. They'd been discussing the Sunday meal that Emilia had served.

"Why do you keep your eyes open at church during the prayer?" Rachel blurted out.

She'd caught her mother in mid-chew. Sophia never talked with food in her mouth.

When finished, Sophia lowered her fork. "Why do you?" she said. That caught Rachel off guard. Her mother was not one to engage the Socratic method. That was a game Rachel played with her father. Rachel answered without much thought, thinking that the quicker the answer, the more truthful it would be.

"I like seeing the bowed heads. The submission."

A hint of disappointment clouded Sophia's face. "But why?" she asked, granting Rachel another chance.

Rachel realized the answer she'd given was a feeling and not an explanation. But she wasn't going to let her mother steer the conversation. Sophia admired that trait in her daughter, although she never got the chance to tell her that.

Rachel took a patient sip of Chablis. She'd been drinking wine with meals since age ten.

"I think you actually hold your head higher during the prayer," Rachel said, pointedly ignoring her mother's question.

"Do you, now?" her mother teased her. "And you?"

"I think my head just seems higher because those around me are bowed."

"And how does that make you feel?"

"Superior, but then I feel bad for that."

Rachel realized she'd answered her mother's question.

"You should never feel superior to anyone," Sophia said.

"Not superior."

"Then don't use that word."

"A better understanding?"

"All those books and that is the best you can do?"

"Affirmation."

Her mother's face brightened. "And what are you affirming?"

"That God created us in his image, so why bow to him? Why ask his help? His forgiveness? Why pretend we've sinned, for if we are in his image, has he, too, not sinned? And why a 'he'?"

"That's a lot of questions."

Rachel shrugged. "Maybe that's why people go to church."

"Do you believe?" her mother asked.

Rachel crinkled her nose. "The whole Jesus thing?"

"Yes, Rachel. The whole Jesus thing."

"Mark Twain said religion started when the first con man met the first fool."

"I'm not interested in what Mr. Twain thinks."

"I believe in wisdom."

"Oh, do you now?" Sophia exclaimed to her barely double-digit daughter. "And what is wisdom?"

Good question, Mom. Wisdom was something she'd been tossing in her mind ever since she'd read T. E. Lawrence's *Seven Pillars of Wisdom,* although she found the title more promising than the content.

"I think," she said, tiptoeing on her thoughts, "that we believe what we are taught, like a language. And that, if we are smart—not smart, courageous—we disbelieve and start over from scratch."

"In a declarative sentence, please."

She rallied her confidence. "Wisdom is knowing it is good to honor tradition and the beliefs of your parents, but it is better to challenge them."

"Not bad. And religion?"

"I find church so . . ."

"So what?"

"Theatrical."

"Yes, Rachel," Sophia said eagerly. "You see, don't you? The robes. The music. The cathedral. The leading actors—for we pay them. It is participatory theater. We stand. We bow. We sit. We sing. We murmur our lines. It is the longest-running show."

"And you? Why do you keep your eyes open and your head up when the priest tells us to pray?"

"It makes me stronger than prayer."

"In what way?"

"It reminds me"—she tilted her head at her daughter—"affirms, that *I* choose what to participate in. No one indoctrinates my thoughts. Infests my mind. I am woman. I bow to no one."

"You don't believe either, do you?"

"It's not that simple."

"Yes, it is."

"No. But don't tell your father," Sophia said.

"No," Rachel said in agreement. "Vargo needs God."

Rachel had taken up referring to her father by his first name, a point that irritated her mother.

"And why do you say that?"

"Because of the business he's in."

"There is nothing wrong with the business he's in."

"He sells drugs."

"He provides us with all we need and far more than anyone deserves. The village you live in would have no church or school without your father."

"A school I was not allowed to attend."

"Still, it is a good school."

"Built with drug money."

"And the clothes you wear?"

"They are beautiful. It would not bother me in the least to return them."

Sophia sensed that the topic they were entering was more important than the one they had just concluded. She leaned back in her chair and bought some time by taking a sip of her wine. Sophia nursed her drinks, rarely finishing them, and was particularly gifted at stretching a solitary glass deep into the night.

"No one is forced to buy his product," Sophia said. "He treats his employees well and pays them even better. Do not be so quick to judge him."

"We go to God's house, and guns follow us in the sanctuary."

"And you think this is bad? You read. Look what they are doing in America."

"That's hardly the same thing."

"Wisdom comes with time, Rachel. Don't pretend it's found between the covers of books."

"Perhaps you should view Vargo as if you're in church," Rachel challenged her mother.

"In what manner?"

"Don't close your eyes."

It was a comment Rachel would come to regret, for her mother had an icy attitude toward her the rest of the day, which was two days before she died.

LIKE THREE SUNDAYS, RACHEL WOULD LEARN THE details of her mother's death three times. It would be the final version that would bring her back to sanctuary. To two women. Standing shoulder to shoulder. Heads high. Eyes wide open. Bowing to no one.

20

E rica the Third called the next morning as I was sitting with Joy between my legs in the shade at the end of the dock. I held a picture book of sea animals, patiently pointing at the pictures, pronouncing each name. An easterly sea breeze scrubbed the boatless bay, the crests of the waves blinding bright in the aggressive morning sun. I'd run Patty over to Harbor House earlier—the goofy duck sat in the seat like a golden retriever. Kathleen was at the college, hopefully not launching herself out a window.

"Can we meet for lunch?" Erica said after I shifted Joy to my other arm. My phone buzzed an incoming text.

"When and where?"

"Downtown. Ford's Garage. You know it?"

I told her I did.

"One o'clock." She disconnected.

The text was from Kathleen. We had an appointment with a private adoption attorney. In two days. I replied with a thumbs-up to the woman who had me conveniently stitched into her back pocket.

I closed the book and situated Joy so that she faced the bay. In a few minutes, I'd take her back to the house. It was my hope that the bay would stay with her throughout the day like it does with me, but we cannot teach such things.

AT ONE-FIFTEEN, ERICA THE THIRD SWEPT AROUND A street corner like an F3 tornado. Baggy pants. Loose-fitting shirt. Sunglasses shielding half her face. A floppy hippie hat —I dug the hat.

I stood when she pulled up at my shaded sidewalk table.

"Sorry I'm late," she said.

"Are we incognito today?"

"Maybe."

"Who are we afraid of?"

"Can I at least sit down first?"

I stepped around and pulled back her chair.

"Thank you," she said acidly. She sat down, plopped her hat on an empty chair, and swiped the sunglasses off her face. I scraped my chair back on the raised sidewalk so that I could angle it and cross my legs.

"Edward sits like that," she said as she adjusted her own chair, searching for even ground on the buckled sidewalk. "As if he only has half interest in whomever he is talking with."

"Are you accusing me of sharing your husband's poor traits?"

She gave the question more consideration than it warranted.

"No," she finally declared. "I was speaking of Edward. I don't know you well enough to accuse you of the same rude manners, although it would not surprise me if your talents ran deep in that area as well."

"Is our whole lunch going to be like this?"

"God, I hope not."

A waiter swung by and took our orders. After he left, she asked why I was still interested in TOTA. I gave her a compliance-approved version of my job. That I was a pair of fresh eyes. I did not mention any of the characters. I kept it light and, a little stung by her rudeness reference, sprinkled in my irresistible charm.

Erica reached for her Diet Coke. She took a sip through the straw, her eyes peering up at me. She placed the glass back on the coaster.

"Why do we use straws at restaurants but not at home?" she said.

"It is a mystery."

"And one that puzzles me. What do you think Edward is involved in?"

"You tell me."

"What do you suspect?"

"Why? So you can report back to your husband?"

"Why are you so mean?"

"I thought I was being charming."

"Heaven help us."

"Your husband deals with nasty people."

"Here's a news flash, Prince Charming: I'm not my husband."

"You're living high off his deeds."

"What do you gain by that line? Is it supposed to make me feel bad?"

"We left feelings a long time ago. A young girl died in a

park. She was likely the victim of a drug war that your husband has a hand in."

"You think Edward had anything to do with that? *Edward?*"

"He might not toot the horns, but he's the conductor."

"Oh, that's just pathetic."

Our lunches came, and we salvaged the moment with small talk. My burger dripped with taste, and I did my best not to tear into it. The fries were crisp. Hot. Halfway through the burger, I ordered a beer. It fit snugly into my rule never to drink before five except on days when I do.

Erica laid waste to her grilled chicken salad; she was not a woman to toy with her food. Her eyes flicked up to my plate. It was not the first time.

"Go ahead," I said, for I'd been in similar situations in the past.

"Go ahead, what?"

"You know. Go ahead."

She kept her eyes on mine, dipped her head sharply, and curled the left side of her mouth. It was the type of move that would take a junior high boy to his knees. Thankfully, this knuckle-dragging fourteen-year-old was sitting.

She reached over and snagged a fat french fry. She dragged it through the ketchup on my plate before sticking it in her mouth.

"I like the crispy ones," I said.

"The doughy ones hold more ketchup." She dabbed her mouth with a napkin. "You have it all wrong."

"It's all about the ketchup?"

"No," she laughed. "Edward. You got him all wrong."

"I'm listening."

"We'll keep it simple. Truthful. Start off on a new foot. Agreed?"

"Works for me."

"Edward is—"

"No," I said.

"No?"

"I ask a question. You answer. Then it's your turn."

"Fine."

"Who were you before you were Erica the Third?" I said.

"I don't like you calling me that."

"My apologies, Erica. Tell me about yourself."

"Edward and I—"

"I didn't ask about Edward. I asked about Erica."

"Geez. You share a fry and think you own the girl?"

"You do know we're engaged, right?"

Finally. An unpracticed smile. She looked at me as if she saw someone different. And in that look, I saw someone different in her.

Erica told me how her parents, both doctors, had little time for her, their only child. She was raised by au pairs and shipped to boarding school. "Why have a kid if you outsource her childhood?" She got pregnant at seventeen—courtesy of her father's best friend. Had an abortion—courtesy of the babysitting money earned while sitting for her father's best friend's children—and attended Vanderbilt University. Majored in theater. "I mean, why not? It was *fun*." She married a doctor. A year after her divorce, her therapist said she never loved the man and was trying "to reclaim lost youth by recreating latent role models and succumbing to cultural expectations." She straightened her life out, did regional theater, and met Edward Giancarlo during a fundraiser for the arts.

Her openness surprised me. Maybe she really was there to help. Or perhaps I'm just a sucker for a woman who hides her shapely figure with tent-size clothes and shares fries. Did I mention the hat?

"He majored in theater," she said. "Can you imagine my shock? I had assumed all theater majors were doomed to a life of food stamps, wet dreams, and bohemian parties where we convinced each other that poverty was the mark of a deep soul. And here was this successful businessman—with the emotions of a rock, I would later discover—who knew and loved theater. We married. Hit a rough patch. Did counseling. Straightened things out but then got all crooked again."

She took another sip of her Diet Coke, reached over, and swiped the last fry off my plate. It was a fat one.

"I left that for you," I said.

"I know you did. Thing is? I can't remember the reason I married him, only the reason I almost didn't marry him. I'm pretty sure he still loves me. But he's locked so tight now, I'm not sure he can escape. We don't even talk anymore. We just speak."

She leaned back in her chair. "Wow. That's enough of me. Your turn. Tell me why you think Edward's to blame for a girl's death because you're just wrong, wrong, wrong."

I told her I suspected that Edward Giancarlo never severed those ties he had when he first practiced law. That those people might have circled back into his life, and I didn't know why, but it might have gotten Liana Castillo killed. I did not mention Vargo, for I didn't want that to leak back to Giancarlo. I couldn't divulge any information about my missing nephew.

A gust of wind rounded the corner and puffed up her

bangs. She brought her hand up and raked it through her hair. "Is that it?"

"That's not enough?"

"It seems more personal to you."

"The child who died at the playground. Do you know her name?"

"The swing set girl?" she said.

I nodded.

"No."

"Her name was Liana Castillo. Her father came to me."

"I see. It is personal."

More than you know.

I leaned back in my chair. "Why did you call the meeting, Erica?"

She dipped her head. "If you'll excuse me, powder time."

She stood and walked inside the restaurant. I settled the bill with the waiter and repositioned my chair, as creeping sunlight had found me. An obese woman walked down the sidewalk with two small children. Her weight shifted with each step as if her feet were too small for her ballast. Her outfit didn't match, but both children, a boy and a girl, were cut from a catalog.

Erica reclaimed her seat, again fidgeting with her chair.

"This sidewalk needs a little attention," I said, standing up.

"I'm fine."

But I was already behind her, helping her scoot her chair forward. As I peered over her shoulder, her loose shirt gaped open.

"Stand," I said.

"What?"

"Your chair's bad. I'll switch it out."

"I think it's—"

"Stand."

"Geez. Whatever." She stood. I stepped into her and ran my groping hand under her untucked shirt.

"What the—?"

I ripped a small microphone off her skin.

"Ouch. That hurt."

"Our engagement's off."

21

I dropped the microphone on the pavement and ground it under the heel of my shoe.

"Hey. You can't do that," Erica spurted out. "It's not what you think. What happened to charming?"

"What happened to sharing fries?" I shot back.

"It's not what you think."

"Is that your only line?"

"Ha, ha. Very funny."

"Who told you to meet me today?"

"Can I at least sit back down?"

We both took our seats. She fluffed out her shirt.

"I'm gathering as much information about my husband as I can, okay? I was asked to see what you knew."

I took a second to process that.

"For your divorce," I said with a slight bounce of my head. I thought it went well with the line.

"The prenuptial is disqualified under certain circumstances. Breaking the law is one of them."

"You have proof that Edward has run afoul of the law?"

"Afoul? Really? I don't know about that, but he's seeing another woman, and that will aid my cause. I confronted him, and he refused to talk about it. Her. Them. Whomever." She paused for a second as if just recalling something. "Lord knows he brought some overweight baggage to the altar. But we were making progress, and he just goes and blows it. Pisses me off."

I couldn't get a handle on Erica. She was one-half actress, one-half spurned lover, one-half loving wife, one-half vindictive spouse, and a solid one-third flirt. That added up to too many people. Maybe that was her problem.

"Who gave you the wire?" I asked.

"A PI firm I hired."

"Try again."

"Guy's name is Salvatore Russo."

"Sally. The man you were searching for at the Mahaffey. But you didn't know what he looked like."

"My lawyer hired him. He told me Sally was the best in the business, but he preferred not to be known by me. Said it was better that way. Some reasoning that it would be better if we were not seen together. He said he would be at the Mahaffey that night to observe Edward. My curiosity got the better of me."

"So, you paraded around asking everyone if they were Sally."

"No. I only asked you."

"And people sitting in the empty theater."

"Oh yeah. Maybe them, too."

"You were pretty stressed that evening. Said someone was turning the screws on your husband."

"Where did you get that from?" Her eyes widened in recognition. "Oh, that's right, I forgot, the stumbling giraffe in the restroom was your wife. What a precious tag team you two make."

"Tell me about the wire."

"I don't feel like talking to you anymore."

"Said the woman who was secretly recording a conversation. Let's hear it."

"Fine." Her shoulders fell. "Sally called and said it was time to meet. When I got to his office, I told him you were snooping around. He wanted to see what you knew. His thinking was that whatever you found might be beneficial in my divorce settlement. You know, piggyback on your efforts."

"You expect a nasty divorce?"

"Is there another version?"

"But you indicated you still love him and he you."

"Those inconvenient truths will be placed aside when we split the assets."

"You're a hell of a dame."

"He's cheating on me. I would *never* do that."

"Like I said, you're a hell of a dame."

She gave an appreciative dip of her head. "Thank you. Want to know the sad thing?"

"Tell me."

"It's going to hurt him more than me. Emotions, I mean. Not money. He just doesn't know it. Men are so stupid."

"No argument here."

We were quiet for a moment, two people adrift at sea. I saw an opening that could benefit us both. Tether our rafts together.

"Let me talk with Sally," I said. "Your premise is good. We may be able to help each other."

"See?" she pleaded. "Is there anything wrong with that?" But I couldn't read the multiple faces of Erica.

"No," I admitted. "But do you see how recording a conversation is not the road to trust?"

She cast her eyes down and brought her hands up to her mouth. I thought she might break, or was it in the script? Top of page eight. Right after "Regardless of taste, always share food off a guy's plate. They fall for that every time."

Her eyes rose to meet mine. "Sally and I are meeting this afternoon. Pioneer Park. Two-thirty. He wanted to know right away what you knew. He also told me he'd found something that would shed new light on everything."

"Any clue as to what he was referring to?"

She swung her head. "He wouldn't say. He wanted to know what you knew first." She paused for a beat. "It's noble of you to care for Liana Padi..."

"Castillo."

"Right. But we both know there's more."

"I'll take that meeting for you."

"Don't push me off."

I reached down and picked up the cracked microphone off the sidewalk. "I'll return his spyware and reimburse him. He'll call you after we meet. You can hear from him whether we have a working agreement or not."

She gave a dismissive tilt of her head. "No. I'm coming with you."

"And risk being seen with me *and* a private eye? You're taking a risk right now. That's why you picked this place. Wore those clothes. You double that if you walk down the sidewalk with me."

She sucked in her cheeks. "Okay."

"Where did you meet him for the wire?"

"Why?"

"In case we don't connect."

She picked up a napkin and retrieved a pen from her purse. She handed me the napkin.

"Here you go. Phone number and address. It's a few blocks from here, second floor. No elevator. It's busted. Thanks for lunch, by the way."

"My pleasure."

"We're a sorry pair if this was pleasure."

We stood. She thrust out her hand, more like an attack than as a conclusionary gesture. We shook, neither of us knowing what to make of the other. A breeze toyed with a loose strand of her hair. It fluffed up her shirt, and I was suddenly lost. In a different place. I wanted to be the wind. I wanted to blow through all the women's hair in all the worlds. Brush their cheeks. Wrap myself around their bodies. Dry their tears and sprinkle their laughs upon the land. Oh, what a good job that wind has.

Her small hand lingered in mine.

"You never told me the reason you almost didn't marry your husband."

"No. I did not."

She withdrew her hand, put on her hat, and trundled away with a purposeless gait. She was swallowed by a group of name-tag-wearing conventioneers invading from the opposite direction. Still, I stared.

22

Pioneer Park is next to the Saint Petersburg Yacht Club and the Municipal Marina. Stately trees shade its benches and crisp sidewalks dissect trimmed grass. Kathleen and I go there after the Saturday Market. We grab a bench, munch on a bratwurst, and nibble a block of cheese we buy from the cheese lady. We share a pastry. ("Just a bite," Kathleen says, and then unapologetically consumes more than half of it. Same with the bratwurst.) I rock Joy's stroller with my foot while Kathleen frets every time a finger of sun reaches down and anoints our daughter's Raphael face.

I'd gotten a description of Sally Russo before I left Erica.

"Short—I don't mean short-short, but not tall. A few too many pounds. Curly hair, cherub cheeks. More Friar Tuck than Magnum, PI. Got it?"

As I entered the park, a woman paraded her dog in my direction. A biblically bearded man reclined on a checkered blanket, reading a book, a pillow supporting his head. An athletic man sat on a bench on the south end. Military hair. Tight jeans. He wasn't my Friar Tuck. Across the park, another man leaned against a tree, smoking a cigarette. He, too, was in jeans and a short-sleeve T-shirt, bulged by his muscular arms.

Both men noticed me. They did not stare.

I kept my head down and strolled across the street into Demens Landing Park. I loitered around the trees on the western edge so that I could observe Pioneer Park.

It was 2:35 when I first crossed the park. At 3:00, the man on the bench stood and strolled over to the man leaning against the tree. They appeared to exchange words. The smoker took out his phone and made a call. A minute later, they climbed into a red two-door sports car and gunned away.

The address Erica had given me was four blocks north. As I trekked under the scalding sun, I couldn't think of a single good reason hired muscle would be in Pioneer Park at the time Sally and Erica were scheduled to meet.

Sally's office was in a former apartment building that had been converted to office space. A directory was inside the door. "S. Russo and Assoc." was listed as 2B. The elevator, as Erica had indicated, was roped off with yellow tape. I took the wood stairs, the temperature rising with each step. At the top of the stairs, a cramped hall led past other offices. Donna Novak Realty. Tompkin's Printing. And finally, S. Russo and Assoc. I doubted anyone was in any of the offices.

I knocked, waited, and knocked again.

The door was unlocked. I cracked it open.

"Hello. Anyone home? Sally?"

The dissonant tone of an air conditioner hummed from inside. I pushed the door a little farther and stepped into death.

Salvatore Russo lay on the floor. Blood soaked his chest.

It puddled around his body. His face was swollen and bruised. His left ear was missing. Like Van Gogh.

Next time, they get their people back in a box. Amazon Prime. A head. An ear.

I dropped to my knees and checked his pulse. None. It appeared he'd been shot in the chest, possibly more than once. Something about him seemed familiar—then it hit me. Sally was the frumpy man I'd observed at the Mahaffey loading his plate with food. I'd been judgmental and felt bad.

I grabbed a paper tissue from a box, closed the door, and flipped the AC unit off. I needed to be able to hear if anyone approached.

Papers and folders were strewn across the planked floor. There was one steel file cabinet as wide as it was high, its drawers open and largely empty. There was no computer, and I assumed that whoever killed him had taken it. But Sally didn't strike me as a computer guy. His office was decorated with black-and-white pictures of Florida and gritty street scenes. A collection of old cameras sat on a dusty shelf. I nudged open what I assumed to be a closet door. It had been converted to a darkroom—Sally liked to develop his own photographs. I wondered how much time he spent PI-ing versus pursuing his apparent love of photography.

The darkroom held a pair of latex gloves. They would be worn so that the chemicals in the developing tray didn't irritate your hands. I stretched them on and methodically started sorting through his lone file cabinet and desk. Papers, folders, and old photography magazines littered the floor. *Art and Photography*. *Modern Photography*. Many of them in like-new condition and dated from the early 1950s to the early 1970s. A monthly calendar lay under a clipping about TOTA Technologies. On today's date, he'd entered 2:30, Pioneer Park.

Did whoever kill him take information that indicated he was working for Erica Giancarlo? Or did his killers go to Pioneer Park not knowing who to expect?

After a fruitless search, I sat on the desk chair. Sally's eyes stared at the ceiling, wide apertures to a world he could no longer capture. It had been a voyeuristic life, a lonely Raymond Chandler PI, hiding behind his camera. While digging for dirt on Giancarlo to strengthen Erica's divorce case, he'd stepped on a land mine. It had cost him his life.

"Talk to me, Sally," I said. "Talk to me, man."

A pair of glasses were against the wall, as if someone had slapped them off his face. I put them in my pocket. I don't know why I did that. I picked up a Kodak Retina Reflex from the dusty shelf where the old cameras rested, although there was no dust around it. 1950s? 60s? A leather case was next to the camera. The Kodak was the only camera poised for active duty.

I placed the camera in the case, stuffed the gloves in my pocket, and peeked out the door. I wiped the door knob with my shirttail and then scuttled down the stairs. I walked at a leisurely pace toward my truck, the camera case over my shoulder.

I punched my phone.

"Talk to me," Garrett said. The man has yet to be accused of a bubbling personality.

"Angel's still in town."

"On my way."

23

I called in Sally Russo's death from a burner phone. I debated telling Detective Rambler but didn't want the hassle. The endless questioning. I knew I would eventually do the right thing—tell Rambler—so why not just do it to start with?

Marcus Knowles had indicated that Jay Parini, the other TOTA employee who was at the warehouse the night of the exchange, might have seen or heard different things than he had. Parini, who had escaped to the Keys for a few days after his harrowing experience, was due home yesterday. After twenty minutes of phone tag, he said he'd be happy to talk to me and that I could find him at a store, High Tide Cannabis and Art, that he and his wife owned.

On the way to the store, I dropped by a CVS to get the film developed. The camera bag had two undeveloped rolls of film in a compartment. Judging from what I'd seen in Sally's office, I'd receive black-and-white prints of buildings and street scenes.

High Tide Cannabis and Art was tucked into the middle

of Corey Avenue in Saint Pete Beach. There wasn't much cannabis paraphernalia. "But that brings the traffic in," Jay said after I introduced myself. The store was tastefully crammed with dish towels, glassware, wall art, and stationary. It was the type of store Kathleen and I would wander into until, bored, I would skedaddle across the street and grab a beer while Kathleen spent an unholy amount of time in the place. I picked up a dish towel—you can never have enough clean ones—when a short, zesty woman of an unguessable age approached me.

"You like that?" She reminded me of an Easter bunny. She was happy, springy on her feet, and her hair a child's failed attempt to color an egg.

"Cheryl," Jay Parini said, "this is Mr. Travis. Jake, my creative muse, Cheryl."

"Thank you for saving my husband's life. If things had gone south that night, I'd be looking for part-time help, and Christ on a bike, it's hell getting good help." She smiled as she spoke, brightening the world with her audible happiness. "I understand you're curious about Jay's last trip to Russia."

"Routine questions."

"I don't know where you flew in from, but there is nothing routine here on Mother Earth.Give him the spiel, honey. I've got some ordering to do. Back in a lickety-split." She hopped off to a back room separated from the main store by a curtain with a picture of a crowded beach bar on it.

While the back half of my mind chastised me for not calling Rambler and identifying myself as the person who found Sally Russo, Jay gave me the same information that Marcus Knowles had provided. "I heard nothing, saw noth-

ing, touched nothing. You know, like those three monkeys."
Jay had decided before the trip to Russia that it would be his
last. He'd already put in his notice to leave TOTA, having
decided to work full time at the store. He and Cheryl had
been contemplating the move for over a year.

"We decided I'd make the leap halfway into our second
bottle on a Sunday afternoon. Come Monday morning,
when your mind's focused on health care, the idea had lost
its luster. Dream drunk but act sober, right? Well, screw that.
I was never cut out for the corporate world. It was a lonely
place for me. As corny as it sounds"—he swept his hand
through the air—"I like this stuff. We're open fifty-two hours
a week, so I can't say it's a reduction in hours, but it's where I
belong."

Cheryl bounced back through the curtain.

"I'll take this set," I said, handing her the dish towel. "I
like your store. I'll bring my wife by. She's a more gifted
shopper than me."

"You plan to see Marcus again?" she asked.

"Not at this time."

"Shame. If you were, I was going to have you take him
the dish towels he designed. No bother, I'll give him a call.
Tell me what you think of them."

She reached under the counter and brought up a dish
towel of a bull with outlandish brass balls. It read "Now,
that's what I'm talking about."

"Ferdinand the bull," I said.

"Well, butter my butt and call me a biscuit—you know
Ferdinand? I didn't show it to the other guy. He didn't buy
anything or say he'd be back with his wife."

"Other guy?"

"That TOTA sent around to check on us."

I hadn't told her TOTA sent me but let it slide.

"Tell me about the other man."

Cheryl flashed her bunny eyes to Jay.

"He dropped in two days ago," he said. "Same type of questions you've been asking."

"And he said he was from TOTA?" I asked.

Jay took that. "Not really. Guess we just inferred he was, like Cheryl did with you. He told us not to mention that he came by."

"But you just did."

Cheryl cut in. "You being the second one in a few days aroused our interest. We trust you. The other man? Not so much. Besides, we're worried, and we gotta confide in someone."

"Confide what?"

Cheryl bit her lip. "Look at us. We're just two kids in grown-up bodies. I'm quirky, and Jay, heavens to Murgatroyd, if you got to know him, is quirkier."

"I like quirky."

She curtsied. "Thank you."

"Tell me about the other man," I said to whoever wished to field the question.

"He said he wanted to know about my interactions with Edward Giancarlo," Jay said. "But Mr. Giancarlo was nothing but good to me."

"What was his name?"

"Salvatore Russo. Said to call him Sally. Nice guy. A little . . . unkempt. Like I said, he popped some harmless questions and was gone. Would have thought nothing about it if you hadn't trailed after him." He shrugged. "That's about it."

The three of us stood there, no one making a move. A song I'd not heard in a long time played on floor speakers.

Recalling what Marcus had told me about the night I exchanged the money for him and Jay, I backtracked.

"Marcus informed me that he was in the little boys' room a lot," I said, realizing I should not have fallen for Jay's botched monkey defense. "Maybe you didn't see evil, hear evil, or speak evil. But you heard more than he did."

"Go ahead, babe. Tell him."

Jay Parini was a man more comfortable with following than leading. A man who, knowing himself, avoided any instance that might require courage. But when called upon, he would step into a role that did not fit him.

"Sure. Fine. Giancarlo was there that night," Jay said, gaining confidence as he spoke. "Talking to Angel. Ten minutes or so before you came. By the time they discovered a door was open and I was within earshot, it was time for the exchange. They didn't have time to question if we'd heard anything."

"You don't find that significant?"

"I got an old-fashioned defined benefit plan, man. I don't want to jeopardize that."

"That's protected by law."

"So was the land they moved the Native Americans to the first five times they relocated them."

"Tell me what you heard."

"Giancarlo was arguing with Angel, telling him he had no right, but what he had no right to, I haven't a clue. I think Giancarlo left. A door slammed, and I didn't hear him again. What was he even doing there? I'm trying to pretend none of this happened. That's why I didn't say anything. And I'd appreciate it if this stays between us."

"You have my word. What else? Even if it seemed inconsequential."

"I just got two out of three words, you know? Angel and some woman went at it after Giancarlo left. She kept defending a man named Vargo."

"Tell me about the woman."

"Not much to tell. A voice I hadn't heard before. She kept insisting that Vargo had things under control. That's it, man. Wish I could help you more. I'm not sure what it's all about. I am sure I don't want to know."

"Did the woman have a name?"

"Never heard one."

"Rachel?"

He shook his head. "Means nothing to me."

"Did you ever tell Marcus this?"

"No. I never mentioned it to him. I mean, I'll tell him, but I just haven't had the chance. He went in the hospital, and Cheryl and I decided we needed a beer at Sloppy Joe's. I thought of picking up the phone—probably should have—and letting him know. But we're both out of TOTA now, and, well, I just haven't gotten around to it."

"Were there any words that didn't make sense? Anything you might have dismissed?"

Jay scrunched his face. "Don't think so."

"Did you ever hear the name Evan Brackett?"

Jay Parini bobbed his head a few times. "Oh yeah. Evan Somebody. Sorry, I forgot about that. No reference point, so I didn't pay much attention. But that dude? Whoever he is, he's in the thick of it. They batted that name around pretty good."

24

My inexcusable decision not to call Rambler had camped out in my mind the entire time I was in High Tide Cannabis and Art, muddling my ability to concentrate. I took a high-top outdoor table at the Chill Restaurant and Bar, ordered a beer, canceled it, ordered it again, and punched Rambler's number.

This came with the first sip: I chastised myself for screwing up so badly with Evan, wondered if Rachel was in town, tried to imagine how Cheryl got her splay of hair to look so attractive, realized another day had slipped away without taking my daughter on a kayak, worried if Kathleen really believed that magic ruled our lives, agonized if Manuel Castillo was still leaking tears, and envisioned my sister's reaction when I told her I found her son and then lost him—maybe for good.

Made me a little wary of the rest of the beer.

Rambler approached me and pulled up a chair. The police station was three blocks away.

"It's not five yet." He repositioned the chair in the shade.

"Will be by the end of the beer."

He couldn't hide his smile. "That's one way of looking at it."

"I got a body for you."

He puffed his breath out. "Why does that not surprise me?"

"Just a coincidence." But my comment sounded so lame, I wanted to redact it.

"Just like last time." He dipped his head at my mug. "How is that?"

"World's best."

"You've sampled them all?"

"I have."

"Really?"

"Would I lie to you?"

"In a heartbeat."

"But for a good cause."

I signaled the waiter and asked for a beer for "my friend."

Rambler's gaze settled on the other side of the street at Serenity Hair Salon.

"I didn't know that hair salon was even there. They just open?"

"No. It's where I go, actually."

He arched his eyebrows. "You go there?"

"They take appointments, and I don't do waiting. She does a good job."

"She?"

"Ask for Valerie."

"I'll give Val a try. My barber is walk in. I used to enjoy the talk while I waited, but no more. It just reminds me how stupid people are. Let's hear it."

I spilled everything about Erica Giancarlo and Salvatore

Russo. He interrupted a few times to clarify specific points. I didn't tell him I took the camera. Nor did I divulge that Walker Percy was missing, and certainly not that Percy was really my nephew, Evan Brackett. I might have left a few other things out as well, my guilt for not telling him sooner lifting like a sea fog at noon.

When I'd finished, he stood, took out his phone, and made a call while pacing the sidewalk.

"Does any of this mean anything to you?" I said when he reclaimed his seat.

"Absolutely. It tells me you have a conscience, but not one deep enough to naturally do the right thing. That, in turn, tells me you are still holding back. You're a real artist at that."

"Thank you."

"It wasn't a compliment."

I raised my mug. "I didn't mislead you on this."

"Twenty-seven years. This is my first beer on the clock."

"Do I get credit?"

"No. My wife does."

"How so?"

"She left me. We split."

"I'm sorry to hear that."

"I don't blame her. I'm not much company. She was for me, but I wasn't for her."

"Any chance of reconciliation?"

"Sure. If I quit my job. Change sex."

"Ouch. Either on the table?"

"Not at the moment. Did you meet with Manuel Castillo?"

"I did."

"And?"

"Now he's cracked both our hearts."

"Remember I told you we found a rented crane? The guy who rented it paid cash. The trail went dead there."

"I didn't think there was an investigation."

"My partner and I are moonlighting."

"Middle of the day," I pointed out. "There's got to be witnesses."

"The neighbors must be cousins of yours. You know, the we'll-only-come-forth-if-we-feel-guilty type."

"Do you want me to make a statement?"

He rubbed his eyes.

"No. We're good. We'll need to talk to Erica Giancarlo."

"What if you can't trace Sally back to her?"

"We will, even if I use you as an anonymous tip. Anonymous—how do you feel about that?"

"I had greater aspirations."

"Don't we all."

"Let me talk to her first. Let her know you're coming."

"Why?"

"She feels cornered, backed to a wall. If she knows you're going to question her, you'll have a better chance of getting the truth from her."

He gave that a second. I wasn't sure I believed what I'd just said but felt I should be the one to tell Erica. "I'm too tired to argue. Twenty-four hours." He checked his watch, then nodded across the street. "It's late. Wonder if they can take me now."

"Give them a try," I said. "You could use a little pampering."

"Like what you've been doing to alleviate your guilt for not telling me sooner?"

"Did it work?"

He coughed. "Damn red tide. It seems farther inland this time." He took a gulp of beer. He set the bottle back on the table and stared at it as he was adrift in the world. "When I took this job? I set out to change the world. Now I'm thinking if I can leave the room with a little dignity, I just might call it a day."

He stood and strolled across the shadowless street to the hair salon. A warrior without a cause. A man without a woman.

25

It was eleven o'clock the next morning. Another rapturously brilliant day in which I didn't know where Evan was. Sleep, like a cat batting a mouse, had teased me all night. During my run, my legs felt heavy. Drugged.

Garrett and I wanted to look around the inside of the warehouse where the exchange with Angel had taken place. Our thesis was that the cartel—possibly Angel—had kidnapped Evan. I didn't think I'd been followed to his cottage, but once Stupid told Evan that Rachel was in town, Evan went searching for her. He was likely caught on a camera.

I described Evan Brackett to the security guard and asked if anyone fitting that description had approached the warehouse.

"Not that I know. But this is a three-shift job," he said. "So, what? A one-in-three chance it might be me? I'm six a.m. to two."

His magnificent nose reminded me of the polished bow of a wooden Chris-Craft. He was incapable, or unwilling, to engage in eye contact and looked past me when he talked.

I asked him if the other guards saw anyone. He claimed they had not. I told him I'd like to peek inside. That my partner and I were the ones who saved the men's lives a week ago.

"I heard about that. But, sorry. I got my orders. No one in."

I offered a C-note. He was unimpressed, forcing me to proffer every bill in my wallet. Three hundred and forty-one dollars. A little steep, I thought, for run-of-the-mill bribery.

"What is it you gentlemen are looking for again?" He stuffed the bills into his pants pocket.

"Lost my car keys," I said.

"Sure. Yeah. I understand. Anything over ten minutes will raise concerns if anyone checks the tape. But seeing as how you were the guys that saved them men a while back, I reckon I can let you take a peek."

"Reckon we appreciate your time."

"No problemo."

I headed into the warehouse, and Garrett stayed behind, explaining to the man with the magnificent nose that we did not trust him and that Garrett would stay with him while he tripped the main box.

Ten minutes later, I was on my way out of the warehouse with nothing to show for my effort.

"Find anything?" the guard asked.

"No."

"I was just telling your mute friend here that I did twenty-five with Tampa PD. A quarter of a century rolling with slime is enough, let me tell you."

I stepped into the man.

"What's your name?"

"What's it to you, pal?"

"That's a long name."

"Darron."

"I need your help, Darron. Tell us about the young man I described to you. Who came a few days ago. I don't care whose shift it was."

He let out a nervous laugh and took a step back. "Easy, guys. We're cool here. Okay? I just didn't know how legit you were, you know? Young man you was asking about? Sure, yeah, he showed up early one evening. Said he helped wire the place. Said he was a security expert and wanted to check something.

"Hector—it was his shift—said this guy knew all about the system, so he figured he was legit. Said the guy spent twenty minutes scouring the place. Had some questions about whether some woman had been here and then split."

"Was there a woman here?"

"No."

"Tell me about when they brought him back and kept him inside."

"Don't know where you got that from. Word was that when they ran the tape, someone recognized your friend. They wanted to know what he said, why he was here, shit like that. Questioned us pretty hard."

"What usually happens here?"

"Trucks in and out at night."

"What kind of trucks?"

"The kind with wheels."

"Drugs?"

"Who cares?"

"After twenty-five years, one would think you would."

"Piss off."

"You ever see a man with horse teeth? Black hair greased over his ears? Goes by Angel."

Fear fluttered his eyes.

"I've seen him a few times, but he don't talk to us."

"Was there a woman here as well?"

"I already answered that."

"The man who came here? He's my nephew. I think they followed him. Kidnapped him. His life is in danger. The man with the dark hair? Name is Angel. He killed a PI not far from here a few days ago. Cut his ear off. The woman you never saw? Her life is at stake as well. You following me?"

"You got a point, just stick me with it."

"You either fight the slime, or you are the slime."

"Thanks for the hot tip. But I'm tapped out here."

I went back to my truck and returned with a burner phone.

"Call me. If it's not your shift, have the other guard call you."

Darron looked at the phone as if it represented far more than he wanted to tangle with.

"Angel's a quarter century of slime rolled into one man."

He took the phone.

There's no way Darron did twenty-five with the police, but I didn't want to call him out on that. I wanted him on my side.

26

Darkness crashed the day, summoning all the fanfare the ancient gods could muster. Arrows of lightning. Timpanis of thunder. Mushrooming clouds, like loose chunks of interstellar black holes, threatened to plummet from the sky. The epic temper tantrum blazed five miles inland as we watched from our box seats on the screen porch.

I'd just put Joy to bed. When I left her room, she was standing in protest, vocally wailing her discontent with a conviction that put the storms to shame. The ancients had it wrong: the gods should be jealous of us. For the smallest among us dwarfs their mightiest warrior.

Garrett, Morgan, and Domingo were joining us for dinner. Garrett was taking a run. He would bunk with Morgan, as he did when in town. Morgan was still at his house, and Domingo was preparing dinner with me in the kitchen.

The clunking water pipes signaled the end of Kathleen's shower. I poured more wine into a saucepan, where puréed carrots and onions had been reducing for over an hour. Kathleen entered the kitchen, her hair wrapped in a white towel, her shower trailing her. I wondered what Rachel was doing at that moment.

"Whose idea was it to have a child?" she said.

"The two tragedies in life," I said. "Not getting your heart's desire and getting your heart's desire."

"This is no time to maul Shaw."

"What is it time for?"

"An old-fashioned. Make it a double."

I got to work constructing her drink as Joy wailed over Frank Sinatra. I like Frank. He lived a fast life and sang slow songs.

Domingo finished the salad and dried his hands on the new dishtowel.

"Mind if I give her a go?"

"Sail away," Kathleen said.

He disappeared into the nursery and came out holding a pinched-face Joy. I gave her a peck on the forehead. Domingo went out the back door. Hadley III came in, froze as if she'd forgotten her purpose, and then dashed away. You never know the mind of a cat. Garrett came in, grabbed a towel, and headed to the outdoor shower, leaving a trail of heat behind him. You never know the mind of Garrett.

"Dare we relax?" Kathleen said. Her double was down to a single. My wife, when on a roll, could shame any stevedore on the west coast of Florida foolish enough to challenge her. I kissed her forehead, still steamy from her shower and about the same temperature as Joy's. A peculiar thing: the steamy foreheads of the two girls in my life.

"What time is our appointment tomorrow with the private adoption attorney?" I said.

She looked around the kitchen as if noticing it for the first time, and—dang, just what do people do here?

"I canceled it."

"Care to explain?"

"No."

"Nothing?"

"No."

"You're not bad with words. Give 'em a shot."

"Bang bang."

"That's it?"

She held up a finger like a barrel of a gun under her mouth. She gave it a long, flirtatious blow.

"How about if I fix you another for the road?"

"It's a long road."

After making her another double—someone's sleeping well tonight—I plucked filets from a different skillet and dumped my reduction sauce into that skillet, scraping the bottom with a steel spatula. I poured red wine into the skillet. It hissed and frothed as the alcohol dissipated.

Domingo came back in with an unconscious Joy on his shoulder, neither of them peeping a word. He carried her into the nursery.

"What's the magic formula?" Kathleen said to Domingo when he returned from Joy's room.

"Her heart is expanding every day. It is hard to contain a beginner's heart."

"But what did you *do*?" Kathleen demanded. It was unlike her to press for nettling details. She was normally content with spiritual mumble-jumble over incontrovertible dogma.

"I sang to her under the stars. It is how my mother put us

to bed on the boat. The tropical night air is nature's melatonin."

"Any song in particular?"

"'Michael Row the Boat Ashore.' That is what my mother and father always sang. There would be more songs. But that was always the last."

"Michael row the boat ashore," Kathleen said softly, as if hearing that combination of words for the first time and being wholly taken by their sound. Their cadence.

"It is a song the heart remembers," Domingo said.

Kathleen took a savoring sip of her old-fashioned, her green eyes flicking in the candlelight. Hadley III darted after a gecko. When she didn't catch it, she slunk away as if she really wasn't interested in the stupid lizard in the first place. God, I love cats.

The sky cleared, and clusters of starry heaven poked pinholes in the darkness. The waxing gibbous moon broke free of a cloud. Soon, it would be the strawberry moon. Kathleen softly hummed "Michael Row the Boat Ashore," Frank having left the stage long ago.

Back to the stars: They say you're not supposed to think of such things. I say, how can you *not* think of such things? What we see is thousands of years ago. How can you be sure you're in the present when you know you're looking at the past? Caesar ruled. Jesus walked. Aristotle taught. No wonder that, at the queerest moments, my senses abandon me and I feel the urge to stick my tongue down Kathleen's throat. Infested with senselessness, I crave something to anchor the moment.

After dinner, Domingo peeled off first. Garrett was next, his body swallowed by the night when he crossed the lawn to Morgan's house. Always one of few words, he'd been even more austere that evening. Morgan followed a few minutes later, although he went to the end of his dock. He would be there, as well, when the sun rose in the morning. Part of him misses the sea, and I pray he never goes back, for I cannot imagine the hole that would create in our lives.

I moved to a lounge chair, spread my legs, and patted the cushion.

"Here, woman."

Kathleen snuggled between my legs, her back on my chest, her head on my shoulder.

"Talk to me, Annie Oakley." She'd been subdued after dinner, more interested in humming than in speaking.

"I don't want us to be diluted," she said.

"Diluted?"

"What Domingo said. I don't want us to ever lose our beginner's hearts. That overwrought romanticism that we make fun of as we age because we can't hold it."

I thought of Liana Castillo's ten-year-old heart that would never know the beginning of overwrought romanticism, let alone its demise.

"Is this related to the child thingy?" I said.

"No. Yes. Maybe. The student I told you about? Who is so quiet?"

"Who writes like a winter storm?"

"Her words just reel me. Her name is China, like the country. I went down to the boat docks the other day to clear my mind—I get that from you. She was there."

The college where she teaches is known for its marine biology program. The school has waterfront property a developer would enslave his mother for.

"She asked if she could complete the rest of the course without coming to class. I asked why. She said she's pregnant. She doesn't want to miss her classes, but she doesn't want to toddle around campus. I gave her permission to continue without attending."

"Did that help—?"

"China doesn't plan to keep the child."

"Oh?"

"I told her what a wonderful gift a child is and urged her to reconsider. She said her parents would never forgive her if she had an abortion, but she's adamant she doesn't want it."

"Did you—?"

"No. Don't you see? I can't tell her. That would be a gross misuse of our relationship. I can't profit from her. I told her to keep the child. That she might always regret giving it up."

"How did that go."

"Terrible. It was a cruel thing to say to her. All I did was load her up on a lifetime of guilt to worry about. But I had to do it. I don't trust myself around her. I'm China's best friend right now, but I'm damned either way, and she deserves so much more. I gave her the name of our private adoption attorney."

"She doesn't know you want another child?"

"She can never know."

"Even afterward?"

"Especially afterward. Her whole life is in front of her. She's a beautiful woman—not White, not Black. Just some skin tone that's totally unfair. She's got this 70s vibe to her, although I can't say why. Oh, and this: she uses the word *shit* a lot."

"Shit?"

"Nothing else from the cussing cousins, but she's fond of that one. Pristine usage. When she ends a sentence with it, there is nothing left to add."

"Look at me," I said. She cocked her head so that our eyes were inches apart.

"What's wrong with win-win?"

"You think that helps me? She's fragile. I'm sure she doesn't think she is, but she is. What if after holding the child, she changes her mind? She'd feel obligated to me. I can't have that on my conscience. Not now. Not ever. Nor is it best for her. She needs to make the decision after she gives birth."

"Then tell her that."

"I did. But she's determined to give it away."

"Did you consider she's not as fragile as you think?"

"It's dangerous for me to consider anything."

"And so you remain silent?"

"I have no choice. I thought of kicking her out of class to remove the temptation, but that's just wrong all over."

We gave silence a few lines, each of us digesting what we'd said. She repositioned herself so that she straddled me. She lowered her head, her hair blanketing my face.

"Promise me," she said, "that we love as we loved from the first. That we never scuff the ashes of our desires."

"Scuff?"

"I'm serious. Where is it written that our hearts are sprinters and not built for marathons? That as we age, we are doomed to suffer the slow bleed of our desires. That's baloney. Pure malarkey. It's just the easy way out."

"You done?"

"I think so."

I kissed the girl.

She took my hand and placed it on her chest. She kept her hand over my hand, and we made love like that, my hand cupping her small left breast, her hand pressing harder and harder on my hand. Later that night I dreamed of kayaking. Every stroke matched a beat of Kathleen's heart. I tried to make the distant shore of milk and honey, but I never made it. A cat sat on the shore. It looked bored.

AT 5:12, THIS WOKE ME: SONGS ARE LIKE LIGHT. STARS. They go forever. Kathleen's soft voice, humming "Michael Row the Boat Ashore," is traveling. Even now. Even forever. It goes deeper and deeper into space, and a thousand times a thousand years from now, across the universe, someone will listen to her. It will be the present.

27

Garrett and I stopped by Sally Russo's old office the next morning, but both Donna Novak Realty and Tomkin's Printing were locked. I googled them. Tomkin's appeared to be out of business, but Donna Novak was still in the game. I didn't want to question her on the phone. Nifty devices that they are, it's easier to reject someone on the phone than it is to their face.

I called Donna Novak and left a message.

We swung by the drugstore and picked up the pictures that had been in Sally's camera. I climbed back into my cool truck and opened one of two envelopes, tossing the other to Garrett.

A woman looking forlornly out to the water. An older man on a park bench, head hung, elbows on knees. A young woman manning her post at an outdoor hostess stand, her face plastered with makeup, her low-cut blouse revealing swollen half-moon breasts. Her eyes distant. Lost. A picture of a young girl holding a balloon, her face bursting with happiness. Sally Russo took that one as a reminder to himself to seek joy, for it did not come naturally to him.

"Nothing here," Garrett said. "You?"

"Not yet."

There were a few pictures of Giancarlo with an attractive woman half his age. She looked vaguely familiar. They appeared to be meeting in less populated spots. Sitting in a booth. Walking a lonely street. They were close in all the pictures, but never touching. It was not either's first affair. Giancarlo was already working on Erica the Fourth. They might be an asset in Erica's divorce proceedings, but they would also break her heart, for she admitted she still loved the man and felt he loved her. But Edward Giancarlo had clearly developed a fresh interest.

Then one picture halted me. "Here we go," I said, placing it on the console between our seats.

A building framed to the right—Sally was not fond of his subject matters being centered. But the building wasn't his primary interest. Across the street, Edward Giancarlo stood talking to a man. A man with black hair greased over his ears.

Angel.

But Angel wasn't looking at Giancarlo or Leonard, who stood behind Giancarlo. Angel's eyes were drilled at Sally Russo. Straight into Sally's camera.

Sally should have developed his film sooner.

28

RACHEL

Interiority

No one talked about her mother's death.

Not Alvaro, the gardener, always quick to greet Rachel in the morning with a smile so sincere she could only wonder if he'd stayed up all night perfecting it. He cast his eyes to the dirt, to the plants, seeking solace in what he knew. Not Emilia, the cook and Rachel's surrogate mother. She became a steel-jawed machine, doubling her time in the kitchen, some random piece of cookery in her hand so that no one would notice the uncontrollable shake that had developed. Certainly not her tutors. Vargo consented; she was done being tutored. And just in time, for what good were nihonium, moscovium, tennessine, and oganesson to a motherless daughter? After her mother's death, such items, while barely sufferable the first time around, became a ludicrous reminder of the folly of the minutes, the brittleness of the days, and the bleak arithmetic of her years.

Vargo told her that her mother died in a car accident.

The carnage also took out the black SUV and the two men who accompanied her. When Rachel had questioned such an encompassing crash, Vargo had snapped at her.

"It was a bad accident. Don't ask anymore."

"I'm sorry, Dad," a suddenly submissive Rachel had replied.

Dad. After her mother died, Rachel had ditched calling her father Papa—and, to the puzzlement of her mother, occasionally Vargo—in favor of Dad. It seemed closer, more intimate, and she craved that connection. She had figured out that one parent down left only one standing. A once-confident Rachel knew she needed more time to grow into the world. It was still too big for her. Too vast. Unpredictable. How can you have a family in the morning and only memories in the evening? Under what subject heading does that fall?

A little over a year after Sophia's death, Vargo insisted they take the plane shopping to a city over a hundred miles away.

"Shopping?" she replied. Her father had never accompanied Rachel and her mother on any of their trips.

"You'd like new clothes, wouldn't you?"

"Yes. But why not where Sophia and I used to go?"

"You mother liked this place better." Vargo was perturbed that his daughter had taken to calling her deceased mother by her name.

"I don't remember her ever mentioning it."

"We'll leave at ten."

Ninety minutes after entering the department store, they exited, the bodyguards hauling boxes and garment bags. They settled on an outdoor café after Vargo had passed on two others that had appeared perfectly acceptable to Rachel.

Vargo took the chair that backed to a wall and faced the street. Rachel knew her father always sat with his back to a wall, his eyes to the world.

They were discussing college and Rachel's quest for a more formal education.

"Do you miss being tutored?" Vargo asked, taking a sip of water. Vargo never indulged in alcohol outside the compound.

"So much," she gushed. "What's a girl to do in a day not filled with Pythagorean theorem and inverted operations? How does a woman live without her daily dose of Boyle's law?"

"Rather nicely, I would assume."

"Oh, the torture."

"Can you live on books alone?"

"Can you live on business alone?"

"You think that is the same thing?"

"Are you going to say they're not?"

Father and daughter discussions favored dueling questions over wordy engagements, neither possessing the patience for windy discourse.

"Thank you for the clothes. I really don't know when or where I will wear them all."

"Your mother never needed an occasion to look nice."

"But I don't want others to think that it means that much to me. It doesn't. Sophia was good at that—looking great without it meaning anything."

He'd had enough.

"Why do you call her by her name?"

She shrugged. "Does it bother you?"

"I haven't decided yet."

"Liar."

Vargo considered the accusation.

"I haven't decided why it bothers me," he said.

"That's better. When I think of my mother, I think of me at the age she died, for after her death, she aged no more. But I'd just begun to know her as a woman, not just as my mother. As a peer. And I need that person. When I think of her by her name, she is unfrozen. She walks with me. Talks with me. Does that make sense?"

"It does," Vargo said, thinking that women are so much more attuned to themselves than men and wishing she'd used a different word than *unfrozen*. He found the word disconcerting.

They were quiet for a moment, the world bustling about them.

"How did you come to see her as a peer?" Vargo asked his daughter, for that detail had not escaped him.

"Just did."

"Was there an event? An occasion?"

"No," Rachel said.

"Liar," Vargo said playfully, adopting her pompous attitude.

She didn't know why she lied other than it was a private affair between her mother and her. It would be easy to get lost in translation, so why bother? Yet Rachel worried. The third Sunday with her mother had started to mythify. Grow fairy tale wings. She needed to set it in stone. If it was ever to be any good for her, there could never be any doubt.

If I don't tell my father, who do I tell?

She dumped the story on her father. The first Sunday. How she took a rebel peek when the priest ordered heads down, souls in submission. The stone-cold beauty of the church floor. The second Sunday. How she saw her mother's head held high, her eyes open, scanning the church. The third Sunday. Mother and daughter, eyes finally meeting, neither backing down.

When she had finished, Vargo gazed at his daughter. "Did you and your mother do this every Sunday thereafter?"

"We did."

Vargo gave a small smile. The class of smile that leaks out of you when you're rearranging the past, seeing it in a new and approving light.

"I see," he said.

"What do you think, Dad?"

"About the two of you disobeying the priest?"

"Is that all you see?"

"I am proud of my two women."

"Why?"

"Must it always be questions?"

"Why not?" she said with a tease.

"Why so?" he ricocheted back.

"Tell me why you are proud," she asked again, careful not to frame it as a question.

"It shows me that you think for yourself and act accordingly. It is a hard thing to do in this world. May I make a suggestion?"

"Please."

"Don't let the priest see you. He is harmless, of course. But allow him his fantasies."

"Sophia said it was all theater."

"It is. You know, I had a role once. As a young boy."

"You?" She could not imagine her father cast in that role, but no daughter ever sees her father as a young boy.

"I was an altar boy. I liked church growing up. After the service, I would go home and read under an oak tree. It was the only day I was permitted to read. I read every Sunday. One day, my father called for me. I put my book down and went inside. He said there would be no more time for reading. That I was old enough to know that work never rests. I was not even permitted to retrieve my book. For all I know, it is still there, under the oak tree."

Rachel wondered if that was why her father tolerated her obsession. Then, from nowhere, this: *Do I have his heart—his boy heart?*

But she didn't go in that direction. Instead, she said, "What work was so important as to leave your book?"

Vargo looked at her sullenly. Ignoring her question, he said, "What do you get from your Sunday defiance?"

"Strength," she said, recalling when she and her mother had discussed the same topic.

"From God?"

"You think that?"

"Please, Rachel. Just tell me."

"From me. From deep inside. Like a safe, where everything of value is locked and protected. When I keep my head up, and those around me bow? It opens that safe. Fills it. Everything I know pours in. All I believe. Even questions are safe there. Does that make sense?"

"You get inner strength in God's house by defying God."

Rachel had never thought of it in those terms, but it sounded good.

"I do."

"Interiority," he said.

Rachel twisted her face.

"Interio—?"

"Interiority," Vargo said. "That which belongs inside. You must nurture it. Grow it. When life gets rough, your mother

—Sophia—will be there for you. Standing next to you. She will get you through your darkest moments."

With those words, Vargo Estrada handed his daughter the tool she would need when she learned of his terrible deeds. When she heard the third and final version of how her mother died. It would not escape her, that moment when hell sliced her, that while her father was responsible for her unimaginable anguish, it was also his advice that would calm her frayed nerves. And—at a most peculiar yet fitting place—steady her aim as she avenged his death.

29

Erica powered her Mercedes convertible out of her driveway. She cut a sharp turn onto the main road, scattering a flock of crows obsessed with a plastic bag. I'd been waiting at the side of the road as she had not returned my phone calls. I followed and pulled into a gas station behind her. She slammed the Mercedes door shut. The bottled anger of her life expressed in a simple act.

"You're following me?" she said. She was dressed for yoga.

"You've been ignoring my calls."

She took a credit card out of her purse and stuck it in the pump. "That's because I wanted to talk to Sally first, and *he's* not returning my phone calls." She withdrew her card and punched her zip code into the keypad. "It's been several days. That's not like him. What did you two talk about?"

She started to lift the nozzle. I stepped into her and placed my hand on hers.

"He wasn't at the park, Erica. I went to his office and found him. He's dead. I'm sorry. You cannot tell anybody that

I found him. I've talked to the police, but no one else must know that I was tracking him."

She looked confused, as if she'd momentarily lost track of her purpose.

"I don't understand," she said, her eyes questioning mine.

"He was murdered."

"Mr. Russo?"

"You need to be careful. Is there anything else I should know that he shared with you?"

But it was too much for her.

"Who would kill him?" Her face flooded with comprehension. "Oh my God. Is it because of what he was doing for me? Is that what you're telling me?"

I debated about how much to tell her about what I found on Sally's camera. I was stuck between protecting her and wanting to see if she could help me.

"I think so."

"You *think* so?"

"You should assume as much. Your name will surface as an active client he was working for. A Detective Rambler will be calling you. I've already talked with him. You can trust him. He's a good man."

Erica stood with the nozzle frozen in her hand.

"Let me do that."

I took the nozzle and stuck the spout in her tank, locking the lever into place. On the pump, an excitable woman eternally trapped in a small TV screen recapped yesterday's sports scores.

"Do you think Edward knows?" she said.

"That you hired Sally to dig up dirt on him?"

She nodded, as if unable to verbally admit as much.

"I would ass—"

"I got it." She hesitated. "Okay, I got it. What a mess. What a fucking mess. What do I do?"

Good question, Erica.

"Why aren't you answering?" she said when I didn't immediately respond. "I'm in real trouble, aren't I?"

"No. Tell Detective Rambler that you hired Sally to find dirt for your divorce and that—"

"Edward doesn't know I plan on filing. My attorney thought I should gather as much information as possible and then ambush him."

The pumped clicked off. I holstered the nozzle back into the pump, silencing the little TV lady.

"He had pictures of your husband with a younger woman," I said.

"Recent pictures?"

"Yes."

She swung her head. "I told you I thought he was seeing someone. I'd hear him on the phone. 'I'll take care of it, honey. Love you, too.' Gooey shit like that. And God, his voice. He really means it. I can tell. When I confront him, he says he can't talk about it, but it's not what I think. Someday, he says, but not now. Do you think men even know the definition of marriage?"

She paused for a beat and then continued. "I didn't really need gas. I just stopped because it was convenient, and I was early for yoga. I don't really like yoga, either. I don't know what I like anymore."

"You'll have better days," I said. Someone had told me that on a bad day a different life ago. Ever since, I'd felt compelled to pass it on.

"Do I tell the police everything?"

"Did Sally show you any pictures?"

"No."

"Did Sally mention any names, give you descriptions of people, places?"

"No. No and no. I assumed that was what our next meeting was to be about."

"Do not lie to Detective Rambler."

"And Edward?"

"That's your call."

She bobbed her head a few times.

"How young was she?"

"It doesn't—"

"Answer the goddamn question, Jake."

"Young."

"Unfuckingbelievable. He's been trying to patch things up, telling me he loves me. That he could explain it all one day. What would that even sound like? Hey, honey, I just needed a little fling, but I'm over that now. It's really been you all along." She swung her head. "Were they happy?"

"Pardon?"

"In the pictures, Jake. Were Edward and his young pigeon laughing?"

I recalled the pictures.

"They seemed serious. No hugs. No hand holding."

"Terrific. They're already past infatuation. Erica the *Fuck*ing Third. What a fool."

30

This is the second time I met the man named Angel.

But first, as I mentioned earlier, you need to know a little bit more about Andrew Keller, my old friend who led me to Elizabeth Walker, who let me to Anna Vargas, whose teenage daughter, Kimberly, gave up her baby to Kathleen and me. That's a lot. I know. But to paraphrase T.S. Eliot, at the end we arrive where we started.

I hadn't taken Keller up on his earnest plea to find Elizabeth Walker. He'd been murdered a few days later. Had I been more sympathetic, he might be alive today. Yet I'd profited from his death, for his murder led to our private adoption. I've learned to live with those mixed feelings. They do not hamper my steps. But I will carry them the length of my life.

I was at the cemetery placing flowers on Keller's grave. I do this every month, although I've never told Kathleen and don't know why. His gravesite is under the arm of a matronly oak tree, its Spanish moss flowing like Rapunzel's hair, its proud leaves shading the sacred ground. An empty plot rested next to his. Andrew had purchased the two lots prior to his divorce. He had no children. And while I prefer to think that Elizabeth and Andrew are together in eternity, the vacant plot guts me every time I visit his grave.

I lied. I often cry at Keller's gravesite. It is my alone place. That's why I've never told Kathleen. I tell you this only because I don't know you.

I bent over the ground to position a vase of flowers. I arranged them to withstand a gust of wind or an encroaching lawn mower that appeared to have recently made its rounds. I dusted grass debris from the base of his stone with my hands. Despite the granite chafing my skin, I wasn't thinking of Keller. Brittany was on my mind. Every day, every hour, that I didn't call her, that her phone remained silent, her life was slipping away. Morphing into a tragedy. *Your child disappeared without a trace, condemning you to a life of incalculable sadness. A life with a line through it. Friends will grow more distant. They will say the same of you. And in the haze of the morning, you'll forget. And then that train hits. Shit. I forgot. Life killed me but let me live. Okay. Here we go. One foot in front of another. Again.*

A few drops of rain dodged their way through the oak tree and tickled the back of my neck. The cemetery was inland from the water, and in the summertime, the relentless Florida heat spawned nervous weather, threatening cloudbursts with little notice. I muttered a few words to Andrew, who, thank God, did not mutter back. As I turned to leave, a black SUV pulled up tight behind my truck. Three doors swung open.

The driver shut his door and opened the door behind him. Angel stepped out. The driver popped open a large umbrella and positioned it over Angel. Two men walked around from the other side of the truck. The four of them strode toward me. The rain picked up its rhythm. I berated myself for not noticing that I'd been followed. I picked a bad time to be engulfed with sentimentality.

Angel stopped a few feet from me, umbrella man at his side. The other two men fanned out.

"You're supposed to bring flowers to a cemetery," I said.

"I'm not here to visit the dead," Angel said.

"Too bad. They can teach you a lot about living."

He nodded at Keller's grave. "You know the man in the ground behind you?"

"I do."

"What does your dead friend teach you?"

"He said heaven's a riot. Every Friday they take a field trip to hell, where they get to watch people like you scream in pain."

"I remember your mouth."

"I remember your smell. What can I do for you, Angel? I've got a busy day, and no one holds an umbrella over my head."

He held up his hand and stepped out from under the umbrella's protection. He reached into his pocket and shoved a photo in my face. It was of me crossing Pioneer Park. One of the two men must have had a camera—*no, there was a third I never spotted.*

"Why you were in this park at two-thirty?"

"I was taking a stroll."

"Who told you to be there?"

"I wasn't anywhere. I was walking. Why the questions, Angel?"

"Who did you plan to meet?"

"Geppetto."

"Who?"

"No one. Do you understand the concept of taking a stroll?"

The rain got serious, driving pellets into my face. Angel made no move to seek shelter under the umbrella.

"You are not a man to stroll through a park. I ask you one more time; why were you at the park?"

"I had lunch downtown with a friend of mine. He's a detective. We were discussing the death of Liana Castillo." I stepped closer to him. The man to my right made a similar move toward me. "He told me they are making progress in finding the scum who would murder a young girl."

"You lie," he said. "That is not why you were downtown."

"Tell me about the drug war that resulted in a young girl's death."

"What did Salvatore Russo tell you?"

"Salvador Dali? He's dead."

"Do you care to join your friend in the muddy ground?"

"What did you do to Evan Brackett?"

He blinked. "Who?"

"If any harm comes to him, I will skin you one inch at a time."

"I do not know this name. But, tell me, who is he to you?"

I didn't want him to know that Evan was my nephew. Didn't want him to have that leverage. That satisfaction.

"Someone I was hired to find."

"I think not."

"I don't care what you think."

"When did you last see this friend of yours?"

"Why do you care? You said you didn't know him."

Angel opened his mouth and ran his tongue over his teeth. He nodded to the man to his left. The man took a swing at me. I slipped his fist and punched him in his solar plexus. I swung around just as the other man's right hand came at me. I jerked my head and caught a glancing blow from his passing fist. I jabbed him with my left fist and then froze when a ten-inch knife parked itself under my right eye.

The man with the umbrella—his umbrella now sporting a blade at its tip—stood, a fencer posed with his foil.

"Do you wish to continue?" Angel said.

"Perhaps on fairer terms," I said, slightly backing my face away from the lethal edge.

The man behind me must have pistol-whipped me, for the back of my head cracked in pain. I stumbled sideways and caught myself on Keller's tombstone. Someone kicked my legs out, and I went down. My head nicked the tombstone. I struggled to hold on to consciousness.

The flowers I'd meticulously placed on Keller's grave had fallen and were now splayed on the ground. A few yellow roses rested on my cheek. I looked at them and they at me. They seemed puzzled that I was at their level. I gazed up at Angel as rain streaked my face, dripping off my nose. I would have given anything to grasp a fork of lightning and pierce his heart with it. Angel positioned his boot so that it was centered on my nose. I tried to get up but was woozy. One of the men stepped on my shoulder. The clouds held nothing back, driving chariots of rain. It doesn't rain in Florida. It drowns.

"Tell me about this man, Evan Brackett," Angel snarled at me. "How do you know of him?"

"Told you. His family hired me after he went missing."

"Tell me more."

"They're not paying me enough."

That got a chuckle from him.

"Maybe you tell the truth. But . . . I don't think so."

He ground his boot into my face. My nose cracked, and blood seeped into my mouth. The grinding sound was worse than the pain. The consistency of blood worse than its taste.

"You told me you fear no man," I said. "What fear brought you here today?"

"None. You misjudge me. I am a compassionate man. I came to tell you that if we never cross paths again, then to enjoy a long life. But if we meet again?—I will not be so kind."

He turned to leave. The man with the umbrella hit a switch, and the blade snapped back into its hiding place. I tried to get up and read the license plate, but my mind teetered on darkness. I slumped back down. The world smelled like fresh roses, warm summer rain, and newly cut grass, and I wondered if Andrew Keller smelled it as well. If so, death wasn't so bad.

31

The morning rain passed. The pain was not as transitory.

After exhausting my mesmerization with roses and the childhood wonderment of fresh-cut summer grass, I went to an urgent care and had my nose reset. It wasn't as bad as I'd feared. Afterward, like a dog curling up in its den, I trekked to Docksides to lick my wounds.

I instructed Keana, the waitress, to keep the beers coming.

"What's up, love?" she said. "You're normally straight iced tea." She smelled like bubble gum.

I'd taken the packing out of my nose, but it was still swollen. "My nose ran into a door."

"I should see the door, right?"

I pursed my lips, shaking my head in resignation. "No. The door won."

"They don't tell you that, but it definitely goes that way."

She whisked away, and I hit Yankee Conrad's number. He

didn't know what to conclude from the picture of Giancarlo and Angel conversing.

"Any news on your nephew?" Yankee Conrad asked.

"Nothing. Any news on the missing DEA agent who might have worked with Levinson in planting the money?"

"He is presumed dead."

"And Levinson?"

"If you're asking of his potential involvement, he claims to have never met the man."

"Do you believe him?"

"I want to."

"That's not the same."

"The best I can do is I don't disbelieve him."

We disconnected. I was mulling his last statement when Rambler called.

"You ever come across a man named Nicky Riggins?" Rambler asked. A dolphin surfaced by the seawall on the far side of the canal. It was followed by two more, surfacing as one.

"No. Who is he?"

"A new level of asshole. Juvie record longer than a giraffe's neck, but since then, nothing we could stick on him. A fellow degenerate, staring at a second trip behind bars, fingered him for Liana Castillo."

"Anything you can confirm?"

"Not yet. But we showed Manuel Castillo a mug shot, just on a chance. He clerks at a Circle K down the street from the playground. He said Riggins was in the store around the time his daughter was murdered. Said he was wired. Jacked up."

"I thought the department wasn't interested in a case it

couldn't solve. Didn't want unsolved murders to drop under fifty percent."

"We're stirring the water a bit. We got a warrant for Riggins's apartment. Found the gun that did Salvatore Russo. It was also the same weapon that killed Liana."

"Riggins did Liana and Sally," I said, sitting up straighter in my chair.

"It might be a plant to frame Riggins. Throw us off the trail. The snitch said Riggins has dreams of being a Hollywood hitman, but he's two dozen IQ points shy of ever making the big screen. Remember, this is from trash who is looking at a return trip to Raiford."

"Your best guess?"

"First, you'd have to be an idiot to take a paycheck to kill Giancarlo's daughter—if that was the case. Remember his nonbiological daughter from a previous marriage was in the park that day."

"And secondly?"

"You sound muffled," Rambler said. "You got a cold or something?"

"Sinus."

"It's pretty sloppy using the same gun within a few blocks and a week."

"He's being framed by the person who hired him?"

Rambler paused, as if he was adjusting his phone. He said some unintelligible words to someone else. A shadow of a bird crossed the water. I glanced up to see the bird, but it was gone. A southbound jet chalked the vaulted sky, its fuselage reflecting the sun.

"Or he's stupid," Rambler said, bringing me back. "The longer I'm alive, the more I favor stupid. It is a prevalent yet rarely acknowledged human trait. Do me a favor? Drop in on Giancarlo."

"Me?"

"We can't touch him. He routes everything through his attorney's office. Tell him we told you we're circling him for the death of Sally. Make up some line about Sally having incriminating evidence of his extramarital affair. But you think he's innocent. Doing him a favor. Rattle him. See if you can get him to commit an unforced error. The guy's hiding something."

"I'll take a swing. How was your haircut?"

"Thirty bucks not including a tip."

"You're not going back?"

"Made my next appointment on the way out."

We disconnected. I reached for my beer and realized Keana had switched it out for a fresh one. I snatched a pen from another table and pulled out a napkin from the dispenser. It was a stubborn little cuss, and I got three for the price of one. I smoothed one out and stuck the others under my plate so the breeze didn't flutter them away.

I wrote:

Evan

Rachel

Liana

Edward Giancarlo

Erica

Sally Russo

Angel

Vargo

Kylie Giancarlo

I considered my sloppy penmanship and then added Manuel Castillo.

I circled Evan and Rachel inside one loop. I underlined Liana's name. Nothing came to me. No sparks. No circuits connected. A pickup truck towing a flatbed of commercial mowing equipment crested the bridge, rattling and banging its way over the water.

"Whatja got there?" Keana asked. I'd not been aware of her. "Got anything to do with the door you ran into?"

"It does."

She planted a hand on her hip and kept her gaze on the napkin. "Tell me about it, love."

I pointed the pen to Vargo and then traced it to the others as I talked. "This man works for a drug cartel and is this woman's father. And she, Rachel, is in love with this man, Evan. But their love is forbidden, and he"—pen back to Vargo—"banished the young man from his land."

She crinkled her nose. "Like Romeo and Juliet?"

"Like them." I moved the pen to Angel's name. "And this guy worked for Vargo. I think he's trying to take the business over. And Giancarlo? I think he's connected to Vargo and Angel and helps them launder drug money. And Liana was in the wrong place at the wrong time."

"Meaning?"

"She's dead."

Keana stepped back. "That's terrible. How old was she?"

"Ten. She was killed on a playground."

"The one I read about? The swing set girl?"

"Her name's Liana."

"You think someone on the list killed her?"

"No. But their maneuvering certainly led to her death." I pointed to Giancarlo. "He seems to be in the thick—"

"Hold on, love," she said. "You're making a mess of it all." She leaned over the table, her Bazooka scent leading the way. Her red-polished nail traced Vargo, Rachel, and Evan. "You say this is father, daughter, and daughter's lover, but they are forbidden to be together?"

"And he's missing."

"Who?"

"Evan. And perhaps Rachel as well."

She straightened up, planting her hands on her hips. "You can forget about that drug money mumbo jumbo. There's the root of your problems right there. Just like that door you ran into, can't be any plainer than that."

"You think—?"

"Money's a powerful thing, but it plays second fiddle to a man's love for a woman, and *that* plays second fiddle to a father's love for his daughter. You think I'm kidding?" She jabbed her finger at Rachel. "*She* is why doors are slamming in your face. Funny, ain't it? How you don't even recognize what hits you."

32

RACHEL

Three men ran.

Rachel had just finished telling Vargo that she wanted to go out that night with some friends.

This was not the first time father and daughter had tangled over the issue.

"Angel will accompany you," Vargo said.

"Angel?" Rachel protested. "No way."

She'd seen Angel around. They'd tossed the knife a few times together. Angel was the only person Rachel knew who was rarely friendly to others and never to himself. She understood the former and was troubled by the latter.

"It is not open to discussion," Vargo said.

"I won't go out with him tagging along."

"Then you won't go out."

And so started the history between Rachel and Angel.

They worked out an alternate arrangement, one she would never share with her father. Is this not what daughters do? Even uncommonly mature ones? Angel would drop her off and pick her up but was nowhere to be seen (so she thought) when she was with her friends. In this manner, Rachel and Angel were joined as fellow conspirators, sharing more than the last two letters of their names. They developed a relationship of trust. Of guarded secrets. She worried whether Vargo questioned Angel and, if so, whether Angel lied. It was not hard to imagine Angel lying. She couldn't put her finger on his relationship with her father. While Angel worked for Vargo, he possessed an independent streak, a daring, both in talk and in his actions. More than a hired hand, he adhered to his own confusing agenda. Sometimes there. Sometimes not. Always on the phone. Some men acted as if they were important. Angel acted as if nothing was important.

One night at a bar, a group of four men settled their eyes on Rachel and her friends. Rachel refused their free drinks, but as the night wore on, it became obvious the men were not interested in her wishes. They shouldered up to Rachel and her friends. Their breath thick with alcohol. Their armpits stenched with the day's work.

"Leave us alone," Rachel said, pushing one of them away. He had snuggled up to her, desperate to suck her neck, to feel her skin between his teeth. For it was the most flawless, the most beautiful piece of flesh the man had ever seen.

He grabbed her. He clamped his mouth on her neck. Angel—*where did he come from?*—rocketed the man across the room with a fist to his head. The man thumped to the floor, dead to the world. Angel drew a knife. He flashed it to the other three men.

They ran.

When Rachel went to bed that night, she wondered what Angel had done. What they knew about him that had caused three men to run.

33

A man with an impressive set of jowls and a cigar in his hand sat to the right of Edward Giancarlo. Droopy took a puff and exhaled, swirls of smoke invading the air. The inconsequential detail of not knowing the man did not prevent me from disliking him. Leonard, Giancarlo's hairy-armed assistant, stood at his home position.

I had called Giancarlo's office and asked if I could drop by his house later that day. William Standiford, Giancarlo's prudish secretary, said no. I'd thanked him and replied that I would arrive at six. Garrett accompanied me.

Giancarlo introduced the man as his attorney but didn't release his name. In response, Droopy, as if extending his business card, puffed more smoke signals in my direction. Giancarlo explained that he knew I was tight with Detective Rambler and was willing to cooperate. He knew of no reason why someone would target his first wife's daughter, if that even was the case. He admitted that Detective Rambler had questioned him regarding the murder of a man named Salvatore Russo but insisted he'd never heard of the man, nor of a man named Riggins, whom Rambler had followed up with.

It was a prepared remark, said in the company of his attorney, who likely drafted it. If it was Rambler's wish that Giancarlo be more forthcoming with me than with him, we were off to a lousy start.

"I'd like to show you a few pictures." I reached inside my satchel.

Rambler had instructed me the previous day that Sally's pictures, camera, and camera bag were evidence and to drop them by the police station. I was surprised that he had not admonished me for taking them in the first place. He was keeping me on a leash, a leash that he was willing to lengthen at his convenience. I'd made copies of the pictures and complied with his request. Some of those copies were in my leather satchel. He also gave me some ammunition to use on Giancarlo.

"For what purpose?" his attorney said. His accent was bred in the south.

"I didn't catch your name," I said.

"Wesley Anderson the fo-ourth," he said. He made two syllables out of *fourth*. His drunk eyes wandered above my head as if to emphasize that I held no interest for him. "Unless you can authenticate the photos, they are useless. If the police had anything they wanted to show Mr. Giancarlo, they would do so. I believe you heard my client's statement."

I directed my comment to Giancarlo. "Aren't you curious?"

"No."

"Yet you invited me in."

"Invite? No. Allow? Yes."

"Earlier today, I dropped the originals off at Detective Rambler's office."

Giancarlo considered my implication. "Proceed."

I took the pictures out and laid them on the table, pointing at the one of him and Angel.

"It appears you are on a first-name basis with Angel, the man who shot your employee, Marcus Knowles, the night of the handoff."

I could have added that he stuck his heel in my face, but a man has got to have some dignity.

No one spoke. I wasn't sure Garrett was even breathing. Anderson placed his cigar in an ashtray. He leaned over and examined the picture. "As I mentioned," he said, "if these digital illustrations mean anything, then we will be approached by the appropriate law official. Until that time arrives, if that time arrives, we have no comment."

"Wait, there's more."

"Oh?"

"Consider these ditties."

I placed two pictures of Giancarlo and the younger woman on the table. In one picture, they were walking out of a restaurant on Beach Drive. The other was in North Straub Park by the water. Giancarlo and the woman faced each other, creating a profile setting and artistic background, just what Salvatore Russo excelled in. In neither picture did they touch each other or appear to be intimate. Kathleen had pointed out that Giancarlo was one cool Popsicle to leave a restaurant with a new lover and not hold hands. I had countered that Giancarlo, in the process of disengaging from wife number three, was proficient in all stages of the courting game.

Giancarlo snatched the pictures from the table and inspected them.

He glared at me. "Where did you get these?"

"I'm not at liberty to discuss my source."

"It was Rus—"

"Edward," his attorney cut in. "The man said he was not at liberty to discuss his source."

Giancarlo took a deep breath, his attorney having just stopped him from mentioning Salvatore Russo's name. "So I have a . . . girlfriend. What is the purpose of you showing me these?"

"These could be damaging in a divorce hearing. You know who took them. That man is now dead."

Anderson positioned himself higher in his chair, a plump little bird puffing its feathers. "Are you suggesting Mr. Giancarlo is in some manner involved?

"Just pointing out the obvious. What were you and Angel discussing?"

Anderson took the question. "That is none—"

Giancarlo raised his hand to silence his attorney. "Mr. Travis is simply trying to stir the waters," he said, keeping his drab eyes on me.

"Tell me about Angel."

Giancarlo leaned forward in his seat. "You're sticking your nose in where it doesn't belong."

"Angel is wanted for attempted homicide," I said, sliding in the ammunition that Rambler had given me. "He's being charged with attempting to kill Marcus Knowles. He was your employee, in the event you forgot."

"You seem to have a close knowledge of what the police are doing."

"We get our hair done at the same place."

"This is no joke."

"It wasn't meant to be."

"They should go after Angel."

"Got an address for me?"

"I'm questioning why I should continue this conversation with you."

"Because you know I'm Rambler's earpiece and you need to give him a reason to lay off. His interest in you is rising by the minute. He thinks you're being framed, but if you're unwilling to help yourself, there isn't much he can do."

Giancarlo sat back in his chair. He picked up an amber tumbler and took a patient sip. He placed it back on a coaster.

"The man called Angel accosted me downtown one evening. He talked nonsense. I told him I had no clue as to what he was referring to." He nodded at Leonard. "Leonard was there. He can confirm our conversation."

"I'm sure he can."

"Prior to that, I never saw the man before in my life."

"That was the only time you met him?"

"That is what I said."

"A door was inadvertently left open the night your employees were taken to the warehouse."

I waited for a reaction, but Giancarlo was unresponsive.

"Do you wish to amend your previous statement?" I asked.

"I do not."

"They heard you conversing with Angel."

Droopy—Anderson—blew smoke in my direction. Little twerp.

"They must be mistaken," Giancarlo said, not backing

down. "I was here at home that evening. Leonard can attest to that."

"Leonard will attest you were on the moon if you instruct him to."

Anderson cut in. "Are you—?"

"I've got it, Wes," Giancarlo said, again cutting off his attorney. "I might have underestimated you."

"Your attorney's smoke can't hide your stink, Eddie. You're moving money for Vargo, your old client from years back. Or did you never break ties with him? Angel and Vargo are in a pissing match. I think the bullet that hit Liana Castillo was intended for Kylie, your second wife's daughter."

Yankee Conrad had gotten back to me and confirmed what I'd been suspicious about; Vargo had been a client of Giancarlo's when Giancarlo started out as an attorney.

"I know who Kylie is," he said bitterly. "The police have shared their theory with me. Is there anything else I can do for you? I've been more than cooperative, but I still have other affairs to attend to this evening."

"We haven't come to the main event."

"Oh?"

"My nephew, Evan. He is in love with Vargo's daughter, Rachel. I think Angel has them both."

His jaw tightened. His eye narrowed as if he could laser me out of his life.

"My bet is that Angel's trying to take over Vargo's operations," I said. "And Vargo's leaning on you for help. Not muscle, but moving money. Angel found out and decided to kill your daughter, but Angel is drug trash; he didn't even know Kylie wasn't your biological daughter and messed up the hit anyway. Salvatore Russo—the name you nearly mentioned—was stalking you for other purposes, and it cost him his life. If you're not careful, they might pin Sally's murder on you."

"We are done here," Anderson said, as if he could dictate events by releasing edicts from his chair.

I leaned forward, pinning my eyes on Giancarlo.

"Manuel Castillo came to me."

"Who?"

"The man whose daughter died on the playground."

"The swing set girl?"

"Her name is Liana Castillo."

Why would he come to you?" he scoffed.

"He was looking for someone who gave a damn."

"And that is what you do? Charge people to pretend you care?"

"There's no money being exchanged."

"I fail to see why you insist on pestering me. I can't help you."

"You're holding out," I said, rising to my feet.

"I don't care—"

I stepped into him and grabbed him by his collar, jerking him to his feet. Leonard lunged at me. Garrett intercepted Leonard with a sharp punch to the stomach. Leonard bent over, gasping for breath. Anderson leaned back and blew a lazy puff of smoke into the air.

Giancarlo glared at me. "Are you done?"

"We're done playing with my nephew's life. I want names. Addresses."

"You just assaulted my client," Anderson pointed out.

I released Giancarlo and stepped back. "We all know nothing here will ever see the light of a courtroom."

Giancarlo straightened his shirt. "In order to find your nephew, you propose becoming the thugs you pursue?"

"If need be."

"I cannot help you."

"You will not help me."

"Juggle the words all day."

"I got Angel having them both, but it didn't start like that, did it? He had to renege on a promise, or Rachel never would have accompanied him in the first place."

"I can't help—"

"Save it."

I changed tack, hoping to trip him up and salvage a small victory.

"Evan said an American questioned him in Mexico. Who was he?"

"Edward," Anderson said. "You do not—"

"Quiet, Wes," Giancarlo said. He hesitated before proceeding, as if he were trying the words out in his mind before articulating them. "He moves the money."

"I didn't ask what he did. I asked who he was."

"You need to look into your own house."

There was something in his pleading eyes, as if no one else was there. No Garrett. No wheezing Leonard. No Wesley Anderson the fo-ourth. Just Edward Giancarlo and me.

"I need more than that."

"Or what? You and your friend bully us around? You're one bad move from being escorted out of here in the back of a squad car."

"Who's the American?"

"I've told you all I can. More than I should, considering there's nothing you can tell me that I don't know."

"I wouldn't be so sure."

"If you think you have something, let's hear it."

"You're close to blowing the best thing that ever happened to you."

"How's that?"

"Losing a good woman who loves you."

"I already know that."

34

The student center at the college where Kathleen taught has floor-to-ceiling glass walls. Those walls look out on a maze of sidewalks that connect intellectual sojourns: history, this way; marine biology, that way; fine arts, straight ahead. Summer session students strolled across the property, their heads bowed in captivity to the electronic devices cradled in their hands.

It was hard not to pine for the stolen days of youth. But I was thankful that I didn't work—or live—in a world where nearly every woman was between the ages of eighteen and twenty-two, sported a pair of runway legs, and refused to stand straight and view the world in front of them.

Giancarlo's comment to look in my own house had rattled me. That's the trouble with going rattling; sometimes you're the one who gets rattled. I sensed he wanted to be on my side, but something was holding him back. Garrett and I had batted around what—or who—Giancarlo might be referring to, but my near-term objective demanded my full attention.

Kathleen said she and China usually met after class for coffee. She had told China she couldn't make it today because she had office hours. I was betting that China still needed that jolt of caffeine.

Kathleen would not approve of what I was about to do. I wasn't sure *I* approved of what I planned to do. But there I sat, nursing a coffee, and there she came, wearing a blouse that flared at the sleeves as much as it flared around her waist. *Skin tone that's totally unfair.*

She went to the counter, ordered a coffee, and headed to an outdoor table.

I stalked her.

"China?"

She glanced up at me.

"Yes?"

I introduced myself, giving her my name and mentioning that I was Kathleen's—Dr. Rowe's—husband.

She cocked her head. "I usually meet her at this time, but she couldn't make it today. Are you looking for her?"

Her voice was smooth. Velvety. Like an unknown orchestra instrument that leaves you peering deep into the reed section, craning to see the source of your enchantment.

"I am not. I was hoping to have a few words with you."

She crinkled her face. "What can I do for you?"

"Can we sit down?"

"Sure."

She was surprised by what I said. She insisted that Dr. Rowe hadn't breathed a word to her. She understood why, and that made her decision easier. But her surprise was no match for my own when she explained what she wanted and insisted it be that way. I agreed and wondered what I'd gotten into. Kathleen said life is an open door. We'll see. We decided to meet again. Not to make a rush decision.

I'll never get over how some little things are so hard, and some big things are so easy. How luck, when she shines upon you, is the most transforming yet unwarranted occurrence.

35

Kathleen, head bent and red pen poised, was reading essays from her class. A neglected glass of wine rested next to her, condensation trickling down its sides like it was crying.

Brittany had called me earlier. No, no new leads. Yes, I'm working on it. Yes, I'll keep in touch. Don't worry. I'm sure he's fine.

I found him. Snuggled up like a rabbit in his writing hut. But I made a terrible mistake, and now a monster has him. Turns out I can't break the family cycle, but I can sure kick that sucker into second gear.

Heavy as that was, it took a back seat to my decision to meet with China. Was I doing the right thing by going behind Kathleen's back? Evan said our truest desire is to have someone desire us. But I believe there are strains of desire. Mutations of lust. We all desire for someone to tell us what is right. To take charge. To act without hesitation, for timidity only breeds regret.

"Penny for your thoughts," Kathleen said.

My gaze was hard on the new bridge across the bay. Its concrete structure arched over the water, its streetlights forming a gilded canopy in the sky. I missed the old drawbridge, its medieval arms rising and falling, the ghost ships of my imagination passing underneath.

"Fine. I'll go a nickel, but not a penny more."

I looked at her.

"You good for it?"

She stood, went to the kitchen, came back, and plunked a nickel on the glass table.

"Speak," she said.

"You haven't touched your wine."

"Now"—she took a sip—"you're out of bullets."

I filled her in on my visit to Giancarlo. A nonstop flight of words with no commas, periods, or paragraphs.

"You think Angel has both Evan and Rachel?" she said when I'd finished.

"I do."

"Why?"

"As blackmail to take over Vargo's business."

"But you're guessing, right?"

"I am."

"And in some manner Giancarlo is helping his old client?"

"Right."

"And you think—what? Angel might have inside help?"

"Giancarlo insinuated as much."

"Any ideas?"

"Just ideas."

"You really grabbed him by the collar?"

"I did."

"How did that feel?"

"Desperate. Stupid."

I hadn't really felt stupid, but after my mistake with Evan, the word popped up every time I referenced myself.

"Well, I certainly got my nickel's worth."

"No refunds." And then, to redirect the conversation to where my thoughts were cowering, I added, "Have you reconsidered meeting with a private adoption attorney, or are you still sticking to your guns?"

"Sticking to my guns. Morgan agrees with me."

Morgan's opinion, on anything, was the OFFICIAL STAMP OF AUTHORITY.

"You both worship fantasy."

"I know," she said in a breezy tone. "But we're happy little believers. It just irks you that we can be right with no reason to be right."

"I don't know what you said, but you said it well."

She leaned over and pecked my cheek. "You'll find him. And Rachel. How's the doorbell coming?"

"Working on it."

Kathleen had been after me to fix the doorbell. I saw no reason, as anyone who ever rang it was either looking to trim trees or sell Jesus. She'd countered that cynicism is not an admirable trait and that there was something basic and civil about someone announcing their presence at your house. Who knows who might present themselves?

Hadley III came in the cat door. She took two steps to her right and sat down with her front paws curled under her. She kept her eyes glued to the screen, searching for geckos, the boundless curiosity of her life. Kathleen returned to her essays, and I made a pass through the kitchen before hitting the bed. A spotless kitchen greets me each morning.

Evan's bloodstone ring rested in the bowl where we place

seashells. I'd left it there earlier and had forgotten about it. I reached in my wallet and took out the picture of Liana Castillo. Next, I retrieved Sally's glasses out of the glove box of the truck. I placed the trio together. I am embarrassed to admit that I—a fully decorated veteran of booze-induced philosophy—pondered their meaning. You'd think I would have learned.

When my eyes finally released the day, I got what I deserved. A real zinger. One for the ages.

A DISCO BALL SPUN SPARKLING WHITE-AND-SILVER LIGHT. Wood caskets lined the circumference of the room. They were closed. Music played, but it was nothing I was familiar with. The tempo accelerated—*accelerando*—until it was a frantic combination of sound and primal beat.

One of the caskets sprung open. Not the whole top, but the half that held the upper torso of the deceased. Victor, a man I'd killed years ago, popped up. His face had a *Shining* Nicholson grin. He fell back in the casket. It slammed shut.

Another coffin lid popped open. It was the first man I'd killed. A man in Afghanistan, a different life ago. He was the enemy, but he'd looked only human on the ground, not enemy-like at all. His upper half sprung upright, still wearing the bloodied battle garments he wore the day I put him in the ground. *Note: Eternity doesn't come with a change of clothes.*

He, too, fell back into his casket. The lid slammed shut.

Behind me. Another casket opened. The man who had kidnapped Kathleen popped up. I wanted to kill him again. Some men are too evil to die only once. The son of a bitch fell back into his tomb.

One after another, the caskets opened. The Cardinal—he crossed himself. Phillip Agatha. *Didn't Garrett kill him?* The dead popped up and down. Laughing. Grinning. Some I'd put in the casket. Others I only felt that, in some manner, I'd been responsible for their death. Andrew Keller was there. I took a step toward him. I wanted to ask him if he remembered that I visited him a few days ago and if he smelled the roses. But he was back in his casket before I could talk. I realized I couldn't talk.

Another casket opened. But instead of a body, the picture of Liana Castillo flashed up, beaming in her school dress. I felt terrible for her, having to be in the circus of the macabre. A carnival of death. She was too young. Too innocent. Sally sprung up, wearing his glasses. A camera around his neck. Food on his lips.

Evan popped up. He quacked.

"No!" I shouted, but I couldn't hear my voice. *Why wasn't the damn thing working?*

I searched for Evan's casket, but it had slammed shut. I couldn't find it. The disco ball spun at a madding speed, the music a runaway carnival track.

The finale: The caskets exploded. Opening. Shutting. Torsos popping up and down. Down and up. And then I saw it: the casket next to Andrew Keller had never opened. *Was it empty like the plot next to him in the graveyard?* I walked to it. I started to open the casket.

"Jake. Jake. Wake up. You're having a nightmare."

Beat it. I need to know. I reached for the—

"Stop it. You're hitting me."

I rubbed my hand over my sweaty forehead, my eyes finally unfastening. The caskets were spinning in my head, but they were no longer caskets. It was the ceiling fan. I lay there, trapped in hypnagogic hallucinations, that bridge between dreams and consciousness, between the world we think we know and the world that knows us.

"You okay?" Kathleen said.

"Never better," I mumbled.

"What were you dreaming?"

"I was at a disco," I said, still coming out of it. "I heard a duck."

"Really?" she giggled. "Hey, remember 'Disco Duck'? Was its something like that?"

It was a disco for the dead.

36

China and I met again at the student center. I wanted to test her resolve. Give her a dozen reasons to back out. I told her that Kathleen might not hear of it. That it might blow up in our face because it always blows up in our face.

"I understand," she said. "But that just confirms that I'm making the right decision. It makes me admire Dr. Rowe that much more." She humped her shoulders. "Besides, you'll bear the brunt of her wrath."

We discussed when, and how, to tell Kathleen, but no obvious choice surfaced. I reviewed legal considerations. Adoption rules. How the courts would favor her if she changed her mind during the first year and that we would support her. I told her I would pay for an attorney to represent her. None of that budged her off her position. She seemed infatuated with the idea of Dr. Rowe raising her child. She seemed more infatuated with, and relieved by, not having to raise a child herself.

"The shit of it is," she said, "I've never been into kids. I've always known that."

When we parted, I was less enthusiastic than when I'd arrived, but I didn't know why.

37

Donna Novak, who had the office next to Sally Russo, finally returned my phone call. I felt a tad guilty deceiving her—I told her I was interested in her listing—but the feeling never grew roots. I'd looked further into Sally Russo and couldn't find any family outside an older brother in Sacramento whom he had not talked to in over two years. Maybe Donna Novak knew Sally, maybe not. But if so, I wanted to know if Sally had uncovered anything else that might shed light on Giancarlo and lead me to Angel. Angel was my path to Evan. Plus, he stepped on my face. I struggle with forgiving.

Donna and I stood on the back balcony of a second-floor unit overlooking a manicured courtyard. It held a small pool that would have frustrated anyone who attempted laps. Donna tried hard to be a refrigerator-magnet-worthy realtor. Lipstick. Sprayed hair. Long earrings. A loose-fitting dress trying to hide a figure that had gotten away from her. Spouting off multimillion-dollar deals as if they were her listings. Her emotional anxiety swung between fear of being exposed and courage to carry on. She toddled in her high heels worse than Kathleen. But her smile was authentic even if her war-paint-mulberry cheeks were not.

"Notice the stainless," she said when we returned to the kitchen. "You won't need to put a penny here, that's for sure." She wore no wedding ring but a collection of bracelets that didn't go with her outfit, as if she'd forgotten to take them off when she switched to her realtor persona. "Where do you live now?"

I wanted to expose myself before we got too deep into the ruse.

"In Pass-a-Grille. But—"

"Oh, I just love it. I'd die to have one of the cottages, but those prices just rocketed. Do you ever get to Eighth Avenue? There's an art shop there. I have some paintings and jewelry there on consignment."

"I've been to that shop."

Kathleen, who had killed every green plant so unfortunate as to have come under her purview, had, years ago, purchased a small sign from the store. The sign read "Grow, Damn It." That was the extent of my wife's gardening skills. But unlike her bafflement with kitchens, I sensed Kathleen harbored a secret desire to be a gardener. To be one of those smiling women in *Southern Living* surrounded by blossoming blue hydrangeas, a spade in their hand—not a speck of dirt on their summer dress—standing in front of a shaded porch. A porch with white couches framed with colorful pillows and a pitcher of lemonade on a pollen-free glass table.

The Grow, Damn It pot sat next to my outdoor shower, a reminder of why I'm totally batty for my wife and a testament that it's okay not to worry about trying to be what you will never be. I wanted to impart that to Donna Novak. But we don't touch people that fast, although that would not be the case with Donna Novak and me.

"Actually, Donna, I wanted to meet to discuss Salvatore Russo. I noticed your office is next to his."

"Sally?"

Sally.

I blurted out that I was working with one of his clients. That I was searching for information that might be beneficial in finding who killed him. I dropped Detective Rambler's name to add legitimacy to my request. Rambler had questioned Donna, but only to the extent of whether or not she'd been in her office the day of the murder. She had not. He had not pressed further than that. I thought that a mistake on his part but would never say as much. Rambler's caseload was nothing anyone would want to punch an alarm clock for.

"You're not interested in a condo?" she said, unable to hide her hurt. I felt bad and wondered when was the last time Donna Novak sold a condo. Or a necklace at the art shop.

"I am not. I need to know more about Sally Russo."

She furrowed her eyebrows. "Because you want to find out who killed him? Why?"

"It's possible Sally was murdered because of what he unearthed while working for his client." Then, as she eyed me with skepticism, I added, "Maybe you can help. Maybe you can't."

"Who is the client?"

"Erica Giancarlo."

"You know Erica?" she said.

"I do. And you?"

She ignored my question. "I don't know how I can possibly help."

"Anything you can add about his work—about Erica—could be beneficial."

"So, you're sorta taking over for Sally?"

"You could say that."

She flashed a sassy smile, uncharacteristic of her. "Then you should have been the one to say it."

"I need your help, Donna," I said with all the sincerity I could muster.

"I told that detective—Rambler—that I wasn't even there that day. I'm rarely in that office. Meaning never. I signed a cheap lease years ago when I had aspirations of being some top-dog realtor. Before I realized there are a hundred realtors for every listing. I'm not renewing the lease."

"You called him Sally."

"We'd pass in the hall."

"You were never there."

We were silent for a moment.

"You knew Erica's name."

She remained quiet, as if we were in a musical, and the composer had written measures of silence.

"They cut his ear off, Donna. Left him to bleed to death surrounded by his pictures."

She turned away from me and teetered over to the patio doors looking out toward the tranquil courtyard.

"Why did you say that?" she said with her back to me.

"I was—"

She turned, her cheeks streaked with tears.

"Why did you *say* that?" she repeated.

"I'm sor—"

"The police never asked me if I knew Sally, only if I was there that day. They cut his ear off?"

"Left one."

"Why?"

"To get him to confess to something he knew nothing about."

Her hand shot up to her mouth. She wiped her tears, smudging her makeup.

"I found some undeveloped film in his office," I said, softening my voice. "I shared it with Detective Rambler. In his work for Erica Giancarlo, Sally inadvertently tripped over men who did not want to be seen together. Men who had nothing to do with Erica Giancarlo getting a divorce. You knew him well, didn't you?"

Her shoulders slumped. "I really was hoping to sell this. You sounded so . . . qualified on the phone. You sure you don't want a downtown condo? Once people move to downtown Saint Pete—oh, they love it so much."

"I'm sorry for your loss," I said, taking a chance.

She blew out her breath and dabbed a corner of her eye with the back of a knuckle.

"The seller's greedy," she said. "She's overreaching and needs to lower the price. But she won't listen to me. The listing will expire, she'll sign with someone else, lower the price, and they'll get the commission." She puffed her breath out. "What a racket. Let's go to my office. I've got some things to show you. Help me get these lights, will you?"

38

We trekked three blocks to her office, discussing how the building started as apartments, converted to offices, and was slated to be transformed back again to residential and how if you live long enough, you witness these cycles and not just in real estate. She was an easy person to talk with.

"How did you and Sally meet?" I asked as she fiddled in her purse for a key.

"When I took the office years ago, he was already encamped. He had a cheerful sadness about him. I think we recognized that in each other." She plucked keys out of her purse and shot me a look. "He brought me flowers."

Salvatore Russo's photographs, the great loneliness he saw in the world, draped the walls of her office. She headed to an under-counter refrigerator. "I thought I'd be spending more time here, but it didn't work out that way. Can I get you something? Coke? Water? A juice box?"

"You don't have animal crackers, do you?"

"Darn, I think I'm out."

"A water would be fine."

"One water and one Coke Zero coming up."

She opened the under-counter refrigerator and handed me a water. She popped the top of an aluminum can and guzzled it like it was the last days of Rome.

My eyes swept the room. "He did exceptional work."

She lowered the can and kicked off her shoes, shrinking by a few inches. She extracted a pair of loafers from under the desk and put them on.

"He had more pictures than wall space, and I was happy to oblige."

"He was working for Erica Giancarlo," I said. "She is innocent in all this. But he saw things that got him killed. Did he say anything to you, share anything, that might help me find who killed him?"

She put down her Coke Zero on a coaster on her desk. She stared out the window, her ample figure blocking most of the light.

"Isn't life a riot?" she said, her back still toward me. "Like these pictures. You look and look and look, and then suddenly you see. Only then do you realize that looking is not seeing."

I expected her to continue, but she stopped, as if halted by her own words.

She turned to me. "I've never been married. Nor he. My life held a futureless future. You regret calling me yet?"

"Not at all."

"You will. Sally and I were staring down a road. That Norman Rockwell road, where you walk hand in hand with another person, and everything is good. I wanted that road. My whole life had been a dream of that road, but I thought I'd done something wrong."

Norman Rockwell: He left the *Saturday Evening Post* in the early 1960s because they refused to allow him to place Black people on his covers. He later rescinded his earlier work depicting the simplistic way of life, stating, "That stuff is dead." Norman Rockwell knew the monorail—which he perpetuated—was a hoax. But who among us has the stomach for such indigestive truths?

"That good road is still there," I said.

"Want to know what low looks like? One Saturday night —this was before I met Sally—I went to the airport just to pretend I was going someplace. I could hardly live with myself the next week. We talked about that. That Lonelyville is a crowded place."

"Is there anything you can help me with?" I implored again, recalling she'd mentioned she had something to show me.

"I don't blame you for not being interested in a fifty-year-old's lamentations on life. Besides, who am I kidding? I'm seventy in six years. Since Sally died, even I've lost interest in me. I'm so lonely I don't even have a shadow."

"You have a lot—"

"That was supposed to be a joke, by the way. Sally said, and I quote, 'If anything happens to me, it might be because of these.'"

She opened the top desk drawer and withdrew a manila folder. She handed it to me.

"You didn't give these to the police?"

"I would have gotten around to it. I wasn't ready."

"Ready?"

"The road, Mr. Travis. I wasn't ready to give up that road. Death had no right. No authority to take it from me. I waited a long, *long* time. And somebody I don't know, who doesn't know me, just takes it? Ends his life?" She cocked her head. "You're going to wish you bought the condo to shut me up."

I held up the folder. "Nonsense. Do you know what's in here?"

"Let's take a look, shall we?"

She pushed aside her Coke Zero and cleared an area on the desk. I spread out half a dozen five-by-seven pictures. They were not from artist Sally, but from PI Sally. Color. Focused. The object of the camera centered in the picture.

And Edward Giancarlo was in every one. It made sense. Sally was hired by Erica to find dirt on him. I did a quick scan to see if any of them also had Angel, but they did not. Most were of Giancarlo coming and going from his office. A few were of him exiting restaurants with people I didn't recognize. I was disappointed.

"He told me these were the only copies," Donna said. "Sally didn't do computers. He has—had a darkroom. Developed his own film, and I don't know why I'm going to tell you this, but here we go: the first time we made love was in that darkroom, and there is no finer place in a city to make love than a windowless room barely bigger than a closet."

I shot her a glance.

"Where was the last place?"

"Last place what?"

"Where you made love."

"Why are you asking?"

"Withdrawn. It's none of my business."

She bit her lower lip.

"My place. In the morning." She paused for a beat and then leveled her eyes on mine. "I woke up with the smell of sex on my fingertips and someone else passing gas in bed, and I thought maybe, just maybe, I was really alive. Any pictures rock your boat?"

I held two photographs, one of Giancarlo entering a church and another of him with his girlfriend outside the church.

"Looks like the Methodist church not far from here," Donna said, maneuvering beside me. "Doesn't look like Sunday. I mean, there's no one else around."

The church was a few blocks away. I'd become acquainted with it when I was investigating the death of Andrew Keller years ago. Anna Vargas, Elizabeth Walker's maid, had lived in the church. She'd sought sanctuary there while her appeal to stay in the United States slowly made its way through a sluggish and overburdened court system.

The picture of the church made me shiver. Life is a circle. That's either true or we make it true, and I'm sure I don't know the difference.

"Look here." She leaned over the table, her finger pointing to a picture of Giancarlo entering the rear door of the church. Webbed plastic grocery bags dangled from his hands. "Looks like he's delivering provisions to someone."

"Did Sally say anything else about these?"

She humped her left shoulder. "He said it was *because* they didn't fit into anything else that he thought they were key to whatever Giancarlo was up to. Sally was hired to find dirt on Giancarlo. He felt he'd tripped over something unrelated and unexplained."

"When were these taken?"

She scrunched her face. "A week ago? Two?"

I flipped through the remaining ones. In one picture, Sally had left his subject, Giancarlo, and instead taken photos of the street. It appeared to be the same day, the same lighting. I moved it closer to my eyes, scrutinizing it. A coffee shop on the right side. A man inside, peering out the window, a newspaper in his hand. The top half of his face visible.

I knew that man.

You need to look into your own house.

"May I have them?" I nodded toward the pictures.

"Please. I hope good comes from them. They are the last pictures he took. I like that they're in color. I also like that the last time I saw him, I didn't know it was the last time. It's best something ends when you don't know it's ending."

She paused and then said, "I ran."

"Pardon me?"

"Through the airport. To pretend I was late for a plane. From the red terminal to the blue terminal and back again because, you know, without a ticket you can't go to the gates."

Her body slumped like a failed dress strap that knew the evening had gone poorly. Her moist eyes were a sad song.

"Is that what I'm going back to?"

I surprised myself and gave her a hug. I expected her to break away at any moment and say she was fine, but she didn't, and we stood like that. Silently hugging each other.

She pulled away.

"You sure you don't want to buy that condo?"

"I'm sure."

She laughed and wiped away a streak of tears.

"Well, damn. I gave it my best shot, didn't I?"

YANKEE CONRAD AGREED THAT THE MAN IN THE window of the coffee shop was who I thought he was. A man

I recognized from the email Yankee Conrad had sent me when he'd first asked me to look into the case.

"And so the impossible moves instantly to the inevitable," he said, studying the picture. I recalled one of Yankee Conrad's contemporaries using the same phrase while I was investigating someone who had found a different way to die.

"You suspected him, didn't you?" I said.

"Suspect? No. Consider? Yes. The only certainty is that nothing is certain," he said, quoting Pliny the Elder. He picked up the picture. "My dear Eugene. What have you been up to?"

39

The dooming bells of the church announced the hour with a solemnity and finality unrivaled in the digital world. Tempus fugit. It was Thursday night. Choir practice. Cars packed the rear parking lot.

The previous day, I'd driven and walked by the church numerous times—hopefully not enough to rouse someone's interest. A car with deeply tinted windows had been parked in the rear of the parking lot. Occasionally, a man would emerge from the vehicle for a stretch and stroll to a nearby sandwich shop. That car was no longer there.

Morgan entered the back door with a group of people, already making conversation with them. Five minutes later, a side door swung open. I slipped inside and joined him. Garrett kept surveillance on the outside.

The church's thick plaster walls made for hushed, stuffy halls. We climbed the stairs to the classrooms, where Anna Vargas had been living after the church granted her sanctuary. Edward Giancarlo had stashed someone in the church. I couldn't stop hallucinating that Evan Brackett would be in one of those rooms. That lightning would strike twice, and I would walk in on him as I'd done at his cottage. This time, I would grab his arm and never let go. That was a long shot, but a man can dream.

The voices of a children's choir, that unmistaken clarity of innocence, echoed the halls. The smell of barbecued beef, like a sustained bass note, accompanied the music.

"May I be of assistance?"

I turned and faced a tanned man with a neatly trimmed mustache. He sported broad shoulders and a relaxed stance.

"We're looking for someone who may live here," Morgan said.

"Our doors are open to those in need," the man said. His sonorous voice was gentle. Kind. "Do you have a name?"

"We do not."

"If I may ask, why do you seek someone you do not know?"

"Is that not what you do in a church?"

The man laughed and extended his hand to Morgan. "I'm Pastor Tim. Who do I have the pleasure of talking to?"

Morgan introduced himself and said we used to visit Anna Vargas in the church.

Pastor Tim arched his eyebrows. "Anna? Yes, she was special."

I thought he would expound, but he clamped shut.

"We helped expedite her case," I said.

"That was so good of you. And you are . . .?"

I introduced myself, and we shook hands. Pastor Tim owned a firm handshake.

"Tell me more about the person you seek who you do not know," Pastor Tim said, shifting his eyes between Morgan and me.

"I observed a man entering and leaving your church. He appeared to be hauling groceries," I said. "I have reason to believe he is visiting someone here. Maybe a young man."

Pastor Tim rubbed his unshaved chin. He smelled like cigarette smoke. He must be eager to get to heaven and test his beliefs.

"Do you know his name?" Pastor Tim said. I thought it odd that he didn't respond by pointing out the obvious: there is a kitchen, and the person might be working for the church.

"Edward Giancarlo," I said. "I believe he parks a car out back, keeping an eye on your church. I'm sure you're aware of this."

"I am not. But I spend much of my time either holed up in my study or visiting church members, often in hospitals."

"If it's all the same, I'd like to continue my search."

He extended his hand. "Of course. Although I am afraid you will not find who you are looking for."

"What makes you so certain?"

He chuckled. "I assure you, I would know if anyone was living here." He extended his hand. "But please, God's house is always open."

Well, that wasn't true. The doors were normally locked, but I didn't dispute his claim.

Morgan and I strolled down the long hall, poking our heads into classrooms. Pastor Tim accompanied us, chatting with Morgan about the expense of maintaining such a cavernous building. We must have been close to the choir practice room, for the air swelled with Peter Lutkin's "The Lord Bless You and Keep You." It concluded with his famous "Sevenfold Amen." The melody took me to a different place, for the song was one of my favorite memories from attending church with my family. We went every Sunday, except in the summers—no sane family did that—until my sister was kidnapped. We never attended again. When I hear choir music, I am confused as to whether I miss the music or the time of my life it represented, which seems far more likely.

"Beautiful choir," I said, scrapping my musings.

"Thank you," Pastor Tim said. "I'm sorry you haven't found who you're looking for. Why, again, if I may ask, are you seeking him?"

"Personal business."

"Concerning what?"

I gave him a weak smile. "Personal."

He let it drop. I wanted to search the basement of the church as well. I was contemplating how to phrase that when Morgan said, "Do you keep in contact with Anna?"

"Who?"

"Anna Vargas. The woman you granted sanctuary to a few years back."

"Oh. Yes, well, I only heard of her. You see, I've been pastor here for about a year."

Manuel Castillo's words came back to me:

We went to our church, the big brick Methodist church down-town. My wife loved that church. The senior minister is kind, and she tried. But there is little she could say to help us.

"Are you the senior pastor?" I asked.

"I am," Pastor Tim said. He folded his hands in front of him.

"I think the minister when Anna was here was Reverend . . . I can't place him . . . Dixon—no, Hixon, is that right?"

Pastor Tim eyed me. "Yes," he said coolly. "He has moved on."

"Who has moved on?"

"Our former pastor. The church likes shuffling us around. Tell me more about this man, Edward Giancarlo. Why do you think he comes here every day?"

Morgan stared at me—we'd never met the pastor when visiting with Anna. I kept my eyes on Pastor Tim. He held my gaze.

"Did I say he came every day?"

Pastor Tim's eyes narrowed. "A simple assumption."

"Perhaps he came for the music," I said. "He loved the piece the choir is practicing. Bach, isn't it?"

"I believe it is." He manufactured a laugh. "But I'm not that good at music. That is what a choir is for, isn't it?"

"Do you mind if I take a peek in the basement?"

"After you."

He extended his arm. I took three steps before he fell in line behind me. Morgan was on my left, keeping his head down.

A table to my right held two tall brass candlesticks and a large glass vase.

I stopped, pivoted, and took a step back toward Pastor Tim, swinging a right-hand roundhouse. But he was ready and easily dodged my fist. He countered with a left jab. I snapped my head to the side, his fist just missing my cheek. He flashed a knife. I grabbed one of the brass candlesticks.

"Good luck with that, asshole," Pastor Tim said.

He thrust the knife forward, and I parried with my candlestick. It was heavier than I anticipated, its weight awkwardly centered. Whoever designed it had not considered its employment as a weapon.

I feigned lowering the candlestick. He came at me again. I dodged to my left, dropped the candlestick, and punched him square in his face. His toupee slid partway off, and I recognized him. The smoker I'd seen at Pioneer Park the day Sally was killed.

He stumbled back but kept possession of the knife. I landed a forward kick to his midsection. He bent over and stumbled back two steps. Morgan stuck out his foot. Pastor Tim went down, taking the table with him. The glass vase shattered.

I stepped on his hand that held the knife and twisted my foot. He let go of the knife. I kicked it away.

I said, "Bach didn't compose 'The Lord Bless You and Keep You.'"

His face scrunched in confusion. "That's it?"

"The senior minister of this church is a woman. And Pastor Tim? No one is really named Pastor Tim."

"Fuck you."

"You work for Angel?"

"You understand 'Fuck you'?"

"You were in the park the day Sally Russo was killed. You did him first and then hit the park to see who showed up. You're one of Angel's boys."

He shifted his weight on the floor, rolling on his side and propping himself up. I took a step back. Morgan picked up the knife and handed it to me.

"Why are you here?" I said.

"Church security."

"Man's name is Evan Brackett. May go by Walker Percy. Where is he?"

"Never heard of him."

I kneeled down beside him.

"Did you ever read Paul's letter to your namesake, Timothy? Because if you did, you'd know that's not you and me.

Guys like us? We're Old Testament. An eye for an eye. A tooth for a tooth. You with me, Timothy?"

He nodded, fear gripping his eyes. But it was a show. He scissor kicked his legs, and I stumbled backward. He started to push himself up. I sprang on top of him, wrapped my left arm around his throat, and brought the knife to the side of his face.

He froze.

"No more stunts. Understand?"

He nodded. I stood.

"Who sent you?"

"One of Angel's men."

"Imagine. You do know Angel."

"Seen him a couple times. He signs the checks."

"You're local muscle?"

"It's a job."

"Why is Angel watching the church?"

"Giancarlo was holding someone here. We spotted him going in and out. He kept a car out back. We set up a watch, but then he pulled out. We never saw him or the car again. But we hung around, saw you casing it—you're not the hot shit you think you are. They put me on standby. Told me to follow you in if you entered."

"The car out back?"

"Ours, asshole."

I'd seen pictures of Giancarlo entering the church, but that was over a week before. I'd assumed the stakeout was his.

"Why were you tailing Giancarlo?"

"Above my pay grade."

"Who did he have here?"

"We never figured it out. But he took food in."

"You come across a young woman named Rachel?"

"No."

"Would the sight of your blood improve your memory?"

"Take all you want. I never heard of her."

"Why did Angel care who was in the church?"

"Like I sit in on the tribal meetings?"

"Tell me again about Evan Brackett."

"Got wax in your ears?"

"Want to keep both of yours?"

Pastor Tim evaluated his position.

"We went to some beach cottage looking for him, but he was gone."

"Gone?"

"Someone beat us there."

Angel doesn't have Evan? Did Evan give them the slip? Mess up his own home to make it appear that he was captured?

"One more. Who murdered Salvatore Russo?"

"Not me."

"You were in the park the day he was killed. The police would love to pin it on you. Close the case."

"We were told to be on the lookout at two-thirty. See who came. You showed up. We figured you knew something we didn't."

"You killed Sally Russo first."

"I don't do that shit. Julio and I was just told to go to the park."

"Who does do that shit?"

He hesitated.

"Is he worth protecting?"

"Rumor is some trash named Riggins.

"He work for Angel?"

"He'll work for a troll. Total wack job."

"You ever hear the name Vargo?"

"No."

"Think harder."

"Nothing, man."

I called Rambler and asked him to send a squad car. Five minutes later, two policemen came in with guns drawn. They holstered their weapons only after Pastor Tim was cuffed. With luck, Rambler would fingerprint him and find something useful. Then we would find out if he knew more than he let on. But they had little reason to hold him.

After the cruiser left, I strode back into the church. Morgan was conversing with a woman in slacks and an untucked black short-sleeve shirt. He said something. She laughed. But her face hit serious mode when she saw me approaching.

"Mr. Travis," she said in a schoolmarm voice. Her hair was pulled behind her neck, her lips pale, her face devoid of makeup.

"Yes, ma'am?"

"I'm Reverend Cyndi-Girard. I understand you brought violence into my house."

"No, ma'am. I encountered a violent man."

"You encountered a violent man," she said, weighing each word. She paused a beat before coming back in. "I'm working late today, Mr. Travis. I have three children at home and a wonderful husband who makes dinner every Thursday. Wonderful Husband just informed me that while reading to our youngest, the oldest announced her intention to have her navel pierced this Saturday, and the middle one, our son, has locked himself in the bathroom he shares with his sisters. My husband suspects he has just discovered self-pleasure. I asked him why he would say such a thing, and he said it was at about the same age that he learned to spank the monkey. We'd been speaking of monkeys, you see, because our dog ate its stuffed monkey and then proceeded to vomit it back up, along with everything else she'd consumed in the last twenty-four hours. Apparently, I am the only one capable of sorting all this out. On top of that, I'm supposed to deliver a sermon this Sunday on Christ's great capacity for forgiveness, but who has time for that when you're googling carpet cleaners? Do you understand I do not have the time or the patience to parry words with you?"

"I apologize for the ruckus I caused."

"Ruckus. Yes, well, I appreciate a good understatement as well as anyone. Morgan, however, has already apologized for you."

"A man named Edward Giancarlo was seen entering and leaving your church last week. I believe he—you—gave sanctuary to someone here. I am familiar with your good deeds in that area. Several years ago, I met Anna Vargas here."

"I know who you are," she said flatly.

"I need to know who Giancarlo was protecting. My nephew is missing, as is a young woman. It might have been either of them."

"I assure you it was not."

"Who was Giancarlo keeping in your church?"

"That is not for me to say."

"But you know?"

"Of course."

"Then tell me."

She took two steps toward me. Her eyes did not challenge mine, nor did they retreat. She was one of those people so inherently comfortable with themselves that you shrank in their presence.

"That is between Mr. Giancarlo and me. If you would be so kind as to go down the hall?"

"Yes."

"On the right is a janitor closet. People do not come to church expecting to see candlesticks and shattered glass on the floor."

"I'll take care of it."

She turned to leave, but then pivoted back around.

"He's a good man," Reverend Cyndi-Girard said.

"Who?"

"Edward Giancarlo. He is a good man. A gentle man. And despite his agnostic beliefs, which we've gone several rounds on, a major supporter of this church. Whatever you're thinking, whatever path your thoughts are leading you on, I strongly suggest you reconsider."

"Can you help me a little more?"

"I gave you all you need to know. As we say in the business—have faith. Goodnight, Mr. Travis."

The Reverend Cyndi-Girard turned and plodded away, in no hurry to go home.

Two minutes later, I was on my hands and knees, cleaning the floor and thinking of Reverend Cyndi-Girard's parting comment. I'm not big on faith, but I didn't dismiss what the reverend had said. It fit with Erica imploring that Edward Giancarlo was innocent.

Morgan went to the kitchen and brought back pulled-pork sandwiches and coleslaw. As we sat on the cool floor, devouring our sandwiches, Garrett called. We'd just hung up a few minutes before, after I filled him in on the night's activities.

"I just got a name," he said.

"A name?"

"The man who killed her."

"Liana?"

"Beth."

Beth.

Garrett's fiancée. I had not heard him speak her name since the night he called and told me she'd been murdered. It was a name from the past that halted the future.

"Where?"

"Still in Cleveland. I arranged a private jet. Saint Pete, Clearwater. Leaves in ninety minutes. I'm outside in your truck. Front entrance."

Garrett had never hesitated when I'd called him. He always had my back. Now it was my turn. Morgan wrapped the sandwiches and texted for an Uber back to his house.

Garrett and I landed in Cleveland's Burke Lakefront Airport a few minutes before midnight, tired, hungry, and thirsty for revenge. Evan. Rachel. Liana. They would all have to wait. The whole world would have to wait.

It ends now.

40

RACHEL

Let's go find seven.

Rachel had become increasingly worried about her father. Her mother, Sophia, had been gone for years, and Vargo had become quieter. Sullen. Not day by day, not even by month. By season. As if something were pulling him under, and that something was winning.

They'd just finished lunch in the shade of the porch. Rachel's eyes rested on yellow flowers in the garden, aflame with the light of the sun. On top of her concern for her father, she was eager to plot her own life. Chase her dreams. *Should I bring it up now?*

"How bad do you miss her?" Rachel asked her father.

"Not as much as I used to," Vargo said.

"Dad!"

"It's not that, Scooter. I feel closer to her now than I did after her death. For, like you, she changes for me."

Scooter. She'd earned the name by chasing rabbits or, as young Rachel called them, baby bunnies. Never mind their age. Their size. The ugliest jack rabbit ever to hop a Mexican landscape was still a baby bunny. She'd dash around the fields, her father impressed with her ability to scoot after the white fluffy tails she had no chance of catching.

"You've not called me that for a long time."

"Haven't I?" he said absentmindedly. His eyes searched the yard for something that wasn't there.

"I need to scoot. I want to go to a university and do graduate work. I'm ready. I think I'm ready. It's what she'd want."

"I'll miss you."

His simple remark of resignation surprised her.

"I'll come home," she said. "Besides, you have your business."

"It is just business. In the end, it counts for little."

"If it counts for so little, then why does it consume so much?"

"Do you think everyone has a choice?"

"I have a favor to ask you," she said. She wanted to keep on subject and not be sidetracked by her father's moping question.

"Anything."

"Before I go, I need to learn more."

"Haven't you tested out of the first two years of college?"

Rachel had taken correspondence courses from the National Autonomous University of Mexico. At age twenty, she was on the cusp of taking graduate courses.

"Three," she said, smiling inwardly. Her father had never been good with the numbers of her life. Her age. What year she was at in her studies. Her birthday—she knew Emilia alerted him when that date was rounding the corner. "I'll be doing graduate work. Before I apply, I need someone to push me. I want to outwork what talent I have. I need to exceed myself."

"Why are you so driven?" Vargo asked, suddenly perplexed by the woman in front of him.

How can you not know?

"I just am." She shrugged.

"Didn't you tell me you were finished with tutors?"

"And you believed me?"

"Why wouldn't I? What were those last five elements again? Wasn't one Arkansas or something?"

"Tennessine, and there were four. Just literature this time. That is where my graduate studies will be. And someone who knows more than me."

Vargo considered his daughter, who had so much of her mother in her that he went from joy to sorrow and back to joy every time he looked at her.

"Okay. When the right person comes along."

THE RIGHT PERSON CAME ALONG THREE MONTHS LATER.

"He is highly recommended by an old friend," Vargo told her. Then, as an afterthought, he added, "Have you ever heard of the theater of the absurd?"

"I am familiar with it," Rachel said. "Why do you ask?"

"Apparently, his knowledge of that sparked the conversation that led him here."

"You know, it's not an actual theater."

"I know that."

"Do you now?" she countered gaily. She had never seen her father so much as pick up a book. "I don't think you know theater of the absurd from a Broadway show."

"I do, Scooter."

"Let's hear it," she challenged him.

"A Broadway show is what we want to be true, and the theater of the absurd is what is true."

Damn. Maybe reading isn't what it's cracked up to be.

THEY MET THE FIRST TIME AROUND THE CAMPFIRE. Rumor had it that a bushy-haired American had arrived earlier that day, but Rachel had not spotted him.

He was a little older than her, and his nervous eyes did their failing best not to lock on her. The wind, particularly excited that night, blew smoke in his face. Rachel thought he was doing an admirable job of pretending it didn't bother him.

But apparently, her tutor wasn't interested in being barbecued. As Vargo talked, the young man picked up his chair. He repositioned it to the other side of the fire, upwind from the flame. Next to Rachel.

While Vargo was talking.

The others around the fire traded nervous looks. Emilia rescued them when, after Vargo finished, she went straight into a story about the time she ran the kitchen at the local hospital, and a dimwitted kitchen hand, after being scolded that the fryer vat was too hot, poured water into it to cool it down.

When she'd finished her tale, the conversation broke into regional pieces.

"Hey," Evan said to Rachel. "I'm Evan. You probably know that."

"I do. But it's reassuring to know that you do as well."

"I don't know what they told you, but I was brought here against my wishes—kidnapped—to tutor you."

"I had nothing to do with that."

"What time do you want to start in the morning?"

"All business, aren't we?"

"I wasn't carted here to roast wieners."

"Wieners?"

"Hot dogs."

"That's good to know."

"What? That I wasn't brought here to roast wieners or that wieners are hot dogs?"

"Wow. I'm dizzy already with everything you can teach me. How is seven?"

"Seven?" Evan said, as if he'd never heard the number before.

"Too early? I mean, the earlier we start, the earlier you can *cart* yourself out of here."

"Seven's fine."

The next morning, Evan was in the living room, sitting by the stone fireplace, at six-forty-five. Rachel showed up at ten, wearing a flowered dress that knocked his head off.

"What happened to seven?" Evan said.

She sat next to him and crossed her slender legs, her perfume rising from her bare neck.

"I don't know, Evan. What did happen to seven? Shall we go look for it?"

He rolled his tongue in his mouth. He'd been told he would be tutoring a high school girl. But this—this *woman*—was clearly no high school girl.

Is this how they come in Mexico?

He popped up. "Sure, Rachel. Let's go find seven."

This one's got attitude. Cute beyond words, too. Can't believe he had the moxie to move his chair next to mine last night.

She stood and faced him. Two strangers at the confluence of their lives. "Where shall we start?"

"In the kitchen," Evan said.

"The kitchen?"

"Seven is the hungriest number."

"That's right," she said with a smile. "I'd forgotten. Seven is known to favor the kitchen."

"The most condescending?"

"Nine."

"Naturally. The humblest?"

"Five."

"Why is that?"

"She must keep the group together." She batted her eyes. "Not easy when seven's always whining about food, nine's bossing the others around, and two's feeling unloved."

Hungry for literature, and for each other, they started reading the sevens. First up was *Smiley's People*, John le Carre's seventh outing. Rachel insisted they read the seventh chapter of *A Hundred Years of Solitude* because when the family patriarch dies, and it rains yellow flowers from heaven, she thought of her mother, and she wondered why heaven did not rain yellow flowers the day it summoned her.

They made a pair of exceptions.

First, *Romeo and Juliet*. It was actually Shakespeare's eighth play, but teacher and student wisely decided to forgo *Henry the Sixth Part Three*. "How many parts did Henry have?" Rachel postured. And second, Irving Stone's *The Agony and the Ecstasy*, his eighth work. When Evan told her that Stone had all of Michelangelo's 495 known letters translated from Italian as research for his book, Rachel swooned with admiration. They were in the grand living room, no one else around. A fire danced in the massive stone fireplace even though it was warm outside. "Four hundred and ninety-five letters," she gushed. "Imagine the time it took. He would have needed a December with more hours than snowflakes, an April with more days than flowers, a summer that—"

He kissed her.

Finally! What took him so long? Isn't there some stupid movie about having someone at "Hello"?

Maybe not so stupid after all, for Rachel had entered the asylum of love with the most unassuming proposition.

Let's go find seven.

41

Friday night. Cleveland, Ohio.

Daniel Morales sat at a bar, laughing with the fellow next to him.

It was those sacred, transitional hours. The workweek just complete. The weekend stretching before you, an open highway of time. A time when old dreams froth and bubble. Worries are an ocean away, and you feel younger. In control. You beg for those days to stretch because it's only forty-eight hours until Sunday night, but you try not to think of that. There are only two nights a week when you don't give the next morning to the man. And that starts now.

Garrett had secured a name, address, picture, and a bar "where he hangs every Friday night until ten, and I don't mean ten-oh-five."

The Pour Choice Bar sat east of downtown on concrete surrounded by the orange-barrel maze of gentrification. A few heads turned when we strolled through the door. We grabbed a corner table. The room had a solitary window, a partially curtained worthless pane of glass opposite the bar.

A shuffle bowling table pressed up against one wall. Small TVs on mute anchored the shelves of dimly lit liquor bottles. A Schlitz beer sign hung on a wall. "The beer that made Milwaukee famous." By the door, it was Stroh's: "Bohemian Beer. Served Wherever Quality Counts." A man, searching for answers, fed coins into a jukebox. Blue Oyster Cult's "Don't Fear the Reaper" came over the speakers. The song was papered on the walls. You could smell it in the air. Taste it in your beer. It played every Friday night at the Pour Choice Bar. One generation passing it down to the next.

Daniel Morales was a twenty-eight-year-old Black man. He lived nearby on South Taylor with a White woman, Nancy Port, whom he was not married to. Morales and Port had three young children in the household. The agency Garrett hired was unsure who belonged to who. Morales had done time for petty theft when he was fourteen and again at sixteen. He'd since managed to avoid jail, but not detection. He'd been a suspect in a rape, but never charged. He'd worked at an Amazon distribution center for the past three years. Nancy Port was a hairstylist. Maybe it wasn't the American dream, maybe it wasn't a dream at all, but it was living.

Twelve years ago, at 11:37 on a Saturday night in February, while five inches of whirling Lake Erie snow gnarled traffic, a gun was fired. Morales, then a member of a defunct street gang, had held that gun. Whether he intended to hit anyone was unknown. A bullet from the gun sailed onto Interstate 90, smashing through the rear window of a car in which Beth McInnis sat. She had been downtown seeing a performance with her parents at the recently renovated Hanna Theatre in Playhouse Square. The bullet shattered the car's window and entered her head—*skull*—killing her instantly.

A casing from the bullet that killed Beth had traces of DNA on it. That DNA matched Morales's when he was swabbed for a rape crime in 2013. He was one of three Black men suspected of blindfolding and raping a White woman in her Shaker Heights home. The police eventually charged and convicted a neighbor, a White man who was subsequently linked to three other rapes. That was after the press published the pictures of the three Black men. The victim's name was never revealed.

Despite the DNA, we could never put Morales within a gunshot of the crime. His gang members all vouched that he was not in the neighborhood that night. The weapon was never found.

That had changed three weeks ago. A man used the same gun to rob a convenience store. Spinning on his heels to leave, he sprinted smack into the chest of a plainclothes detective stopping by to purchase a lottery ticket and a lidless coffee—they were out of lids. Upon seeing the gun, the detective purportedly declared, "Not today." He tossed the hot coffee in the robber's face.

The gun had a history. And those who were tied to that history scrambled to cut deals. To look out for number one. A man bargaining for reduced jail time fingered Morales as the man who "took out that White bitch in the back of her car years ago." Such unsubstantiated statements are often thrown out to reduce jail time. But then another man stepped forward as well. Morales's former gang members— at least the ones who could be located—were no longer eager to vouch for him. We had the gun. We had witnesses. It was as close as we'd ever been.

DNA traces on bullets, shell casings, and guns do not mean the person whose DNA is on them actually pulled the trigger. Garrett and I had discussed that on the flight. He was noncommittal as to his course of action. Without saying it, we both wished the man didn't have a regular job, children, a woman, and a bar he went to every Friday night and left at ten sharp. Those items didn't make him a good man.

They just made it harder to kill him.

Garrett and Beth McInnis had planned to get married after she finished medical school. After she died, he teased death. Baited it. Mocked it. He'd rise at three a.m. and run five miles, angry at the road. He eagerly awaited my calls. He threw himself into his career—he was a utility lawyer with an office in downtown Cleveland, not far from the Pour Choice Bar. His humor, never his strongest suit, went underground.

Beth had been dead a long time. Now we were bringing her back, and I didn't know whether that was good or bad. I suspected it was neither, but something altogether different than I was familiar with. We'd made a good pair over the years: my heavy conscience and Garrett's superficial lack of one. But my conscience wasn't as pristine as I pretended, and his conscience was far more active than he let on.

At least the Garrett I used to know.

At nine-fifty, I took a final sip of my Bohemian beer and reached into my wallet to settle the tab. The picture of Liana Castillo spilled out. I hastily put it back. We slipped out, unnoticed by the celebratory Friday crowd. We had different plans, depending on whether Morales emerged by himself or with others.

We settled in our rental. A solitary streetlight, fending off the night, loomed like a weary star over the lineless parking lot.

Ten o'clock sharp. Morales walked out. Alone. Not stumbling, but with purpose. Time to go home. He marched to a late-model four-door sedan in the rear of the lot. Garrett and I exited our rental.

"Daniel Morales?" Garrett said.

Morales turned. "That's me." His eyes darted between Garrett and me before settling on Garrett. "What can I do for you, brother?"

We kept walking. Garrett planted himself a few feet in front of Morales. I settled off to his side. Morales, aware of our positioning, cut me a nervous look.

"My name is Garrett Demarcus."

"Afraid I don't know you."

Morales was tall and thin, more pole than man. He had a tenor voice and a mess of hair that, on second look, might have been by design. He wore a Hanford Dixon long-sleeve T-shirt with a few yards on it.

"Beth," Garrett said, as if the word had leaked out of his pores.

"Pardon?"

"Beth McInnis."

Morales's eyes widened in the dim light. His mouth drew tight. He knew. How many nights did he lie in bed and wonder if this day would ever come?

"Don't know the name, brother," he said. His voice strained. Higher.

"Don't call me brother."

"Sorry I can't help you . . . dudes. I gotta go home."

There are times in our lives when we need a change, to break the routine. But there are also times when we want nothing more from the world than just to leave us alone. To allow us to withdraw and cuddle in the harmless monotony of our existence. Daniel Morales's home, a few blocks away, was now a distant land, the sacred rhythm of his days, his hallowed monotony, forever gone.

"You pulled the trigger of the gun that killed her," Garrett said. "Not far from here. She was in the back seat of a car. Maybe you didn't mean to, but you killed her."

"I don't have a clue what you're talking about. You got the wrong man."

"We were engaged."

"I'm sorry, bro—dude. But like I said, you got the wrong man."

"I don't think so."

"I don't care much what you think."

He reached for his door handle.

"Don't," I said.

Morales glared at me. "Or what? You gonna jump me?"

"Nothing that pleasant."

He cut his eyes at Garrett. "Listen, man, I'm sorry for your loss, but like I keep sayin', you got the wrong man."

"She was twenty-six. Her whole life was in front of her. *My* whole life."

"How do—?"

"I was on tour. Know how you get the news in the service, *brother*? Your CO calls you in. You're thinking he wants intel on your last mission. Prep you for another. But that's not what it's about. You walk out the door. You don't understand. You will never understand."

Morales gnawed his lower lip. "Look, man. I mean, thanks for serving and all, but I don't—"

"They found the gun," Garrett said, taking a step toward the man. "The ballistics matched. We got two men who say it was your gun. They—"

"Why you believe—?"

Garrett put his hand up. "You were dumb muscle for a drug gang. You fired it that night. You killed her."

Morales shifted his weight and took a step back, bumping into his car. He glanced toward the bar, but it was a continent away.

"I don't know what you're talkin' about. I never killed no one."

"You think she was no one?" Garrett said, his temper boiling. He took one last step forward and was on the man, chin to chin.

"No, man. I ain't sayin' that uh-tall."

"What *are* you saying?"

"I didn't—"

Garrett thrust his hand out, his arm shadowed with roped muscle. He grabbed Morales by the neck, thrusting him off the ground.

"You killed her," Garrett shouted.

Morales gasped for air. He started to weep. Slow at first, and then without censor. As if something pressing inside was finally gushing out. I thought of Manuel Castillo crying at the bar, how all men cry alone, and I knew that Daniel Morales had retreated to a place no one could follow. I felt great pity for the man but tried to squelch that non-warrior emotion. I had witnessed what the death of Beth McInnis had done to my friend. My ticket was punched for revenge, not forgiveness. Old Testament time. Let's bring that good book on.

"I was a kid, man," Morales choked out. "I didn't mean to kill no one. You gotta believe me."

Garrett released him. "And she was a young woman riding home with her parents."

"What you want?" Morales said, battling his tears.

"Wanna know where I came from? I was East Side shit the second I was born. I spent my whole life trying to be anything other than what I was born into. I ain't the man who killed your girlfriend. I've been runnin' from that man my whole life."

"It doesn't work that way."

"I got kids, man," Morales said rubbing his neck. "A woman. A good job. I swear, man, I never wanted to hurt anybody my whole life."

"You didn't hurt her. She never felt a thing."

Morales's face pinched in pain. "Don't be sayin' that. What you want from me? You gonna kill me? You go ahead. Do it now. Then you go tell my woman. Tell my kids. That what type of man you are?"

"You could have turned yourself in."

"At sixteen, *brother*? You tell me you would have done that."

"I never would have shot her."

"Fuck that, man. You got college written all over you. You just a White man in a Black body. I got the street on me. Yeah, I knew. I read about her death the next day. Figured it was my bullet. What was I to do? Go to some white-ass police and say I jus' tryin' to be tough? Show them older boys that I belonged, wasn't afraid to pull a trigger? Fuck that, man. But I wasn't aimin' at nothin', man. I've been sorry every day of my sorry life. Can hardly look my children in the eyes. You know what it's like reading a children's book when you got that shit on you? You got no idea what I carry. I work hard to be who I am, not who I was."

He paused and took a deep breath.

"I read she was engaged to some man overseas. I knew

you'd be coming. I *knew* it. And here you are. So do it. Just fuckin' do it."

"You could have turned yourself in," Garrett repeated. He was at the crossroads of his life.

Morales wiped his tears away with his forearm. He glanced at the bar. "I'm sorry, man. So fuckin' sorry. But I can tell you this: the horror of what I did made me a better man 'cause I had no chance of being much of anything when I was born. So you tell me—what you want from me?"

"What do *you* want from me?" Garrett said.

"What?"

"You heard me."

Morales battled his tears. "Ain't no way you ever going to forgive me. But what good does killin' me do?" He swiped the back of his hand under his nose. "I got kids, man. My woman. My goddamn job. Goddamn Amazon. Fuckin' forty minutes each way. But it pays, man. Puts food on the table. I'm a good worker. You ask 'em. I'm a real good worker."

Garrett's bald head reflected the pale light from the lone streetlamp.

"We're good here," he said.

Morales wheezed his breath in through his nose.

"You playin' with me?"

Garrett glanced at me. "Let's roll."

"Hey, you mean that?" Morales said.

But Garrett had already turned his back to Morales and was hiking away. I fell in behind him.

"Oh no, man," Morales yelled. "Don't you be walkin' away from me. You just gonna pick your time and drop me when it's convenient for you. I know how this shit works. I ain't waitin' around for you to show up. Ain't no way for a man to live. I tol' you—you do it now. You too chickenshit for that? I'll meet you anywhere. Anytime. Let's get this done. You hear me? *You hear me, you motherfucker?*"

Garrett turned and strolled back up to him. Morales shrank under the dim light. His Hanford Dixon T-shirt draped over his bony shoulders. His tearstained face twisted all to shit.

"We will never meet again," Garrett said.

"You just gonna send someone else?"

"Go home, Daniel Morales. Read books to your children. And remember, she is watching you."

Garrett Demarcus reached out and squeezed Danial Morales on his shoulder. I thought of the Reverend Cyndi-Girard, and isn't the goddamn Rock and Roll Hall of Fame around here someplace?

I CLAIM NO RIGHT TO PREACH, SO PROCEED WITH CAUTION —skip it if you wish. But it seems to me that hate is easy. Love is hard. Evil didn't kill Beth; randomness did. You do not react violently to randomness. Garrett knew this. Most of the world does not.

As for me? I didn't think the compassion card would bring Evan back. Break my family curse. Resurrect Liana Castillo from her child grave. I didn't see Angel settling down, getting a job, renouncing his past, and reading *Goodnight Moon* to his children.

Lucky me. I had the easy way out.

42

China and I decided to avoid campus. We met at Paradise Grille on the Gulf of Mexico. Bickering gulls circled above summer tourists lined up to place their orders. Cobwebbed fish lines prevented the dirty birds from dive-bombing the tables. The air was drugged with humidity. I coughed repeatedly. I craved a cold beer but had a steaming cup of coffee in front of me.

"Thank you for the coffee," China said as I handed her a Styrofoam cup.

"Would you rather have a beer?" I asked.

"Shit, yeah."

I waited in line—again. Although it was not as busy as I would have thought, for the blossoming red tide had thinned the crowds. A frenzied breeze whipped off the water, pouring through my shirt. Greenish-gray splashes of white-caps tormented the Gulf, as if the great body of water threatened to wash itself up on the shore. Massive clouds, darker than night, blocked the sun. On the west coast of Florida, hell comes from the south.

I returned with two cold cans.

"To morning drinking," I said.

"To morning drinking."

She put her beer down but kept her hand on it.

"I had my ultrasound," she said, her eyes flicking up to mine, as it to make certain I was still there.

"Oh?"

She told me.

She went on to patiently explain what she wanted. No exception. It has to be this way. Don't you see? She was firm in her demands. Solid in her thinking. Concrete in her convictions.

"Will she be okay with this?" she said.

"Yes."

"Are you sure?"

"I am."

"How can you be?"

"I know her."

"But you said she told you she would never approach me."

"That's why it has to be this way."

"And you?" she asked. "Are you certain?"

"I think so."

"Think?"

"Only a fool would be confident at this point."

"I'm confident," she said.

"I wish you weren't. Remember, you can change your mind any time. You don't know how you'll feel afterward."

"You've said that before."

"I just said it again."

"I know. I mean, I know I don't. But I envision it, and that's not me. Not only now, maybe never. I'd be no good—

just full of resentment. She deserves love. Does that make me bad?"

"Not in the least bit. You can change your mind. That's what I'm saying. You understand that?"

"We've been over this."

"But do you under*stand*?"

"Yes. You've said nothing?"

"That is correct."

"When are you going to tell her?"

"I don't know."

"You know the oven's on, right?"

"I'm aware of that."

"So when?"

"Maybe at the end. Not the end, but at the very beginning for her."

"Can I be there?"

"I think it would be best."

"I've thought about it, and I do as well. So, we have a deal?"

"We do."

"Shit, this beer tastes great."

"It does."

The wind blew like it was never going to blow again. In the shallows, a young girl jumped in the waves, throwing herself against the foamy sea. She laughed with glee, her arms flaying at the jagged surface as if she were conducting the wind and the water. Nearby, her mother kept a watchful eye, shouting at her not to go out too deep, to stay in the shallows. But there was no need for the mother to be concerned, for the girl understood.

The chaos comes to you.

43

Eugene Levinson, the CIA agent who worked with the TOTA Technologies employees who traveled overseas, strolled out of the Birchwood Restaurant on Beach Drive. He headed north toward the Vinoy Hotel, his long strides eating up chunks of sidewalk. Levinson's home was four blocks north of downtown, in the historic district. It was nine forty-five, Saturday night. He'd just had dinner with Yankee Conrad. I checked my phone as a text came in from Conrad:

He knows.

Eugene Levinson was the man I recognized in one of Sally's pictures while meeting with Donna Novak. He was in a coffee shop across from the church where Giancarlo was sequestering someone. Yankee Conrad had confirmed my suspicion when I showed him the picture in his office. Eugene Levinson also matched the description Evan had given me of the man who had befriended him in Mexico: angular face, all forehead, and Lincoln ears. And pale, like his ancestry roots ran deep in the British islands.

Evan Brackett was the only person who could tie Eugene Levinson to Angel and Vargo. If I was right about Levinson, Evan was a threat to him and had to go. Maybe Levinson had Evan. I fell in step behind him. He stopped at the crosswalk directly across from the Vinoy Hotel.

"Mr. Levinson?"

He did not acknowledge me.

"I'm looking for Evan Brackett. I'm his—"

"I know who you are, Mr. Travis," he said, keeping his head straight. "And you can tell Yankee that I knew he wasn't interested in dinner. I do find whatever you two are up to rather amusing."

"Where's my nephew?"

He turned his head toward me. "I assure you I have no clue."

"I assure you I don't believe you."

"Believe what you wish." The light changed. Levinson took off. I matched him stride for stride.

"Why were you in the coffee shop across from the church watching Edward Giancarlo?"

"You have the wrong man," he said, not granting me his attention.

We'd crossed the street. He stopped and faced me. "Is there anything else you wish to pester me with?"

"I don't have the wrong man."

"Delusional beliefs will not solve your problems."

"How did it start? You picked up something from TOTA employees years ago and decided to dip your hand in the well?"

He sucked in his cheeks. "Again, I have no idea what you are referring to."

"Are you protecting Angel or promoting him?"

"I have no—"

"You're going to need a new line."

"And you're going to need to excuse me. Have a good evening, Mr. Travis."

I did not follow him. I'd accomplished what I wanted.

A HALF HOUR LATER, EUGENE LEVINSON EXITED HIS house. He entered a black SUV that was waiting for him on the street, its parking lights glowing the pavement. I gave it a block and a half and started my engine.

"Not too close," Garrett advised.

Here's a strange consistency in our lives: Garrett's always afraid I'll trail too close, and I'm paranoid that I'll fall too far back.

"Same vehicle from the cemetery?" he asked.

"First three letters match."

"You'd think they'd be more careful."

"They're not worried."

The SUV swung left on Second Street North. I gunned the truck through a yellow light. My phone rang. Rambler.

"Talk to me," I said, my eyes scanning the street for the black SUV.

"You in a hurry?"

"Trying to tail a man I think is the eye of the storm."

"Anyone I know?"

"No."

"Your Pastor Tim is bad company. He violated parole by carrying a gun. Second offense. He's looking at going back to the can. That jogged his memory."

"He had a gun on him?"

"That's what I said."

Rambler paused to make certain I understood what he was really saying.

"You okay with that?" I asked. Rambler was not someone to cross the line.

"There're a lot of things in this world I'm not okay with, starting with Liana Castillo's death being ruled an accident and ending with my wife moving in with another woman."

"Ouch. How long's that been going on?"

"Didn't ask. Angel put the hit on Sally Russo."

"Pastor Tim knows this?"

"He was there. Riggins pulled the trigger. He also postmarked the ear."

"To whom?"

"Giancarlo."

"Any message?"

"Another ten or your daughter's ear is next."

"Pastor Tim gave you that?"

"Car! Car! Car!" Garrett shouted. I swerved to miss a car.

"Man's real name is Orlando Reichert. Nothing in life to make his mother proud. Says he overheard they put a hit on Giancarlo's daughter and then demanded extortion money to protect her. He paid, now they want more."

I spotted the SUV and took a hard right on Central.

"So Giancarlo's adopted daughter was the target at the playground the day Liana Castilla was shot?"

"If you buy it."

"And they're still extorting him? Something doesn't make sense."

No touching. No holding hands.

I saw another possibility, and it fit. It fit so damn well. Explained so much.

"There's another," I said.

"Another what?"

"Gotta go. Sorry about your wife."

"I'm not. We're becoming good friends. That beats a cover marriage."

We disconnected. I took a hard left, away from the black SUV.

"Change of venue," I said.

"We'll lose Levinson," Garrett protested.

"We'll find Evan."

44

I ordered the guard to open the gate or Giancarlo's next guest would bring his daughter's ear. Giancarlo met us in the courtyard, his face lined with years that weren't there a few days ago. Leonard stood behind him, a gun in his hand, his eyes on Garrett.

"Why are you disturbing me at this hour?" Giancarlo demanded.

"Where is Erica?"

"In her room."

"Get her."

"Why should—?"

"You know why."

Edward Giancarlo studied me for a moment. His chest rose and fell.

"I don't know what you—"

"She needs to know."

He hesitated. "You can put the gun away, Leonard." He turned and marched into the house. He returned a few minutes later, barefooted Erica in tow.

"Mr. Travis," she said. "This better be good. I was reading *The Shepherd's Life*. Jesus, does that man like sheep."

"Can we go in where there's light?" I asked.

Giancarlo paraded us into his house. I laid pictures on the marble table in the foyer. They were photos that Sally had taken of Giancarlo and his girlfriend.

"What's the purpose of this?" Erica said with disgust.

"Tell her, Eddie," I said.

Giancarlo's right thumb dug at his forefinger. It was too much for the theater major who'd gone to law school. Who did what he had to do to pay the bills. Who started a company, grew it to a lucrative enterprise, only to have a client from years ago circle back into his life.

"Tell her what?" Erica demanded. "She's pregnant? Oh, I know; how's this—you *love* her, right?" She turned her wrath to me. "Get out of here. Better yet? I'm leaving. I've had enough sheep shit to last a lifetime."

She turned theatrically to Giancarlo.

"Goodbye, Edward. I'm sure we had some good times. Perhaps someday I'll recall one or two."

She started toward the hall.

"Tell her, you fool," I implored Giancarlo.

Erica spun around. "Tell her *what*?"

"He still loves you," I said.

Her shoulders slumped. "Oh, for god's sake. Does anyone here have half a brain?" She focused on Giancarlo. "Edward, I'm sorry it didn't—no, screw that. I would never, *ever* cheat. I deserve better than you."

"She's my daughter," he said.

"What does Kylie have—?

"The woman in the picture—young enough to be my

daughter? She is my daughter, Erica. My biological daughter."

45

I t was now a two-person play. I had but eight words.

"I don't understand," Erica said, her eyes desperate on her husband.

"I had her years ago. Her life is in danger. I've been trying to protect her. Hide her."

"From who?" Before he could answer, she added, "Why didn't you tell me?"

"I wanted to. But for everyone's safety, I felt it best not to."

"Who is after her?"

"I had a client years ago, a man named Vargo Estrada. I represented—"

"He wants to hurt her?"

"Please listen. I—"

"What's her name?"

"Let me—"

"What. Is. Her. Name?"

"Clarissa. My daughter's name is Clarissa. Vargo and I met when we were both young. I represented him on some business deals. He's not a good man, but there are worse. He deals with drugs. Some very bad people are after his business. He turned to me for help. Moving money. They discovered I had a daughter and went after her. They took a shot at Kylie. They didn't know that she was not my biological daughter. Not that it mattered; I'd do anything to protect her. I paid them to leave us alone. I was a fool to engage with them. I brought Clarissa closer to protect her. I've been hiding her."

"Hiding her?"

"In a church."

"A church?"

"Yes. In a children's classroom."

"A children's Sunday school room?" Erica was repeating words like you do when they're coming too fast, and you need time to process.

"Yes."

Erica took a second to process that. "Is Kylie safe?"

"I've made arrangements. But they have no interest in her now."

"What are they after?"

"They want me to turn on Vargo. I am ... privy to some of his financial holdings. I said no. They threatened me."

"So turn on him. He's not worth your daughter's life. Either daughter."

"I owe the man."

"Owe the man?" Erica said. "What possibly for?"

"My life. Years ago, he let me live."

"Why would he have wanted to harm you?"

"Sophia."

"Terrific. Who the hell is Sophia?"

"Clarissa's mother."

"And what does she have to do with all this?"

"She was Vargo's wife."

The air froze with silence.

"He only let me live because he did not want to kill the father of his wife's daughter," Giancarlo explained. "Clarissa was raised in Europe but moved to Naples a few years ago. That's why I've been going there. Telling you it was for business. We were never close, but we want to be close and are closer now than we have ever been. She's been thinking of moving up here. After the near miss with Kylie, I took action."

Giancarlo shifted his attention to me. "Vargo is nearby. I told him you were here. He wants to see you." He shot a glance at Garrett. "Alone." Back to me. "He is desperate to find his daughter, Rachel. They're picking us up in ten minutes."

"Who has Evan?" I asked.

"You and Vargo will talk."

"Does Vargo have him?"

"Ten minutes."

"I'm going back to my sheep," Erica said. "What an absurd mess you made, Eddie. At least so far, no one's been hurt."

"Liana," I said.

"Who?" Erica said, her face twisted with puzzlement. "Oh yeah, that swing set girl. You got a thing for her, don't you?"

46

I sat blindfolded in the back of an SUV, my mind a thrumming mass of chastising thoughts. I'd once thought that Evan had staged his own disappearance or that Angel had him. Maybe even Levinson. Fool. No. Stupid. Rachel and Evan were currency to be traded by men with conflicting goals. Find one, and the opposite party has the other.

The SUV came to a halt. We got out, and I was marched into a house. We were on the island across from my island. I know this because after climbing a high bridge, we'd gone through a roundabout, and there is only one roundabout in Tampa Bay at the end of a high bridge. With proprietorial pride, I know my land. My water. The salt-congested air that borders my life. I coughed. The red tide bloom now commanded the atmosphere, clogging my throat.

Someone removed my blindfold. Two men with guns stood in front of me. Another man was behind me. Soothing classical guitar music played from speakers. Another man sat in a chair facing us. Giancarlo stood behind him, off to the side, as if he was not worthy to be in the man's eyesight. The man in the chair held a cigar fatter than his fingers.

"Vargo?" I said.

"You are Evan Brackett's uncle," he said.

"I am."

"He looks like you."

"I've been told."

"Evan created a lot of problems for me."

"He fell in love with your daughter, and there's not a better man in the world for her. Your choice of business is the source of your problems."

Vargo tapped his cigar on the ashtray, keeping his slit eyes on it as if the act warranted his uncompromised attention. Like the other men, he was dressed in black, but his silk long-sleeve shirt gleamed under the dimmed overhead lights. He sat deep in his chair, like a man who'd been on the road a long time.

"My daughter, Rachel, gave you a note," he said.

How would he know that?

Either Evan told him or Rachel did. If it was Rachel, Vargo would have hightailed it back to Mexico with her.

"You have Evan," I said.

"He is safe."

"The warehouse?"

"When he appeared, we followed him. Angel was an hour behind us."

"How about if he and I skedaddle out of here."

"I'm afraid I cannot allow that."

"Am I to assume that Angel has your daughter?"

"He does. He told her he was coming to Florida. She left in the night without consulting me. It was foolish of me to underestimate her resolve to be with Evan, and she was a fool to trust Angel."

"Where does that leave us?"

"Bring me Angel's ear. Then you can have your nephew."

"Who am I, Dorothy?"

"Rachel watched that movie often when she was young, although the monkeys scared her terribly."

I dipped my head toward his small army. "You seem well equipped. Why not storm the palace yourself?"

"I'd rather you risk your life."

"I'd rather it the other way around."

"You have no vote."

"Tell me about Eugene Levinson. How did you get a CIA man in your pocket?"

"He is not loyal to me."

"He's Angel's man?"

"Levinson frequented Vegas. He drank too much. Talked. One night, Angel picked up conversation that Levinson worked for the US government. A G-man, someone said. Angel was—is—a hit man. But not one without street instincts and brash ambition. He knew he could move up in the cartels if he bagged a G-man.

"Angel followed him back to his hotel room. He forced himself in. He'd brought a young girl with him. A professional. He showed Levinson the pictures the next morning. Levinson has been on Angel's payroll ever since."

Vargo tapped his cigar on an ashtray. As if giving it a second thought, he left it there. He kept his eyes on me. "Edward?"

Giancarlo, properly summoned, took a step forward. "In our work with Levinson, some of my employees became suspicious. I warned them not to say anything. We didn't need the trouble. Levinson told us he was planting money in a sculpture of a bull in an attempt to trace it. I alerted Vargo. He learned that Angel was aware of this, which told us Levinson and Angel were talking. Experimenting with methods of laundering money. That is why I withdrew my company."

"Why wouldn't Levinson take Angel out?" As I spoke, I knew the answer.

Vargo took the question. "Angel dies, and the pictures are released. But there is more. Levinson has grown addicted to power. Money. It is a game to him."

Vargo raised himself out of the chair and walked to a bar cart. He poured himself a drink. Neat. He took a sip and paused as if to enjoy the brief interlude.

"Angel brought Levinson to my compound. You know this, yes? Evan said he told you. Freddy, the American."

"Wasn't that foolish of Levinson?"

"He was unaware, at that time, that Rachel and Evan had fallen in love and that I would not allow anyone to touch Evan. But now, Evan can expose him. Mr. Levinson dearly wants your nephew dead. This is why you will find my Rachel and eliminate Levinson and Angel."

"You just added Levinson to your bucket list."

"Do you have any idea of your debt to me?"

"You rushed Evan out of Mexico to save his life. Levinson and Angel knew he recognized the DEA agent's head in the box."

He nodded.

"Who ordered the hit on Giancarlo's adopted daughter?"

"Why do you ask? The shooter missed."

"A girl died that day. Liana Castillo. Her father came to me."

His eyes scanned my face. "Angel. He thought he could turn Edward against me. He didn't know that when two men love the same woman, they share a sacred bond."

"With all respect, I think I'll pass."

"Pardon?"

"You're no threat to Evan. You've demonstrated as much. You can perform your own dirty work."

Vargo looked at me as if I'd failed a basic pop quiz.

"Come," he said. "Let us enjoy the night." He pushed back a heavy sliding door and stepped onto a balcony. He took several paces away from the door. I coughed.

"Do you cough because of the red tide?" he asked.

"I do."

"It does not affect me. How unfortunate for those who are sensitive to it. How long does it last?"

"It moves on its own terms."

"You cannot fight it?"

"No. There is nothing we can do."

"Is there any reason for it?"

"It is meaningless."

"How does it form?"

"They don't really know. But pollution draining into the Gulf makes it worse."

"With all our science, we are still ignorant."

We were quiet for a moment. When he finally spoke, his voice was firm. Quiet.

"My men cannot hear what we say here. They are loyal men, but any sign of weakness, and they will act in their best interest."

"You indicated Angel was an hour behind you, in going after Evan."

"Such information, Evan's location, could have only come from one of my men."

"You have a leak."

"Do you love a woman, Mr. Travis?"

"I do."

"Do you have any children?"

"A daughter."

"And do you love her?"

"I do."

"More than life? More than the coughing air you breathe?"

"Without thought."

"Then you know. I would sacrifice everything for her."

"Not just for Rachel. But for your wife, Sophia, as well."

"What do you know of my love for my wife?" he said with a bite.

"He is not a lover who does not love forever."

He cut me a sharp look. "That is you?"

"Euripides, I believe."

"Ah, the Greeks. Rachel told me there has been nothing new since then, although I suspect your nephew was the source of her knowledge."

"Let me have him. It does you no good to keep him."

"He demanded more money."

"Angel?"

"Payment for another week of Rachel's life."

"And?"

"I paid him." He shrugged. "Was it the right thing to do? Who knows? He is not an honorable man. I paid him only to limit my regrets. What is it they say—give peace a chance?"

"Evan is of no use to you."

"I cannot release him until my Rachel is safe, any more

than the moon can outshine the sun." He turned to me. "That is the only way I will get your best effort."

"You know nothing of me."

"We are the same man."

"I hardly think so."

"Why? Because you judge the blood you've drawn to be more deserving than the blood on my hands? You might feel morally compelled by your actions, but you are still responsible for them."

"You think it's that simple?"

"I've seen them together," he said, ignoring my question. "I assure you, their love is as strong as a love can be. Maybe stronger, for I am older and do not remember the rawness of my feeling for Sophia when we first met. It is important for you, yes? To make sure Evan and Rachel are together?"

"It is."

"I want to ensure that my daughter's future is free from the violence that broke my heart. You will represent me, help me broker a deal. In return for information on Eugene Levinson, your government will allow me freedom in your country. I will retire. Perhaps be a grandfather one day. And we will meet at—what do they call it?—family functions."

His Hail Mary plan had little chance of succeeding. Men in his profession do not retire.

"We have the same goal, yes?" Vargo said, seeking confirmation.

"We do."

He gave a solemn nod. "Good. To a father growing old, nothing is dearer than a daughter. Do you know who said that?"

"I do not."

"Your friend, Euripides." He smiled weakly at me. He

sighed, as if it were his last sigh on earth. "Age holds little promise for me. I fear that in my blind rage, all I have done is distanced my daughter. I have financed the devil. I have heard the screams of a hundred mothers. I have destroyed my daughter's capacity to love me. Who would aspire to such things?"

He paused. I was going to ask him what he was referring to when he continued.

"She knows nothing of which I speak. But Angel will tell her. He will poison her against me. He will hurt her more with his mouth than with his hand."

We were quiet a moment. I suppressed the reflex to cough.

"Have you ever read the book *Hatchet*?" he asked.

I searched my memory, for it had been decades since I'd picked up the book. "Long ago. Why do you ask?"

"I was reading the book when it had just come out. I was interrupted and never got the chance to finish it. Tell me, how does it end? Does Brian survive?"

More searching.

"He does."

"Did he tell his father that his mother had an affair before their divorce?"

Coming back to me now.

"He does not."

His chest rose and fell. "That is good. Tell me, as a father of a daughter, to a father of a daughter, do I have your pledge?"

"You do."

"I hope I enjoy my retirement, although it was nothing I ever believed in."

. . .

HE FELL TWO DAYS LATER, GUNNED DOWN ON THE REAR balcony, the sun gently extinguishing itself in the Gulf of Mexico. I wondered if his last thoughts were of joining his wife or of leaving his daughter, for he seemed to love both very much, but if he believed in Euripides, joining his wife would not heal the pain of leaving his daughter.

Garrett and I stormed the house after Rambler called. Only one detail bears mentioning: Evan was gone.

47

RACHEL

Interiority redux

Do they not know?

Angel and Rachel were having dinner on a crowded sidewalk in downtown Saint Petersburg, tides of people swelling the streets. Angel was trying to keep the conversation light. Breezy. But, at that moment, Rachel Estrada believed the world to be a humming nervousness of existence. The whole production just a moment away from an inglorious finale. One big whistling mass of humanity, skipping past the graveyard. Look at their smiles. Hear their laughs. Smell their cretinous ignorance.

Do they not know?

At any moment, a young girl might lose her mother.

Do they not know?

Yellow flowers do not fall from heaven.

Her thoughts settled on her father. The last time she'd seen Vargo, he was a defeated man. A man stooped by a galactic sadness he could no longer bear. She knew that his business problems only grew, but couldn't you say that about any business on any day? Why now? He'd been such a gallant warrior for so long, she could not place the source of his faltering. At first, she thought his downward spiral was related to her mother's death, his sadness metastasizing over the years. But she now felt it might be something altogether different. Something foreign. Unknown to her.

The enigma of her father manifested itself with a twist of a fork, a shovel of cold peas, a tepid attack on a salad left largely unappreciated.

"You're supposed to eat it," Angel said.

"Pardon?"

"Your food. You are supposed to eat it."

The gentleness in Angel's voice didn't fool Rachel. He was not a man. He was a rabid dog. She'd always known this. *What had he done to make three men run?* But he'd been a willing coconspirator for years as she blew through youth. That knot, coupled with her mission to reunite her heart with Evan, had created her current predicament. She blamed no one except herself.

"I'm not hungry," she said, thinking that the number seven would never admit as much. But that candied memory only darkened her mood.

"Would you like to go to another restaurant?"

"Would I be hungry there?"

Angel wiped his mouth. He pushed away his empty plate and swept his arm in the air.

"Leave. Stand. Go now. I won't stop you."

"Not without Evan."

"I told you, I don't know where he is."

"You lie."

"Why would I lie?'

"Why? You're dishonest. You're a thug. A killer."

Angel took a moment with that, mostly to calm Rachel. Her last comment had earned the interest of a nearby table, two women eyeing him suspiciously.

"Did you ever learn how I came to work for your father?"

"I'm not interested," she said, staring in contempt at his baleful face. She suddenly doubted every decision she had ever made. *What brought me to this point in time?*

"I thought you liked stories."

"I wouldn't trust anything you say."

"And you trust your father, Vargo?"

"He is honorable, something you will never be."

"Tell me Rachel, is lying honorable?"

"No."

"Never?"

"I'm not playing games with you."

"How old were you when your mother was murdered? Ten? They told you it was a car accident, correct?"

"I'm not discussing my mother with a rat like you."

"You didn't mind this rat when I'd take you to town and turn my head in the evenings."

"My father would not approve."

"You did."

"I wasn't paying you."

"Did you ever tell your father the truth?"

"We never discussed it."

"You lied by silence."

"It's not the same thing."

"You're right. It is far worse. They told you it was a car accident. They lied."

"I was young. My father was protecting me. He told me the truth when I was older."

"And what did he tell you? That another family did not like the way Vargo did business. They did this to her—to him—to teach him a lesson. This is what he told you, right?"

Rachel lowered her eyes. *Car accident.* That was the first version. Then Vargo had told her how her mother really died. How her bullet-ridden SUV was found in a ditch, her body inside. None of the men in the SUV behind her were even able to escape their vehicles. Sophia, her driver, and the two men behind her died in a bloody ambush.

Vargo had her SUV destroyed. He told Rachel that her mother likely never felt a thing. It was a quick death. Around town, it was never discussed.

"He told you she was ambushed, right?"

"I know how my mother died."

"You know the truth now because you are old enough, correct?"

"Get to the point, if you're capable of one."

Angel gave an uncharacteristic nod of his head.

"Do you know how I came to work for Vargo?"

Tired of his questions, Rachel could only look dully at Angel. Two couples, each walking a dog, approached each other. When they met, the women fell to their knees and greeted the dogs like it was the second coming of Christ.

"Both of my older brothers were gunned down when I was six. One of my earliest memories."

"I'm sorry for your loss." There was no sincerity in her words, but she thought a little sympathy might shut the rat up.

"We were poor. My mother tried to wash the blood out of their clothes. It did not come out. When I was older, I had to wear those clothes."

"You didn't have to."

"True. I could have gone naked through the world. A choice that, by birth, you never had to make. Vargo hired me to carry out his revenge. To kill those who killed your mother."

"Good. I hoped you killed them slowly."

Those words were equally insincere. But she felt the need to toughen up, suspecting that Angel had something up his filthy sleeve.

"There were five men who ambushed her SUV that day."

"I said, I know the story."

"It was not as he told you."

"And I'm going to believe you? If you have a different version, keep it to yourself."

"I do not blame Vargo for lying to you. You were young."

"I know he settled the score."

"You don't even know the game," he spit out. "You only know what he told you. I would have done the same if I had a daughter."

"God won't let men like you have daughters."

Angel tightened his jaw. Enough of this sass. Of this bitch. He'd been taking her attitude since she was thirteen and never as much as laid a hand on her. Never a thank you. Did she not think he knew how she looked at him? The disdain? The condescending mockery? Stupid cunt.

"The ambush did not kill your mother."

Something dormant stirred inside her.

He leaned forward. His voice low. His words intended for one person only.

"She did not die in the ambush. They took her to a shed. They raped her. Five men. And then five more. And then fifty times fifty planted their seed in her. Death was her only friend."

Rachel's heart, beating wildly against her ribs, surrendered all sense of rhythm. She felt herself being swallowed, her body cannibalizing itself in an effort to shut out Angel's words.

"It was meant as retribution against Vargo, for he had gotten greedy. I was eighteen. There was not a man in the world I feared. When you wear the bloodied clothes of your brothers, you wake up every day eager to settle the score. He turned to me. But Vargo had no intention of evening the score. He wanted to send a message that no one ever touch his family again. His family, Rachel. There was only you. What I say, he did for you. I did for you."

Rachel's eyes locked on a potted palm on the sidewalk.

"Look at me."

She kept her eyes on the potted palm. *Looks like it could use a little water.*

"Ten men. Every man who touched her. Do you think that is fair?"

"It is done," Rachel said, struggling to control her breathing. She didn't want to see this pig see her sweat. That her mother was raped before she died must have been why her father could not meet her gaze when he told her of Sophia's death. *I can hardly blame him. Perhaps he could not even say the words.*

"But I didn't kill ten men. Your father asked me to find out which of those men were married with daughters. Three. Three of the men were married with daughters. I was told not to kill them. Look at me."

Rachel kept her eyes on the potted palm. *Maybe a little fertilizer as well.*

"I did as your father instructed. I let the men live."

"No," Rachel said, unconscious of her own speech. It

would be the last word she spoke that evening. She stood in a large building. Someone stood close to her. Someone who radiated indestructible love.

Angel spoke.

"Did you ever wonder why no one in town would talk to you about this? Why they looked down when you approached? Crossed to the other side of the street? My men raped them. The three mothers of the three men who were married with daughters. We raped them until we could rape them no more. They said your mother never called out when she was raped. Never cried. But these women? They screamed. This was done so that no man would ever lay a hand on you. To this day, the village where it occurred calls it the night of a thousand screams. The sounds of mothers—"

She tried to close her eyes only to discover they were already clamped shut. She went so deep inside herself that if you were passing on the sidewalk, you would see a man with greased black hair flared over his ears like demonic Cadillac fins. His teeth too large for his mouth. Sitting alone at the table. Babbling to an empty chair. A total nutjob.

Her surroundings came into focus. Her mother stood next to her. They towered over other people, a mumbling, bumbling mass. Mother and daughter looked into each other's eyes. Silent. Stoic. The world, with all its demented absurdities, its discordant realities, could not touch them. She understood this now. She did have her father's heart, for he'd lost it. Then—as dreams do, changing scene and soundtrack with no warning—she and Sophia were outside. They stood in a field of yellow flowers. Beyond them, in the shade of an oak tree, a young boy read a book.

48

This is the third time.

Euripides also said, "When a good man is hurt, all who would be called good must suffer with him." He did not tell us what a good man was. I felt no guilt being saddened by Vargo's death. All I knew of the man were his plaintive words, his palpable love for his daughter.

I knocked on Brittany's door. She deserved to know that I'd found Evan, and then lost him. That I believed he was still alive, and I would do everything I could to bring him home. She was so relieved that I hadn't arrived to inform her that her only son was dead—*God, Jake, when I saw you driving down the driveway*—that she casually dismissed my role in his abduction. I called Manuel Castillo and told him I hadn't forgotten about him. He thanked me for "talking to me." I told Yankee Conrad about my tête-à-tête with Vargo. His death. He said Eugene Levinson was in the wind. He doubted he could be found. "Imagine," he said with a bit too much admiration for my taste, "right under our noses."

China called. I put her off. I couldn't deal with *that* right now.

At eleven-thirty-seven on the second evening after Vargo fell, my phone rang. It was the number of the burner phone I'd given to Darron, the guard at the warehouse.

"Talk to me," I said.

"I got a line on your man. Word is they got some woman and man, been shuffling them around. But the whole regiment's cutting out. Got a plane to catch. Tonight."

"Where are they? The warehouse?"

Garrett and I had been keeping eyes on the warehouse and Levinson's home. Low probability odds, but we had to cover the bases. Combat the boredom.

"Don't know."

"What do you know?"

"Hey, I'm just trying to help you out here."

"And I appreciate that, Darron. What can you tell me?"

"I told a few of my buddies to be on the lookout for slime that goes by Angel. Said he might be responsible for that swing set girl that died. That stokes our furnace. My good buddy Kurt's a night watchman at this other building. Just got off the horn with him. He said they were there, but he overheard they was heading to church."

"Church?"

"Go figure, right? They said they didn't want to hang around the warehouse—cameras and all. Kurt said your guy, Angel, admired how someone used some church to hole somebody up in. You know, hide 'em."

"Did they give you the name of the church?"

"Negatory."

"Anything else?"

"He thinks they're on a schedule. Advice?

"Shoot."

"If I was you, I wouldn't be yapping to me."

"Thanks."

"No problemo."

WE PARKED TWO BLOCKS FROM THE METHODIST church where Giancarlo had sequestered his daughter. Morgan and Domingo came along for extra sets of eyes. They were together, as they had planned to go night fishing. An empty black SUV sat by the rear door. A man leaned against it. It took me a second, but I placed him.

Julio and I was just told to go to the park.

I marched up to him at a crisp pace. "Julio, what's shaking?"

Surprised, Julio stared, trying to place me. By the time he did, Garrett, who had maneuvered behind him, calmly instructed him to raise his arms. I frisked him and took his gun. We gagged him, bound his legs and arms, and stuffed him in the truck. That was after he told us who we would find inside, along with their schedule. Angel and his band of Merry Men were waiting for a private plane to land at Albert Whitted Airport. The downtown airport, jutting into Tampa Bay, was less than five minutes from the church.

Garrett and I left Morgan and Domingo behind with instructions to keep an eye on Julio and text if they saw anything. We slipped inside and kept low and against the church walls. There were draped with colorful celebratory banners. Victory in life. Victory in death. No wonder this stuff sells. You're a winner either way. We split. Garrett headed to the kitchen. I scampered down the hallway to the main sanctuary.

A woman screamed, followed by Angel's angry and unintelligible words. My heart jumped. I assumed the woman was Rachel, and Evan would be with them as well.

I texted the group that they were in the sanctuary.

I tried to remember the layout from the few times I'd been in the church. I sprinted down the hall until I was at the front of the sanctuary. A door to my left was open to the choir pews, a beam of light escaping as if it knew.

Do I confirm with Rambler? Wait for Angel to leave and have the men in blue waiting? But now that Vargo was dead, and Angel had his money; what need did he have for Evan and Rachel? I envisioned the Reverend Cyndi-Girard strolling into her church and finding two bloodied bodies. And she thought she had domestic issues.

A gunshot jolted my thoughts and made my decision. I dashed through the door and into the chancel, ducking behind a choir pew.

Angel, with his back to me, stood on the main floor of the sanctuary at the bottom of wide steps. Evan was on the ground. Rachel kneeled over him, her hand supporting his head. He appeared unharmed. The three men who had accompanied Angel to the cemetery stood to his side. A fourth man, smaller, stood in front of Angel.

"Take them, Riggins," Angel said to the smaller man. "I don't want their bodies found. Ever."

"I want twice as much," Riggins said.

"Why would I do that?"

"You said one, and now it's two. See how that works?"

"Would you like to make it three?"

"A big mess like that would leave a lot of clues."

"You're a stupid man. I made a mistake hiring you."

"We part ways tonight," Riggins said. "No one will ever

find these two, and that's what's important. Double or nothing."

"Fine."

I didn't really know Angel, but I was familiar with the breed. Riggins had made a tactical error.

"Now," Riggins demanded.

"I don't have it on me."

"Guys like you stuff it up your ass. Now, or one of them is your problem."

I drew my gun, for I feared Angel was contemplating killing Riggins, Evan, and Rachel and being done with the whole business.

"Pay him, Rodrigo," he said, glancing at the man who had wielded an umbrella at my neck. "The way we honor our business deals."

Rodrigo reached inside his jacket and pulled out a wad of banded bills. He counted them, or pretended to. He picked up a leather satchel that appeared to already have some heft to it, unzipped it, and stuffed the bills into the bag. He tossed it toward Riggins. It hit the floor and slid to a stop at his feet. Riggins picked up the satchel. When he looked up, Angel had a gun pointed at him.

Angel shot Nicky Riggins twice in the legs. Riggins went down, shrieking in pain.

Angel took a few leisurely steps until he towered over Riggins. "If I killed you quickly, you wouldn't have suffered. This way, I know you feel pain before you die." He glanced at Rodrigo. "Our pilot?"

"Fifteen minutes." Rodrigo dipped his head at Rachel and Evan. "What do you want to do with them?"

Evan struggled to his feet. He stood with his arms around Rachel, more of a huddle than a hug. Rachel looked up.

Rachel. From Hebrew. One with purity.

It was as if my friend the wind had circled the globe, caressed a thousand faces from a hundred centuries and sculpted one of youthful fortitude. Of simplicity. Of elegance.

"We bring them," Angel said. I exhaled quietly, unaware that I'd been holding my breath. "We can dump them over the Gulf of Mexico." He looked at Rachel. "I meant to dispose of your father that way, but it proved too bothersome."

Rachel screamed and broke free of Evan's arm. She launched herself at Angel, her feet flying off the ground, her hands clawing for his face. Rodrigo intercepted her. He wrapped both arms around her. One of the other men pointed a gun at Evan, who had bolted after her.

"What did you do to him?" she yelled at Angel.

"Nothing that does not happen to us all in the end."

She kicked her feet like she was bicycling in air. But her rage was no match for the muscles of the big man who held her.

"You said you'd let us be. That if I came with you, you would let him quit."

"You heard what you wanted to hear."

"Liar!"

"Liar?" He shook his head with humor. "Vargo promised me he would turn his operations over to me. But he had no intention of doing so."

"That's because you killed the DEA agent. You are a murderer, and he knew it."

"Did you not hear a word I said the other night? And you think your father was a saint? I didn't even tell you what he did before you were born."

"He wasn't that man anymore."

Angel strolled to Rachel. He reached out and traced a finger over her face, running it down her throat.

"Once you did not return on the promised date, it was only a matter of time until Vargo came looking for you. Vargo wanted to die. To atone for his sins. To silence the night of a thousand screams. He killed to protect you, and by doing so, he sacrificed himself. Pity you didn't see your role in this."

Rachel spit in Angel's face.

"Do that again, and we will rape you like they raped your mother. You will beg to join your father."

"You're a pig," she said.

Angel stuck his tongue out and rolled it around his upper lip, searching for Rachel's spittle.

"Rodrigo," he said, keeping his eye on Rachel. "Tell the pilot we will be an hour late."

"We should keep on schedule."

"Do it," Angel barked.

Rodrigo reached inside his pocket. A shot cracked from the back of the sanctuary. The man not holding Evan went down.

The other man tackled Evan and dove behind the front pew. Angel squatted, fumbling for his gun. Rodrigo dropped his phone. He wrapped both his arms around Rachel. He pivoted and faced the rear of the sanctuary, using Rachel as a shield.

I aimed at his back just as Morgan and Domingo pressed against me. I'd been so intent on the action in front of me, I'd not noticed them enter. When I glanced back up, my clear shot was gone.

"Is that you, Jake Travis?" Angel yelled at the rear of the

sanctuary. "I was hoping we'd meet again. You want to trade bullets? I think not. Throw your gun out or Rachel . . . no, it's Evan, isn't it? He's not just a job. A relative, perhaps?"

A gun came sliding down the aisle.

The sanctuary was quiet as Angel calculated how easy that had been. He spun his head and looked at Rodrigo, who was still holding Rachel.

"The Black man. He is here, too."

Rodrigo hit the floor next to Angel, leaving Rachel exposed. Evan sprang free and darted to her side. He wrapped his arms around her. Seized with indecision, they stood exposed at the base of the steps. The man who had held a gun at Evan stood. I sprang up, shot him twice, and ducked back behind a choir pew. Angel spun and shot at me, his bullets splintering the wood around me.

"You get the back," Angel yelled, keeping his eyes toward the front of the sanctuary.

Rodrigo drew a knife. With a knife in one hand and a gun in the other, he slithered down the aisle toward the back of the sanctuary. Angel started for the altar, standing tall, eager to share his bullets with the world.

Garrett sprang from a pew and tackled Rodrigo. Both bodies tumbled to the ground. The knife skidded toward the front of the sanctuary.

Angel gave a quick glance behind him and then continued toward me.

"Mr. Jake? I hide my face from no man."

I sprang up just as Rachel threw herself on Angel's back. She screamed and clawed at him, pulling out clumps of hair. Angel spun, trying to dislodge Rachel. Evan rushed him, but Angel whipped him with his gun, sending him to the floor. Like a mighty demon, Angel torqued into an unhuman form, flinging Rachel away with one arm, her body sliding until it stopped at the first step to the chancel.

I'd kept my gun on Angel. He kept his gun on Rachel.

"Shoot me. As I fall, I will take her to hell with me."

Rachel grabbed something off the floor. She stood. She marched toward Angel, as if she'd become detached from her body. Chin up. Shoulders back. Eyes alert. Her left arm behind her.

"You'll get there first," she said.

In one smooth motion, Rachel Estrada flung Rodrigo's knife, planting the blade with precision in Angel's torso.

Angel tottered. He looked at his stomach. He glanced at Rachel. He smiled. He raised his gun and pointed it at her. Garrett and I both fired, rattling his body with bullets.

Morgan, and then Domingo, flew through the air like twin skydivers, arching their bodies over Rachel.

Angel's finger, like a beheaded snake, kept squeezing the trigger of his gun, the evil in him seeking another host.

Morgan was younger and quicker than Domingo—a name that means born on Sunday—and that is why Morgan landed on Rachel first, and Domingo landed on Morgan and took two of Angel's errant bullets in the back. I rushed to his side, that Sunday morning, but there was nothing I could do. I hummed "Michael Row" and held his hand so he did not cross alone, and now he dances with his father and rests next to Andrew Keller under the fresh-cut summer grass.

49

Manuel Castillo sat on a bench facing the Gulf of Mexico, a paint-by-numbers sunset transfiguring the sky. The red tide bloom had moved offshore, and I no longer coughed. But it was still out there, for it never really leaves us.

I told Manuel the man who shot Liana was dead. That his name was Nicky Riggins. That Riggins bled out on the floor of a church sanctuary after Angel shot him. That in the end, we had tried to save him. For while I did what I could for Domingo, Garrett had called 911. My biggest fear was that Riggins would live and Domingo would die, and doesn't that just sound like life? I didn't tell Manuel that just before the medics arrived, I'd whispered a few words into Riggins's ear. Made the medics' job a little harder. But we're not going there.

Manuel listened without apparent interest. As if words no longer held meaning. Perhaps they never had.

When I finished, he thanked me.

"For what?"

"Caring."

"She can never be replaced, but this will help. Please, take it."

"I don't want it."

"Why?"

"It would only be a painful reminder of her."

"You're wrong."

"Oh?"

"She wants to see you happy. Your wife and other daughter. I feel so bad. I do not know her name."

"Stefanie."

"She wants Stefanie to go to college. For you not to work until your dying day. Your wife, her name is Theresa?"

He nodded. His eyes locked on the sand between his stubby feet.

"She wants a house. You told me that. Stainless steel. There is enough here. Live as Liana would want you to live. You don't need me to tell you that."

"*Si.*"

I left him staring at a squadron of pelicans gliding effortlessly over the water, their motionless bodies moving. On the bench next to him rested the satchel of money that Angel had intended for Nicky Riggins. It had been Rambler's suggestion. Said the hell with dignity, he wasn't done trying to change the world.

50

Three months later, I rang the doorbell I'd recently fixed. She thought good things might come to the front door. Let's see.

The door opened.

There she stood. My Florida morning. My fantasia. The tidal pull of my heart. My untitled passion. My seashell-collector-high-heel-hater-directionally-confused-kitchen-bewildered-can't-grow-a-damn-thing lover.

She looked at me. She looked at China. Her face contorted with confusion.

I'd purposely refrained from rehearsing an opening line and now saw the error of my thinking. I held a baby girl in my arms, clueless as to any of it.

China stepped around me. She planted herself between Kathleen and me.

"This is the way it's going to be, Dr. Rowe. So don't give Jake and me any shit."

EPILOGUE

I pull Joy's floppy hat down to shield her face. She touches everything. Floats her hand over the side of the kayak. I stare at her small hand and think of Scott's line in "Lady of the Lake": "The rose is fairest when it's budding new." Every second of her life is blazed with wonderment. Curiosity. A child reboots your soul. Helps you, again, to live resplendently. To breathe the million miracles the sun unwraps each morning. To forget, if only momentarily, the temporariness of life. Yesterday, over cocktails, Kathleen was aflame with excitement over family trips. How old do they have to be before we teach them to hurtle down a mountain of snow? At what age can they go to Europe and get something out of it? The heck with Europe, when can we sail the Caribbean in Morgan's boat? But, man-oh-man, that's a lot of sun. And how about Disney? Think about it: the Magic Kingdom is only ninety minutes down the road. Hot dog! How many people can say that?

"Do they still have that ride—It's a Small World—or did

it close? And how about that monorail that goes into the park? The girls will love that. Hey, are you listening to me?"

ABOUT THE AUTHOR

 Robert Lane is the author of the Jake Travis stand-alone novels. *Florida Weekly* calls Jake Travis a "richly textured creation; one of the best leading men to take the thriller fiction stage in years." Lane's debut novel, *The Second Letter*, won the Gold Medal in the Independent Book Publishers Association's (IBPA's) 2015 Benjamin Franklin Awards for Best New Voice: Fiction. He is also the recipient of the Eric Hoffer Award for Best Mystery. Lane resides on the west coast of Florida. Learn more at Robertlanebooks.com.

Receive a free copy of the Jake Travis series prequel, *Midnight on the Water*.

As much mystery as love story, *Midnight on the Water* is the saga of how Jake and Kathleen met, tumbled into love, and the drastic measures Jake, Morgan, and Garrett take to save Kathleen's life—and grant her a new identity. *Midnight on the Water* is available only to those on Robert Lane's mailing list. The newsletter contains reviews of books, music, and television shows across a wide range of genres. It also includes updates from the next Jake Travis novel.

Enjoy Midnight on the Water.

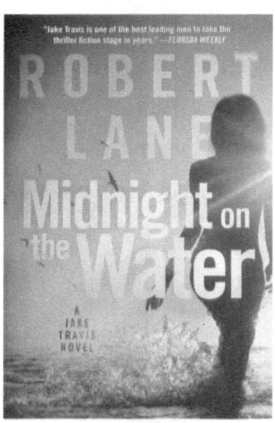

Also be sure to read these other standalone Jake Travis novels:

The Second Letter

Cooler Than Blood

The Cardinal's Sin

The Gail Force

Naked We Came

A Beautiful Voice

The Elizabeth Walker Affair

A Different Way to Die

Visit Robert Lane's author page on Amazon.com: https://www.amazon.com/Robert-Lane/e/B00HZ2254A

Follow Robert Lane on:

Facebook: https://www.facebook.com/RobertLaneBooks

Goodreads: https://www.goodreads.com/author/show/7790754.Robert_Lane

BookBub: https://www.bookbub.com/profile/robert-lane?list=about

Learn more and receive your free copy of *Midnight on The Water* at http://robertlanebooks.com.

www.ingramcontent.com/pod-product-compliance
Lightning Source LLC
Chambersburg PA
CBHW021203250626
47155CB00008B/2647